FOLLOW THE CROW

VANISHED, BOOK ONE

B. B. GRIFFITH

Griffith Publishing

Publication Information

Follow the Crow (Vanished, #1)

Copyright © 2020 by Griffith Publishing LLC

Ebook ISBN: 978-0-9899400-5-4

Paperback ISBN: 978-0-9899400-4-7

Written by B. B. Griffith

Cover design by Damonza

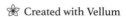 Created with Vellum

To Mom.
For everything.

Strange—is it not?—that of the myriads who
Before us passed the door of Darkness through,
Not one returns to tell us of the road
Which to discover we must travel too.

- Omar Khayyám
Rubaiyat
(Edward Fitzgerald, trans.)

1

BEN DEJOOLI

If you drive due west from the city of Albuquerque, New Mexico, for two hours and then cut north before you hit the city of Gallup, you'll see a big stretch of glass—flat nothing dusted with sand, slightly lighter in color than the rest of the Red Rock Country to the north. It's called the Chaco Flats, and it'll go wavy on you in the distance, give you an unsettled feeling in your gut and make your eyes water to look at it if you catch it at mid-day. If you were tempted to turn back at this point, to get yourself back to humanity in Albuquerque or to cut northeast to Santa Fe, you wouldn't be the first. You might even be tempted to keep going west, straight on to what passes for civilization at the shithole Nevada border towns, and if you did, I wouldn't exactly blame you. But if you have enough gas in the tank and want to see one of the greatest feats of social engineering the United States ever attempted, head north through the flats and keep driving until you hit the Chaco Navajo Reservation.

You can't miss it. Drive far enough north and all roads eventually lead to Chaco. Whether or not you'll be happy you came is another matter entirely. I promise you'll find the rez. But that's all I can promise. You'll know it by the dented sign that says Welcome to the Navajo Nation. The dents come from buckshot fired by drunk kids with nothing better to do. For years we kept replacing it only to find it shot up again the next morning. Nothing says "shoot me" like a pristine white tribal sign leering at you along a seven-mile straightaway. I'm a tribal cop, and even I know that. But don't let some shot-up sign scare you away. There's plenty that'll scare you, mind. Just not that.

So say you drive from Albuquerque, and say you got the gas and the morbid curiosity once you hit the flats, and say you head north and pass the buckshot welcome sign, then you'd hit the welcome center. It's nice. Renovated just last year. Come on in and take a seat, and we'll show you a pretty video and an entire wall full of educational pamphlets about what it means to be Navajo, from patent (proud nation of warriors and statesmen) to present (it's complicated). There's a gift shop there too, and directions to our popular stopovers, including the Tribal Museum, Old Town, and the Wapati Casino.

The employees at the welcome center won't tell you this, because it's one of the cushiest jobs in the rez and they don't want to lose it, but we *really* hope that you hit the highlights and bounce out of here, hopefully a few bucks lighter. Maybe with a nice arrowhead collection or a little plastic tomahawk for the kids. Stick to the main road. Because if you don't, you'll start to notice things.

For instance, if you were to turn left off the main road about a quarter mile past the welcome center but before the turnoff to Wapati, you'd see that the cleaner houses and apartments sort of disappear on you. You duck your head to check the car radio then look up, and all of a sudden you're at a row of tract homes. This is the Painted Sand development, and it's not that bad, actually. What's bad is another quarter mile south, where there aren't even homes. Just metal boxes. Like a bunch of semi-trucks dropped their freight containers off the side of the road and left them there to slowly rust out but before that happened about six people moved into each one. This place doesn't have a name. At the station we call it Boxes. You go there with your partner, and you keep your gun hand free.

Today, if you were to drive past Boxes where the concrete turns to packed gravel and the gravel turns to dirt and the dirt turns to mud, you'd find a bar called Sancho's. And today, if you were stupid enough to walk inside, you'd find me, Ben Dejooli, officer of the Navajo Nation Police, and my partner Danny Ninepoint. And if I saw you, I'd usually tell you to get the hell out for your own good, especially if you were white. But today I've got worse problems, and it looks like you're along for the ride anyway. Maybe you're a stubborn one, like me. Like most of us here at Chaco. Don't get me wrong, we have a lot of nice places on the rez. Places that are beautiful and peaceful and welcoming. It's just that the cops don't go to any of them.

Today, some poor Navajo ended up dead in the storeroom of Sancho's, strewn out on the floor amid empty bottles, the sick still damp on his face, and a needle still stuck in his arm. His rubber tie-off dangles loosely from around his bicep. He's purpled and stiff.

"Found him when I opened up," says Sancho, a ruddy-faced Navajo with a round, bearish head and a banded tail of black hair halfway down his back. I check my watch. Bars open early in Chaco, and the sun is already high in the sky.

"That was almost two hours ago, Sancho," I say. Danny gives me a quick, wary look from under the flat brim of his hat. Danny thinks I talk too much. Or maybe it's that I just say the wrong things. He's usually right. Danny was an NNPD veteran back when I started, and that's going on six years now. He doesn't like to let me forget it. But when things go south, there is no better Navajo to have your back. He usually finishes things before they start. They call him Ninepoint because he was already as big as a nine-point buck back when you're that age when kids start giving you nicknames. So you can imagine how big he is now. He carries around a scalp knife with a bone hilt and a beaded leather wrist strap. He keeps it where his gun should be and his gun where his stick should be. It's a clear enough warning: mess with Danny Ninepoint and he's going straight for the knife.

Sancho glares at me for a half second longer than a civilian should rightly glare at a cop. And a couple seconds longer than he'd ever glare at Ninepoint.

"We didn't find him 'til later. We called you boys as soon as we stumbled 'cross him." He sounds like he's talking about a raccoon that got stuck in the ducts. I squat down to get a better look at the dead guy. He's puffy and mottled, but I recognize him as one of the old regulars who works the Wapati penny slots. He's even got a Wapati Casino jacket on, muddy and frayed. Probably a comp. You sit for five years pumping coins into a box, and they'll be happy to give you a buffet voucher and a jacket. The jacket looks well-worn. The guy's old. Well-traveled. He doesn't strike me as the type to overdose on heroin like some teenaged tweeker, but I keep that to myself for now.

"You normally let your customers shoot up in your back room, Sancho?" I ask. Sancho doesn't answer me. One of the barflies shifts forward in his chair. He doesn't get up, exactly, but he's letting me know he could get up and over real quick if he wanted to. He's staring at me through the mirror behind the bar and rolling an empty shot glass. Danny sees it too and steps in.

"Now just hold on here. Nobody is saying anyone did anything." He points at the barfly. "And you, big fella, if I see you get up from that seat, I'll paste you to it. You hear me? Mean mug the mirror all you want, but you stay set."

"Sorry, Ninepoint," Sancho says on behalf of the bar, but he's looking right at me. "It's just that your partner's been known to run his mouth, and I like my bar and my life here just fine." His eyes glitter. He knows what he's saying.

See, Sancho doesn't like me. Neither do any of Sancho's regulars. Or most people on the rez, for that matter. Your average Navajo isn't exactly buddy-buddy with Navajo Police, no different from the US cops and the civvies on the outside, but they'll abide a steady presence like Danny. They know Danny. They trust Danny. Also, Danny doesn't give them much of a choice. With me it's different. There are two things a Navajo cop gets known for. The first is killing another Navajo. That's bad, but people know that sometimes bad things happen. Hell, sometimes they'll even allow that the other guy deserved it. The other is banishing a Navajo. That's worse. Danny never did that. As far as I know, nobody on the Force has done that. Nobody but me.

Technically NNPD can't banish anyone ourselves. Only the tribal court can do that. When you're banished it means you are no longer Navajo. It means you've been thrown from the Navajo Way. Our path is no longer yours to walk. Your soul has been untethered from the souls of the People, and you are now a wanderer. It's a heavy hand. The heaviest. The only time it's been used in Chaco in recent memory was in a case I helped build against Joseph Flatwood. A case that didn't make me any friends, and that took away the best friend I had.

This isn't the first time someone's jabbed me about the banishment like this. It won't be the last. Still, it gets to me. It's not like I don't think about it every day already. That case ripped my family apart. It ripped my life apart. Flatwood and I ran together. He was my best friend right up until the second I decided to banish him. Now he's dead to me, but sometimes, when I dream about the old days, we're still raising hell together.

I know I should back down from Sancho, but I can't. I've never been very good at letting things be. "I cut Joey Flatwood loose, and he and I were friends. Imagine what I'd do to a shitbreath old pusher like you."

"Now Ben—" Danny says, but stops when the big fella and the man to his left, both of them built like fire-hydrants, get up from their seats. We're trained to defuse situations, but I never liked Sancho, and I never liked his bar. And right now, I just don't feel like defusing.

"You're what's wrong with this rez, Sancho," I say. "If it was up to me I'd dump you and your drunk fuck friends out in the middle of the flats then come back here and burn this place to the ground."

When I get in Sancho's face he backs down, even though he's a good foot taller than me. He wasn't lying when he said he cared about his business, such as it is. But the big fella and his friend don't back down. They're the type to get liquored up at ten in the morning hoping for something like this to go down. The type who think Navajo cops aren't real cops. The type who think Indians shouldn't police other Indians. There are a lot of people that think like these two, and for them, this is payday.

The quiet one decks me first. I shoulda known. It's

always the quiet one. To my credit, I do stay on my feet. I'm small, but I'm wiry. I can bend. He damn near knocks me to the floor, but I pop back up like a toy and jack him once in the throat while I reach for my stick. He clutches his neck, and I flip my baton from its holster. Sancho is screaming something in Navajo that I know I should understand, but everything starts to spin and I don't recognize this type of spin. I've been hit plenty of times, even knocked out a time or two, and I know that spin. That's a suck-the-world-out-from-under-you spin where one second you're on your feet and the next you're on your face. This time it's sort of like when you stand up too fast, but worse. Like if you stood up too fast with a hangover and a sack of sand around your neck. There's a high-pitched ringing in my head. It's so loud I feel like it's coming from my face where he popped me. In my daze I think that maybe if I cover my face it'll mute the sound, so I do. I almost fall over, but I steady myself on a bar stool.

Under normal circumstances I'd probably be in for an ass kicking, hitching up like that in the middle of a fight like I need a tap out and a glass of water, but I've got Danny Ninepoint with me. By the time I shake the spins from my head, Joe and his quiet, sucker-punching friend are sprawled out on the floor, and Danny is pulsing one fist like it's just warming up and pulling his long black hair back around with the other.

"You alright, Dejooli?" he asks, and I can tell he's none too happy with me either.

"Yeah, just...wasn't expecting that."

"Maybe you should have," he says, and it's a reprimand and it stings, still, even after six years. But the good thing about Danny is that's where it ends. I try to straighten up, but the buzzing lingers and Danny must see it on my face.

"Watch the door," he says. "I'll write all this up."

I nod, grateful for some air. I hadn't noticed it before, but Sancho's smells like sulfur. Which is fitting, I suppose.

Outside I wave away a few of the rig monkeys fresh off the night shift looking for a drink, and they grumble but leave all the same and wait in the shadows for us to finish up. For some reason the smell is slow in going away, and maybe it's the adrenaline, or the knock to the head, but everything around me is intensely bright. The ruts in the dirt are sharp and clean, the rust on the cars looks like rich mud. The dirt-spackled yellow of the tenement houses seems saturated, almost like it's glowing. When the fall sun breaks from the clouds, I can barely feel the heat it gives, but it flashes like a bomb of light. I cover my eyes and I turn away until it's cloudy again. When I turn back, a crow sits on top of our squad car, on the light array, and it's staring right at me.

The Navajo have a rhyme and reason for every living thing under the sun, and I'm going to be honest with you, I forget most of them. And if you were to point out a crow on any given day and ask me what it *means* I'd look at you like you're a lunatic. But this crow is different. This thing is massive, almost as tall as the driver's side window, and the flashing hazard lights don't faze it at all. Its eyes glisten black, then yellow, black then yellow, in time with the lights, and as it shifts in the light I see a peculiar coloring, almost like it's striped in dark red underneath the ink black of its outer feathers. I realize I'm expecting it to do something, like talk to me, or point the way to an ancient secret with its bony beak. Instead it takes a huge shit on the squad car, then squawks once and flies away just as Danny walks out of the door. He walks out alone. The fire behind his eyes is calmed. His face is wide and smooth and unknowable once more. Sort of like the Chaco flats.

"Can't help but notice you didn't arrest anyone," I say, resisting the urge to massage my temples.

"If we arrested every drunk Navajo we came across we'd have paperwork out the ass. You know this."

"How about every drunk Navajo who assaults a cop? How 'bout that, Danny? In a sane world that guy is in jail."

Danny Ninepoint gives me that flat gaze that says I still don't understand. I'm not sure how I still can't understand after six years, but I somehow don't. I'm trying, but I keep not understanding.

"Sancho's run that bar for almost twenty years now."

"So?"

"So you tell me what happens to guys like the big fella and all his drunk friends when they get their stipends and show up at Sancho's only to find we've shut it down because some boozebag swung at a cop. I booked the big guy once before on a disturbance call because he was hopped up on paint thinner. I let him out of the tank the next morning, and he asks for a ride right here. These are the type of guys who ask cops for rides to bars, Ben. I'd rather they be Sancho's problem."

I see his point, but I'm not willing to concede it yet. "And the dead man? We just gonna let that one slide too?"

Danny looks away, and for a split second I think he's gonna say yes. But then he shakes his head.

"Of course not. I reported him to IHS. They'll give us the autopsy. I know what you're thinking, but Sancho isn't a pusher. He's an asshole, but he's not a pusher. He's not lying when he says he wants to keep his business. He's not stupid. This place is his life."

I know Danny doesn't mean to bring up Flatwood.

Danny doesn't hold it over me like the rest of the rez. It was Danny who told me to stick to my guns in the whole mess, to see it through, to take the stand against Joey. But it still stings.

"Look, the point is this is just what it looks like. That old gambler probably lost a bit too much at Wapati, went to a place he knows, Sancho or one of these guys forgot to check the back, and he settled in for one last kick. That's it. No need to get anybody arrested."

I still don't feel right about the whole thing, but my head is killing me and the place smells like a million matches, so I nod. Danny claps me on the back with his bowl of a hand. In the car, the radio buzzes from dispatch, crackles a code, and waits for a response.

"C'mon, we got shit to do," Danny says.

On the drive out I look for the crow. I see a lot of crows, but I don't see the one from before. I think I'd recognize that one if I saw it again, even at a glance.

2

BEN DEJOOLI

The rest of the day I'm thinking about Sancho's and that dead gambler. Danny and I go on a few more calls after lunch—routine stuff, a minor wreck outside of Wapati between an uninsured beater and some poor family in a minivan who cut through Chaco on their way to Farmington up north. We drove down along the floodplain to make sure it was all clear, meaning no tweekers or squatters. Sometimes people think the rains are done by this time in the fall, but we usually get one or two more big ones before the end of October, and they'll sweep that entire flood channel clean in a second. Dirt, debris, animals, people, all of it.

The whole time we're making rounds I want to bring up Sancho's, but I know Danny is done with it. He's old school. After he files a thing away in his mind, it's over. He's also seen a lot more dead Navajo than me. But it's more than just the OD. It's the whole scene back there. It was bad all around. The drunk and the dead and the smell of burning. Nobody should spend their last seconds on this earth holed up on the floor of Sancho's back room. And then there was the crow. And how I almost pitched over. On my drive home after our shift, some guy catches me spacing out at a stoplight and honks. I'm thinking about how palsied the gambler looked, like he was clawing at the needle with his last breath, and how sad it was that all the guy had to his name was a Wapati jacket, dull gold and dirty. Nothing at all in his pockets, no rings, no necklaces. Not even a shitty bead bracelet. Nothing.

I can feel my eye swelling up where the quiet one sucker-punched me. That'll be a fun little reminder of how I punked out when it counted, staring at me in the mirror for a few weeks. This is one of those days you should try to put behind you as soon as you clock out, but it just won't leave me.

The way I've been talking about the run-down tenements and shacks on the fringe of Chaco, you may think that where I live is a world away. You'd be wrong. My home is one half of a split duplex a quarter mile north of the police station. I live there with my father and my grandmother, which is pretty standard around here. People live with their families under one roof their entire lives. Believe it or not, with just the three of us there's a lot of space. We each have our own room, and there's a small kitchen and a yard out back that we share with the neighbors. Just one bathroom, but by now we all know the routine and nobody bumps into anybody else. In fact, it's downright spacious considering that when we first moved in, back before I joined NNPD, there were five of us. Back then it was my sister Ana and me in my room, and Mom and Dad in theirs, and my grandmother content in the small storage room off of the kitchen. But then I lost my sister, and because I lost my sister I lost my mom, although in a different way. She still stops by every now and then, but for the most part she's long gone. She lives in a studio apartment in Albuquerque now and has a job as a caretaker there. You could say that she banished herself.

It's late by now, and since the night quickens even earlier in the fall, it's nearly full on dark by the time I get home. But it's a false dark. You can't trust the early dark of fall. You want to think the day is over, but it's not.

As soon as I get in, I get a beer from the icebox. I'm not even going to try to hide it. Gam would know anyway, because she always knows. Dad's different. I could eat dinner with an icepack plastered to my face and my father wouldn't notice until it was brought to his attention.

I'm sitting in the kitchen eating a reheated mole stew and holding a cold beer to my puffy eye when Gam comes in. She mostly cooks and knits these days, and the kitchen is her domain. She seems to know any time anyone crosses the small threshold she's carved out for herself there. When she sees me with the beer pressed to my face, she pauses. Her face darkens, then she sees that I'm eating lukewarm mole on rice and takes it from me, shooing me out of her space. She gestures for me to sit at the small table across from the refrigerator while she puts the stew on the stove top and takes a smoked chicken breast from the refrigerator. She shreds the breast with two forks while the sauce heats and then adds the chicken. All the while, she's quiet, waiting for me to talk, but I don't feel like talking, not least of all because she makes me do it in Navajo, and despite her best efforts, my Navajo has always sucked. She refuses to speak English. I have a hunch that she's fluent, but if you don't speak Navajo to her, she won't answer you. She stirs the stew and stares at me with that benign, blank expression her generation has. The look that says they've got all the time in the world to sit right there waiting for you. She's small—the top half of her body barely clears the counter—and her long black hair has gone entirely grey, but that look is still strong.

I sigh and set the can down, then I crack it open and take a big swig.

"Bad day at work," I say, in Navajo. She nods and plates the stew and sets it in front of me.

"Did you catch them?" she asks. I don't know how to explain the Sancho's situation in English, much less in Navajo, so I just grunt and give a weak nod. She watches me placidly, and I know she can see right through me, but just then Dad comes home and she stands again, ready to dish up another plate.

"I'm going to bed," he says in Navajo, waving her off. He slurs just a bit, and I can see Gam's slight frown.

"You should eat dinner," Gam shouts.

"I'm not hungry right now," he says quietly, and softly closes the door behind him. Gam covers the stew and sets it back in the refrigerator. Dad will eat it later tonight when he pads around the house, usually from one in the morning to three or four. He's up every night at the witching hours. Has been ever since Ana disappeared. Most of the time he just watches television, but every now and then I catch him out back where Ana used to play. There's a pile of rocks in a little sandbox there that she loved to stack and arrange. Mostly he just sits and stares at that, too, like it was the television, although a couple times I've seen him talking to it like it's a shrine of some sort and not a six-year-old pile of rocks. He looks hunched these days, and since he's as short as I am it doesn't do him any favors. He's been drinking more, too. Gam and I know it, even though we haven't said anything yet. He only works part time at the hardware store south of the welcome center, but he's gone the whole work

day. He's not the type to go to Sancho's, but he's probably at some place just a step up. Which isn't saying much.

Gam looks down at the ground and says everything without speaking a word. Oren Dejooli is her son, and she is embarrassed by him. She never forgave my mother for leaving him and still refuses to be in the same room with her on the rare occasions she comes through the reservation. Gam's generation took everything on the cheek and kept plodding, especially as it concerned their husbands. The idea of leaving everything and running away to the city like Mom did is foreign to her, but more and more I think she's beginning to understand how strange Dad has become.

I made a conscious decision not to dwell on Ana. Every day I tell myself to file it away. Do like Ninepoint does. You can see how well that's worked. Like talking to Gam in English. You can say whatever you want, but you're not gonna get any results. Over the six years since she went missing her name has become an all-encompassing thing that hangs over the house and follows us around every day. Our lives have been shattered and then rearranged into pre-Ana and post-Ana. The line that separates them is Ana, too. She's everywhere you look around here, but nowhere to be found.

I want to keep Gam around. The thought of her shuffling back into her room to pick up her knitting strikes me as unbearably sad just now.

"*You know Sancho's?*" I ask her. She frowns and makes a spitting motion. She knows it all right. Gam knows just about everywhere on the rez and just about everyone. And their parents. She speaks of people in terms of 'the kid of so-and-so," or, more likely, "the no-good kid of so-and-so."

"*A guy died there last night. An old Navajo. He was always at*

Wapati, or walking along the roads by Wapati in a gold jacket. He was a..." I struggle to find the words, but Gam finds them for me.

"Alone," she says, and a brief flash of genuine sadness bows her face. It throws me for a second. She says something in Navajo that I don't catch completely, but I think it's an old prayer. Something about a last visit and the end of a journey.

"You knew him?" I ask. Already she's composed herself again, and she waves her bony hand dismissively.

"He was old, like me. Old people know each other in small towns. That's all. How did he die?"

"Drugs," I say, in English. I don't know the Navajo word for drugs. I'm not sure there is a Navajo word for drugs. Gam pauses in her stirring of the pot. She furrows her brow, then shakes her head.

"No," she says, simply.

"No?" I ask, incredulous. Gam shakes her head once, sharply. I laugh. I can't help it. I'd spent this whole day trying to convince myself that there was nothing wrong with an old timer overdosing in the backroom at Sancho's, and I'd basically done it, too, by the time I walked in the house, so it annoys me that she throws open that door in my mind again. Especially when there's nothing I can do about it. My laugh sounds harsh and hollow. Gam frowns at me.

"I guess you're pretty sure of that," I say in English, not expecting a response, not wanting one.

"Die at Sancho's?" she says, stirring the pot again. *"No. Not him."*

"Oh yeah?" I ask, fully switched to English now. "And where was he 'supposed' to die, then?"

Gam watches me calmly.

"Where is a man supposed to die?" I ask.

"At home."

"He lived out of his camper, Gam. He had no home."

Gam shakes her small, round head in soft rebuke. Her bun flops.

"The gambler's home is the Arroyo," she says.

The Arroyo is just like it's advertised. It's a wash at the far end of the floodplain, due south of where Danny and I swept through today. It's also the prime car camping spot on the reservation. If you live out of your car in this country, there's a good chance you'll get robbed if you're on your own. A sleeping man in a car is a prime target. Lock your doors and they'll smash your windows. If the tweekers and the drunks see something valuable inside, it doesn't matter if you're in it or not. If you're a camper, it's best to stick together. 'Course, it's best not to sleep in your car at all, but for most of these folks that's not a choice, so they park in a half-circle around the top of the Arroyo. It's gotten to the point where it's become a neighborhood in its own right.

Danny said when he first started that Sani, the chief of police, wanted them gone. Said they were unsightly, and ramshackle neighborhoods often come with ramshackle "businesses," most of which aren't remotely legal. When an old camper blew up and took a pair of Navajo with it, two more casualties of the meth businesses, Sani told Danny and his partner at the time to clear them all out. The two of them blew into the Arroyo like a whirlwind and screamed and thumped cars (and a few people) with their sticks. The cars left for a day and then pulled back in the next night. That's the thing about neighborhoods on wheels. They're tough to catch.

"The Arroyo is nobody's home," I tell Gam.

"The Arroyo," she says again, nodding. End of discussion. She picks up her bowl of stew, goes to her corner chair and

sets it carefully down on a pull-out tray. She takes a bite, then she picks up her knitting. It's the beginning of a blanket, and it's gonna be a beautiful one, too. As I watch her, I see her hands shaking, and not for the first time I wonder if that blanket is ever going to get finished.

That night I don't sleep. I sort of fade in and out of consciousness, but I wouldn't call it sleeping. When I'm alone in my bed I realize that the ringing in my head that started at Sancho's never really left me. It was perched behind my forehead and murmuring to me the whole time; it just took complete quiet to notice. Every time I start to drift, the sulfur smell comes back to me and I blink myself awake, scrunching my nose. My eye feels tight and puffy, and my head throbs in time with my heartbeat. I already know I'm getting the brawler's wink.

I'm not sure exactly what makes me shoot out of bed, but some time near midnight I come around and find I'm already standing by the window, panting, with my heart in my throat. After my blood slows and my eyes adjust, I see my dad standing outside in the moonlight, staring at Ana's shrine. There's also a skittering on the roof. My first thought is it's a squirrel my dad somehow disturbed on his nightly excursions about the house, but on second listen this thing sounds too big. There's a sharp tap, and then I hear the explosive fluttering of wings. Big wings. Crow wings. I look up and out the window and strain my eyes to scan the sky, but the moon has thrown everything above ground into inky black relief. It's as if the bird, or whatever it is, is absorbed into the fabric of the night as soon as it leaves the roof. I turn back to Dad. He doesn't seem to notice anything but the rocks in front of him.

I sit back down on the bed, take some deep breaths, and listen hard for the ringing. I think it's gone, which is a relief, but in its place is a strange quiet. And the quiet is made worse by the fact that my dad is in the back yard sitting on the dry grass and staring at a cairn my sister made six years ago like it's a totem pole rooted to the secrets of her vanishing. I remember when Ana built that thing. She attached no significance to it. She was messing around in the back yard, digging up weeds looking for "fossils." She plopped some rocks on top of each other on her way to the next door of her imagination, the way nine-year-old girls do. Dad has made them far heavier than they were ever meant to be. After another fifteen minutes of listening to this silence, I give up, throw on an under-shirt, and go downstairs. I move by the light of the muted television, not wanting to wake Gam, and I sit at the table again, drink an entire glass of water, and stare at my father, trying to make sense of him. The stew pot is empty and meticulously washed. Dad is a fastidious man. He doesn't want to disturb anyone with what he's dealing with at midnight on the back lawn. He doesn't want to disturb us with Ana. He knows each of us has our own Ana to deal with, and he's a hardline Navajo in that. His problems are his own.

Gam and I know he goes outside like this. Gam thinks it's far more normal than I do, and she thinks the fact that I find this type of ritualistic meditation strange is proof of a creeping white influence. Usually I just let him alone with his grief. But tonight I'm not getting back to sleep, I already know it, so I slide open the door and step outside. The porch light catches my motion and flicks on, and Dad is startled. He jumps up and backs away from the light. He doesn't meet my eye.

"The rocks saying anything to you tonight?" I ask.

I think my dad was expecting some sort of scolding, so

when he hears the soft tone of my voice, he steps forward and looks up at me.

"Stranger things have happened," he says. "But no. They are quiet."

"Rocks can't tell you where Ana is," I say, and then, because I think the day still has its fingers in me, and because somewhere I feel that fucking crow still watching me, I say, "Flatwood might have been able to, but he's gone now. Is that why you're out here? Is it because of me? Because I got rid of him? Because he was never going to help us, Dad. Whatever he knew he took with him when he was banished."

Dad seems to snap out of his fog, and he shakes his head, his face imploring. "Is that what you think? That I'm out here blaming you?"

"The thought has crossed my mind, yeah. Everyone else blames me for Flatwood. And I've had a shitty day. Another day in which people who have no idea what happened that night somehow hate me for agreeing to testify against the guy who abducted my sister. Like I'm the bad guy."

Dad steps forward into the full flush of the floodlight, and I can see just how pitted and hollow his eyes are. "Not me, Ben. Never me. Do you understand me?" His eyes still have a touch of liquor to them. He grabs me by the shoulders for a moment, and I'm struck by how much we look alike. He has the same sharp features that I do and the same softly sloping eyes. It's just that he looks hollowed out, and he's shrinking. It's hard to watch. Some part of me thinks a son should never grow taller than his father.

Dad turns his head back to the cairn and drops his hands from my shoulders. "I was the one who left him alone with her. I was the one who stepped out for a quick drink. I was the one who thought I needed a drink because she'd been in the hospital for nearly a month and it was draining on me. I was the one who dropped my guard."

"Dad—"

"—and I was her father, Ben. You did your duty. In front of the court and the elders, you stood like a man. All you did was tell them the truth. I was the one who failed her."

"Nobody failed anybody, Dad. Joey was practically a member of the family. Things that bad don't happen because you step out for a drink. Things that bad happen whether you step out or not."

Dad walks back to the cairn and moves out of the way so the light washes over it. He cocks his head at it like an old dog.

"I think I see her, sometimes," he says.

"So do I. Every day."

"But only when I watch a thing until my eyes stop watching. Only when I drift. That's why I come out here. Because I can drift."

I understand where he's coming from, but I also think the whisky I can still smell on his breath might be helping with his "drifting." It's not that I'm not sympathetic. It's just that if I kept hanging on to Ana the way he does, I'd have driven myself insane by now. Sometimes I wonder if that's not the route Dad's heading down, and sometimes I wonder if he's not doing it on purpose.

"Are you gonna come inside?" I ask.

"No, you go in. This is my time."

So I leave him. But I don't go back to bed either. I spend the next hour listening for a bird on my roof, and at one in the morning I feel more awake and restless than I did outside talking to Dad. Whenever I don't know exactly what's bothering me, I tackle the first thing that I think of, and the first thing I can think of is Gam saying the word *Arroyo* like it was the answer to everything.

I get up, splash some water on my face, throw on another layer of deodorant, and button myself back into my uniform. I strap on my belt and holster my gun and grab my keys and my flat-brimmed hat. Danny Ninepoint would hate me going to the Arroyo alone, but Danny would also hate me waking his ass up at the birth of the morning to chase after a dead man he was over and done with the second we left the bar. So I don't call him.

The road to the Arroyo is winding and barren. It's past Main Street, and past the tenements, and past the fringe, and past the stretch of desert beyond. After a good dust storm, the tracks can sometimes be hard to follow, but I've been here more times than I can count, and I know my way. It's only when I get into the velvet black of the desert at night—when the headlights of my old truck get swallowed up five feet in front of me—that a small part of me wonders if this was a smart thing to do at all, much less alone. And the buzzing begins again. But it's not so bad, and I've come this far already, and I don't think I can stand turning around and finding my dad still staring at a pile of rocks, so I kick into low gear and creep my way out into the desert.

The Arroyo appears in front of me like a shelf on the ocean floor. The drop-off beyond the campers that ring the ledge is steep, and at this hour looks a shade darker than black. In the daylight it's a trash pit, but right now it seems like a swirling door to the worst Chaco has to offer. Almost all of the cars sit silent and cold like boulders, but a handful are lit from within, and I can see shapes shifting about like genies in lamps. Danny and I have been here in the dead hours before. Usually this group knows enough to let a patrolling cop be, but then again, I thought that about the men at Sancho's up until today too.

Already I see blinking eyes peeking out of makeshift curtains like coyotes caught in my headlights. A van nearby starts its engine. That's to warn those still awake that a cop is here. In the daytime they aren't so subtle. It's three honks. Nice that they're considerate to the sleeping vagrants, I suppose.

I'm looking for a memorial of some sort. If the gambler was really a part of the Arroyo, they'll know he's dead by now and will have set up something to mark his passing. They're addicts and drunks here for the most part, but they are a tight community and they watch their own. It's been that way since Gam's time. The Navajo don't like death. Old school Navajo, like many of the folks at the Arroyo, still think death is a thing that's catching, so they'll have cleaned and purified his camping spot and gathered anything he may have left about for burial. It takes me nearly a full pass before I find it.

In the darkness it just looks like an empty spot between camps, but it stands out like a lost tooth and I slow down. When my headlights glint off the small pile in the center of the space, I know I've found the right place. I throw my truck into park and check the perimeter. There's a rusted out camper to the right that's as dark as a cellar closet. To my left is a flatbed truck with a tarp stretched over it. A one man job. But that one man is out in the night leaning against his truck and smoking a cigarette. The cherry burns like a demon's eye in the blackness. He stares me down as I hop out. I can't tell if he's being surly or if he's bored. Around here it's most likely both.

I close the door to my truck gently, keeping one eye on the smoker. He's dressed in a faded Cleveland Indians baseball jersey and tear-off gym slacks, and he's swimming in them. He's not wearing shoes, and his head lolls a bit toward the ground, like he's watching me out of the top of his eyes.

"Officer," he says. He doesn't sound condescending, but he doesn't sound happy to see me, either. "Funny seeing your kind at this hour."

Guys like this don't worry me. What worries me is if he causes a scene and brings the whole shithole camp down on me. I'm hoping he knows the drill and doesn't want anything more than a late night smoke.

"A man showed up dead today," I say. "He was an Arroyo man. In fact, unless I'm way off, I'd say he lived right here. People knew him as the gambler."

The smoker is silent, but that tells me as much as I need to know.

"You're holding vigil," I say.

"I am. Not that it would matter to an apple like you."

The Navajo who live at the Arroyo are probably the worst off of any of us, but they're fierce nationalists. You get some of the most hardline Navajos living out of vans on the edge of the desert out here, and they stick to the old ways. They respect the purification periods and observe the holy days and practice the chant ways, and they look down on anyone who doesn't and still calls themselves a Navajo. I try not to take it personally when he calls me an apple. I think he'd call any Indian who didn't live hand-to-mouth right next to him an apple. It means red on the outside, white on the inside.

"His name was Oka Chalk," he says. "He'd been here longer than any of us. He only became the gambler because of fuckers like you and the shit you bring into our land."

A lot of people lump NNPD in with tribal politics and the dealings of the council and the elders. Never mind that we have nothing to do with Wapati or the finances of this rez. We're just tasked with trying to keep it together.

"Easy," I say. "I'm just trying to figure out what happened to the man.""Seems clear. He died," says the smoker, staring blackly at me.

"Yeah, I got that." I stare right back at him. "Thing is, what's a veteran Arroyo man doing dying like a common smackhead?"

This throws him. His glower cracks just a bit. "Smack?" he asks.

"Yeah. Smack. The gamb...Oka Chalk died in his own puke propped against the backroom of a dive bar near the fringe. So I'ma ask you something, seeing as you're on vigil and all and that probably means you and him were friends. Does that sound like the guy you knew?"

The smoker takes a big drag, and it washes over his head in the white of the moon.

"Smack?" he asks again, and I know he's speaking to himself. And I already know that's not how the gambler died. I also know I'll never get a straight answer from this guy. They have a code around here, and it doesn't include working with "apple" cops like me. Instead, I take a look at Chalk's camp site.

It looks like the gambler lived his life out in a fifteen-foot square of dirt where he parked his car. I look out beyond the Arroyo drop-off and try to give the dead man the benefit of the doubt. I say to myself that there was probably some beauty here, in the unfiltered sunsets and the endless plains, but I can't sell it to myself. Right now this patch of dirt reminds me a lot of the prison cells we have down at the station. And at least there you have plumbing.

There are tokens in the center of his spot, left by the Arroyo community. Herbs and flowers mostly, and piñon and juniper branches. Things meant to purify the space. There are also other gifts with no Navajo significance at all. A carved wooden whistle and a tattered stuffed rabbit. There are folded notes, as well, and a collection of coins. The tokens form a big pile, about a foot high, in the dead center of the spot. I get the feeling that the gambler was well liked here. I turn back to the smoker with a new appreciation. I see now that the man looks bereaved. And here I was about to come out swinging. I decide to come clean to the guy.

"Look. Something about this doesn't sit well with me. About this whole thing. I don't know what yet, but I'm trying to figure it out. All I know is he shouldn't have died that way."

The smoker watches me for a good fifteen seconds in silence. Then he speaks.

"He used to give me a spare can of beer every now and then. That's all. But around here, that's enough. I said I'd hold vigil because I think he was a man worth it. I don't know nothing about him more than that."

I nod. Sounds about right. Sounds like the end of a poorly placed hunch.

"But I do know this," the smoker says, and it sounds like he was debating telling me this thing, this one thing, from the second I said I was out here trying to place the gambler on the right side of the books. "He started this token pile," the smoker says.

This throws me.

"What? You mean he knew he was gonna die?"

"Don't know nothin' bout that. Just know the last time I saw him, after he pulled out of his spot in that van of his, he got out, walked back over here, and set down the first token. Then he left."

I cross my arms and turn to the token pile. I walk over to it and kneel down. I gently move pieces of the pile, and the smoker doesn't seem to mind, so I go digging. I set each piece in a row to the left of the pile, flowers, beaded jewelry, bits of pounded leather, coins, braided strips of hair, until I get to the very bottom, and there I find a totem.

A totem is a powerful thing for an Indian, especially an old-timer, for whom these things generally mean more than for your average young buck. The Navajo believe that a person and an animal can be connected and that connection is unique and powerful. We don't carve any totem poles or anything like that, but if a Navajo believes strongly enough that they are connected to an animal, sometimes they carve it out of rock or stone and make it into a totem that they keep on them, usually in a pouch by their side. Different animals mean different things, but the connection is always personal and symbolic. I feel like I used to see more totem pouches on people when I was young. I even thought of making a totem myself when I was a kid. I wanted a bear. The bear is popular because it stands for power and courage and great strength, all things a little boy wants. The problem is, you don't choose your animal. Your animal chooses you. I've never seen a bear in my life, and I don't much care to, and I'll be the first to tell you I don't exactly have "great strength," so there went that.

If a Navajo has a totem, he never parts from it, which makes it strange that the gambler would leave his behind. And the gambler's totem is a crow. A solid turquoise crow, about the size of a walnut, and beautifully detailed. The marbling of the turquoise makes it look like it's in mid-flight even as it sits in the dirt in front of me.

The crow is a strange animal in Navajo lore. It's not that the crow has negative connotations or anything, but it's not exactly the type of animal you see carved into totems. In fact, I'd never seen a crow totem in my life. The crow stands for spiritual strength, but it's also a symbol of change. In Navajo stories, the crow is often tricky, and sometimes he's actually a shape-shifter. You never quite know where he's coming from. And if we count the tapping on the roof, which I do, this is the third encounter with our tricky friend I've had in the past twenty-four hours. I'm not exactly a spiritual man, but I'm not blind, either. I look up at the smoker, who watches me calmly. The buzzing in my head gets louder.

"It's a crow," I say, lamely. He nods.

"Don't touch it," he says, but he doesn't need to worry. You don't touch another man's totem. It's wrong. Even I know that.

I carefully bury it once more and then stand, too quickly. I stagger for a few steps until I right myself on my truck. The smoker is still watching me, and an image of him peering, cigarette limp in his mouth, spins around my head. The smell is back again, but it's stronger, almost like plastic burning. I gag with the intensity of it.

The smoker says something to me, but I'm holding on to my truck for dear life and I'm not listening anyway because all of a sudden I see thousands of crows and I realize that the night sky has been a patchwork of oil-black feathers all along. They seem to wave gently like heat coming up from tar on the road. The leather and bones and coins in the pile seem to dance, like the crow totem is trying to work its way out. I look up at the smoker to see what he thinks of all this, and he's still trying to talk to me. His brow is furrowed, but his words sound like gibberish. I have an irrational urge to grab the crow and steal it for my own, an abhorrent thing for a Navajo to do to another Navajo, especially one who has just left this world, but right at this moment it doesn't seem strange at all. It seems right. My vision is constricting, but still the crow calls to me, like light shining through the holes in a black button.

And in a brief moment of clarity I realize I'm going to pass out, and this is about the last place in the world a guy should pass out, especially a cop. I try to get into my truck, but my body is floating away from me bit by bit. I paw at the com on my shoulder, click it on, and mutter into it.

"Danny. Danny, I'm at the Arroyo. Danny, I need..." What do I need? Whatever is coming from my mouth is distant and muffled and certainly doesn't sound like my voice. I drop my hand from the com. The white noise that comes back from it floods over me, and I drop to the ground. My head bounces off the runner of my truck, but I'm too far gone to care.

Then everything is black.

3

CAROLINE ADAMS

I always get slammed with work at the end of a night shift. Like, half an hour before I'm supposed to go home. And it takes all of the Nurse-Fu I've accumulated over the past two years working here not to rip my hair out. It's not even the late admission itself, or that it's an ER overflow. We get overflow admissions all the time here on the oncology floor. Albuquerque General is constantly overflowing, and it's usually the same people spilling in and out. No, what gets to me most is the cutesy way my nurse manager says it: *Car-o-line, we got one more for ya!* As if she was out looking for four leaf clovers on my behalf. I try very hard not to express disappointment. I know better than that. I feel like she watches me for it. Mary Ellen is the kind of manager who swears by the power of a positive attitude even as she pisses everyone off. Or maybe it's just me. Although I don't think so, because I've seen other nurses scowl after her, some doctors, too, although they're doctors and they can get away with it. I tried to bring it up once in the break room, but I didn't have the words to explain what bothers me so much, and I felt like the other girls there were waiting expectantly for some ammo to use against me. So I talked about how I felt like I'd gained ten pounds since starting night shift, which set off a round of the usual *Oh my God I know*s and brought us back to safe ground. Sometimes I don't know about this floor. For nurses, a lot of my co-workers can be quite uncaring. Exhibit A is that I have no friends here. But again, maybe that's just me.

If our ER gets a late-night rush, it's usually because of the Navajo. I'm not being racist here or anything—nurses don't have time to be racist. It's just a fact. And if we get an overflow case and it's a Navajo, they usually give it to me. Maybe they think I'm better with Navajo patients because I spend one day a week working at the Chaco Health Center inside Chaco Rez and should therefore have some sort of connection with the Navajo. I have no such thing. I've tried, but the Navajo are a close people. Or maybe I'm a bad nurse. I waste a lot of time obsessing over things like this, in case you can't tell. And since we're being honest, I think I might as well tell you that the reason I work one day a week at CHC is because it's a condition of the government grant that put me through nursing school. I find it rewarding, don't get me wrong, but it's not like I came out of school on some crusade to help the Navajo. That's just what ended up happening.

When Mary Ellen tells me about the new admission, I'm already taking care of one Navajo who happens to be detoxing from alcohol, and it's not going well for either of us. Alcohol withdrawal is a mess. Detoxing from opiates or stimulants can be bad, but going cold turkey won't kill a drug addict. Detoxing from alcohol can kill you, so we have this step-down system that tapers the patient over a long period of time in which they tend to threaten your life and spit in your face.

I don't blame patients for what they say when they're detoxing. I know they're not in their right minds. I try not to take it personally when grizzled old men with purple noses call me a cunt or tell me I'm a waste of time and to get the fucking doctor. I'm getting better about it, but for a while I stayed up late wondering if I *was* a waste of time. Or, more specifically, If I'd wasted my time becoming a nurse. Those were early jitters. I hardly have those any more. Still, when you have to have the CNAs restrain the patient and strap a face-mask on the guy to keep him from spitting at you while you take his vitals, you do wonder. And this guy is taking it to such extremes I feel like I might start laughing.

"Any tingling in the hands or feet?" I ask.

"Cunt."

"How about your stomach? Do you still feel nauseous?"

"You cunt!"

"If you have any appetite at all it'd be really good if we could get something in your stomach."

"Yoouuuuuuuuuuu..." he winds up, puffing his chest out like a mangy goose. "Cuuuuunnnnnnnnnnntttt!" he finishes, whooshing out like a whoopee cushion. The CNA in there with me, a big Mexican woman named Inez, smiles kindly at me.

"Well," she says, "at least we know there's no shortness of breath."

I let out a sharp laugh before I can cover my mouth, which sets him off in a string of babbling. This is the kind of laugh that threatens to go manic, so I have to excuse myself from the room and take some deep breaths. Naturally that's when the attending doctor walks by. I have a moment of panic when I see the long white coat and here I am leaning against the wall trying to keep it together, either about to laugh or about to cry. But then I realize it's Doctor Bennet and I relax again, but only a little. He's a floor favorite, but he's still a doctor.

Doctor Bennet is a tall, thin redhead. I'm a small girl myself, and I'm pretty sure we have the same waist size. He's a foot taller than me, too, so I think I have him beat in the thigh and calf muscle mass as well. He wears well-fitted slacks when he's attending, and trim white shirts with thin ties of every color. I'm not sure I've ever seen him repeat a tie, which is impressive, and every one of them is as thin as a ruler. A thick tie would look like a dinner napkin on him. He's holding a medication cup between his thumb and fore-finger, and he holds it out to me.

"Caroline," Bennet says, in his formal way, although he does smile. "I was glad to see you on the schedule tonight. This is from the pharmacy. Benzos for your detox patient."

I take the cup and thank him, bobbing my head wearily.

"How's the night been?" he asks.

"Cuuunnnnnnnnnnt!" comes a throaty reply from inside the room. I blush and reach over to close the door softly. I look about and see that two nurses at the nearby charting desk are staring at us.

"About like that," I say.

Doctor Bennet doesn't laugh, but his eyes do. "I see," he says, putting his hands on his flat hips.

"And I have another admission," I say. "I don't think I'll be leaving any time soon."

Bennet checks his watch. He knows night shift switches over soon and that if I haven't admitted my last patient I haven't done any of my charting. And that means I'll be here well into the morning.

"Tell you what," he says, and he gently plucks the medication cup back from me. "I'll take care of our friend here. You get to your admission."

I could hug him. Then I blush again because of how totally out of line that would be. Wouldn't the girls at the charting desk like that? God knows what kind of firestorm that would set off. Thankfully I'm already sweaty and red from the general work day, so the blush blends right in. I give him a breathy thanks, and if he sees how desperately relieved I am, he doesn't let on. He glances briefly at the pills, nods at me, and just walks right into the room.

"Now that's quite enough of that," he says, and his voice is hard and final, and it works. The patient shuts up. Another thing about Doctor Bennet. He may look like a reed, but he's got an incredible bedside manner. He sets patients right. Sometimes that means he cracks down on them and sometimes that means he's gentle, but either way it's always what they need.

But I'm already gone, down the hall, into the next room and to my admit. And not a second too soon, either, because when I knock and open the door he's already sitting up and probing his IV line, looking to pull. It's a miracle the bed alarm didn't go off. That might just have been the straw that broke the nurse's back.

"Whoa, whoa! What are you doing?" I ask, a little too desperately. "Let's just sit still for a second, shall we?"

I skid over and grab his arm and check that the line is secure, and I'm so flustered that it takes me a minute to realize that he hasn't said anything at all. I look up at him and realize he's as surprised to find me holding his arm as I am to find him trying to pull his IV line. I can tell he's a Navajo, and what with the late hour and all the nastiness with my last patient, I brace myself for more trouble, but it never comes.

"Sorry," he says, and he takes his fingers off of his line. His face is smooth and dark, not ravaged or ruddy like some of the Navajo that I come across, and his eyes are clear and deeply brown. The kind of brown that is at the bottom of a jar of honey. I suppose *eye* is more appropriate, since one is wide and alert and the other looks like it caught a baseball. He's also young. My age. Maybe younger. And short. Shorter than me. But cut in that stringy, athletic way. And by now I realize I'm staring.

"...It's just, I don't think I need to be here," he says. "I didn't want to bother anyone. Thought I might just slip out."

He has a touch of the Navajo accent, the careful emphasis on each word, and I can't help but smile. This smile is nowhere near the manic smile I was fighting down in the hallway outside. This one relaxes my face.

"Slip out? You can't really 'slip out' of a hospital, I'm afraid. We have to sign you in and out. Plus, you just got here."

"I feel fine, now, really," he says. And now that he's not going anywhere, I pick up his chart from the foot of the bed.

"Ben Dejooli," I say. "Navajo?" Whenever I see a patient uncomfortable, I start talking. Sometimes they don't even answer me, but it does settle them more often than not. If anything, it's simply better than the sterile white noise of a hospital. "What's Dejooli mean, if you don't mind me asking? I work at the Chaco Health Clinic once a week. I like to hear about Navajo names."

This stills him, and he looks at me with a newfound interest.

"It means 'gone.'"

"Gone?"

"Well, it means 'went upward.' But things in Navajo have a lot of different meanings. I think it's more like 'gone.'"

He seems distant all of a sudden, and I wonder if I

screwed up by going down this line of conversation, so I bring it back to the task at hand.

"Says here you lost consciousness on the reservation. A Daniel Ninepoint called in the ambulance, and when you were non-responsive they bypassed the clinic and brought you straight here."

Ben looks down, and I can see that he's ashamed. A lot of Navajo men are ashamed of illness. They associate it with weakness.

"I woke up in the ambulance. Tried to get them to turn around. They wouldn't listen. I'm fine. I don't need to be here. I just passed out is all. Haven't you ever passed out?"

"Not that I can remember," I say. But the answer is no. I would remember. I remember everything. And I would be such a hypochondriac about it that I'd probably check myself into the hospital as soon as I woke up. "It's most likely nothing, but we still need to check some things. See if you concussed yourself. I see you have a black eye."

"That's from before. So Danny found me?" he asks, grimacing.

"Don't know about that, but he called the ambulance."

"Great," he says, shaking his head.

"I take it he's not a friend of yours."

"He's my partner."

Wonderful, I think. *He's gay. Naturally.*

"I'm a cop. He won't be too happy with me. I wasn't supposed to be where I was when I passed out."

I blink. *A cop.* Why am I so relieved he has that kind of partner? What is going on here?

"Where was that?" I ask, to keep him talking.

"The Arroyo." He rubs gently at his face and taps softly around his eye. "Never mind. Look, I really need to go. I gotta straighten this out."

I've found that when a patient tries to derail an admit—which happens often because there are a whole litany of questions I'm supposed to ask—it's best just to power through.

"The black eye is from earlier? Before you passed out at the Arroyo?"

"Yeah."

"Is it from a fall?"

"Yeah. I fell into a fist." He says this looking down at his lap, but I laugh. Then it strikes me that he might be offended, so I cut it off with a cough. I'm still working on Navajo humor.

"Well, sometimes concussion symptoms show up late. Did you feel nausea, or light headedness after you were hit?"

"He didn't knock me out," Ben says, a little defensively. "He only got in one punch."

"Sometimes people can lose consciousness for only a second and don't even realize it. Usually there's disorientation and nausea afterwards. "

Ben pauses, and I can tell he's not telling me something. It's very hard to fool a nurse. We may miss things on our own, but we can usually tell if you keep things from us.

"No nausea," he says softly. "But..."

I wait.

"But I was...I don't know. Things got blurry and I couldn't talk, so I sat down for a second. But it cleared."

"And this was before the Arroyo?"

"Yeah. Yesterday morning. It was a rough day." He eyes his uniform, folded, with his belt and badge hanging neatly from the chair nearby. His gun he'll have to get from the checkout desk at the front entrance. He looks uncomfortable, more than just embarrassed. He's swallowing and brushing at nothing on his forehead. He looks up at the hanging bag he's connected to and then down at the bed. He crinkles the sheets, and he starts breathing faster. I've seen this before too. White Coat Syndrome. I think some part of him is terrified of the hospital.

"Listen, Ben, we'll get you out of here as soon as we can, but—"

"Do you smell that?" he asks.

"What?"

"That smell, it's like a...a burning smell. Is something on fire?"

I look around myself and even try a subtle sniff of my armpits while he's ghosting his head back and forth.

"Nothing's burning, Ben. It's okay. You're okay."

I do something I rarely do uninvited, which is step forward and lay a hand on his shoulder. He reaches up and tries to wrap his fingers around my wrist. I'm expecting him to throw my hand away, but when he grips me he just holds on. All the while he's sniffing, moving his head a fraction of an inch and sniffing again. He looks out of the small window as if he's expecting to see someone there, then he blinks several times, and all of a sudden he's under control again. Or at least faking it well. He looks up at me and even manages a shaky smile. He plucks his fingers away and sets his hands in his lap.

"Like I said. Tough day, that's all."

I unclip a small pen-light from my breast pocket and look into his pupils, and he allows it. There is no delayed dilation, no trouble tracking. None of the symptoms of a concussion. But rather than make me feel better, this gives me a cold, clammy feeling. Like water is dripping down my back. I'm an oncology nurse, and two things here raise huge red flags for me. One: he smells a smell that is not there.

Two: when he tried to grab my hand, he missed by a good six inches on his first attempt. Like he was swiping at a missing ladder rung.

"Ben, was that time after you got hit the first time you smelled something burning?"

"I think so. Near enough, anyway."

"How many times have you had to sit down to get your bearings?"

Ben shrugs. "A few. I don't drink as much water as I should, and I think I'm kind of dehydrated—"

"Think with me here. More than twice?"

Ben nods.

"More than five times?"

Ben nods.

"More than ten times?"

Ben thinks, then shrugs. Which might as well be a nod. I swallow.

"It always goes away," he says, but he's eyeing the equipment again and picking lightly at the skin on the back of his hand. He's trying to look around me and out the door.

"Ben...are you alright?" I ask.

His face finds mine and softens. "Yeah, really, I am. I just...I don't like hospitals."

"Not many people do," I say, by way of reassurance, but it comes out sounding condescending, and I shake my head. I'm not normally like this around patients. I keep the second-guessing and endless over-analysis out of the patient rooms. Usually it hits me around three in the morning. Or three in the afternoon. Whenever I'm supposed to be sleeping.

"Sorry. What I mean is that it's normal to feel stressed out in a hospital. It's a proven effect. It's called White Coat Syndrome. It skews a lot of our blood pressure readings."

Ben nods and manages a half smile. I can tell he knows about White Coat and that he also knows what he has is worse, but I don't want to press him. He's eyeing me with this soft, tired, lopsided wink, and it's ludicrously endearing. Probably because he doesn't mean it to be.

"I don't even know your name," he says.

"Caroline."

"Caroline," he says, nodding. "I know you're just doing your job. But I'm fine, and I really want to go. No offense."

When you work on a cancer floor, you see cancer everywhere. Melanoma on arms and backs at the gym, liver cancer in the pallid, red-nosed strangers you pass on the street, lung cancer in the chronic, wet cough of someone next to you in line. You learn to dampen down the desire to smack some medical sense into these people, but the urge never really leaves you once you've worked on an oncology floor. Right now I really, really want to grasp Ben Dejooli by the shoulders and tell him to hell with what he wants. What he needs is to get an MRI immediately, and if he's lucky, it'll say that all he's having are cluster migraines or that it's vertigo or something.

But that's me running away with myself again. That's three a.m. Caroline. If I let her loose, it's all over.

"How would you even get home?"

"I'd take a cab."

"A cab from here to Chaco? You know how expensive that is?"

He taps his teeth together and nods.

"There's nobody you can call?"

"There are people I can call. But I'd rather take a cab."

I shake my head at the stubbornness of men in general.

"Well, if you really want to go, you and the attending physician have to sign an AMA form."

"What's that?"

"It's a form that says you're leaving against medical advice."

"Whose?"

"Mine."

He ponders this, and me, for another moment before nodding. I take a big breath and throw up my hands.

"All right. I'll get the doctor."

I leave the room before I can say anything else. I don't know why this guy is affecting me like this. I'm acting like a nursing student, not an experienced RN. Actually, I'm acting more like a pining teenager, if I'm completely honest with myself.

I find Doctor Bennet at the computers drinking a large, black coffee. He's both hunched over and tucked under the desk, and he makes the chair he's sitting in look like it belongs in a kindergarten class. He looks up at me and presses his lips together. No doubt I look like a flustered hen. Except sweaty. It's amazing how working nights throws off your internal temperature. I'm freezing one second, then I'm clammy the next.

"What's up?" he asks.

"The patient is nine seventeen wants an AMA."

"That was quick."

"He's insistent. I think he has a problem with hospitals."

"And what do you think? Should we let him go?"

This is another reason why all the nurses love Doctor Bennet. He asks us what we think. Yeah, I know, it doesn't take much. But you would be absolutely flabbergasted at the number of doctors who treat us like hospital accessories about on par with the vending machines.

"They brought him in because he blacked out, but I can't find any evidence of a concussion. He's responsive and alert, aside from the paranoia. He's not complaining of any pain."

"Well, if he wants to go and he can go, we gotta let him go."

I deflate a little at this, and Doctor Bennet sees it.

"What's the problem? I'd have thought you'd be relieved." He checks his plastic Timex watch. "You're already here past shift change."

"It's just...he's complaining of a burning smell. And I think he may have some visual impairment. Depth judgment issues."

"Is he driving?"

"No."

Bennet creaks back in his chair and crosses his long arms over his white coat.

"And this isn't his first episode. He said he's had at least five of these incidents in the past."

"You think he may have a brain tumor," Bennet says.

I don't answer him, but that's answer enough. It's always a strange thing when you pull out the word 'tumor' in a diagnosis. It's such a heavy word. Nobody wants to say it. We get as used to it on the oncology floor as I think anyone can, but it's still heavy, even to us.

The other reason I stay quiet is because technically nurses aren't supposed to diagnose anything. That's what the white coats are for. I know a lot of doctors who would laugh my concerns off as the nervous ramblings of a young nurse, but like I said, Bennet is different.

"You're serious about this, aren't you." It's not a question, it's an observation.

"I know it's not really my place to say—"

"Of course it's your place," he says, stopping me as he gets a call on his phone. He snaps it from the table and answers it with a gruff "Bennet." He's quiet for a moment, and I look elsewhere. There are about a million things that I should be doing, but none of them seem all that important at the moment. Bennet says, "Can they wait?" and then he waits for a moment. "Then they'll have to wait," he says. He clicks the phone off and looks up at me, and his brow softens again. As he unfolds himself and stands tall, he grabs his stethoscope and drapes it around his shoulders.

"Let me get a look at him," he says.

When we walk in to Ben Dejooli's room, Bennet has the AMA clipped to the board in his hand.

"Hi, Ben," he says, pulling the low stool out with his foot and sitting down in front of the bed. He grabs Ben's charts and flips through them, and there is a silence that would have been awkward if I was the only one here with Ben. But Bennet makes it seem like an expectant silence. Like a conductor about to take the stage.

"So you passed out," he says.

Ben nods. I can tell that he is weary. He doesn't want to go through all of this again.

"Did Caroline tell you that she wants to count out a brain tumor?"

Ben widens his eyes. Which is an amazingly restrained response. I have to lean back on the door frame, but Bennet moves on. His delivery is so straightforward it's as if he's told Ben that he might be allergic to cats. And because Bennet doesn't treat the elephant in the room like an elephant, it doesn't become an elephant.

"No," Ben says, looking up at me. I can't hold his gaze. This is the first time I can ever remember turning away from a patient like this.

"And I have to say, Ben, after reading her admission, I agree that it's a concern. Something is giving you trouble."

I never gave him an admission, but that hardly matters now.

"So I'm gonna do a couple of things here. First, I'm going to sign this AMA. You're free to go. We aren't liable for anything that happens to you." Bennet wipes his hands across the air as if to shoo the legalese away.

"Second, I'm going to write up a referral to the CT clinic. Indian Health Services will take care of your costs." So Bennet knows he's Navajo too. It shouldn't surprise me. The doctors at Albuquerque General have a program where they rotate at the Chaco Health Clinic. I've seen him there once or twice. He's smiled at me.

"What's a CT?" Ben asks.

"It's a brain scan," Bennet says, grabbing for the pen and pad in his front pocket. "We just want to rule out the worst, that's all."

He rips a page from his pad and hands it to Ben, who looks at it like it's written in a foreign language.

"Just take that to the clinic, second floor."

"I really can't today," Ben says, and I can see he's gone a little pallid, but it's more than that. His general color seems to be fading. "Maybe in a couple of days," he says, half-heartedly.

"The referral is good for a month, but I really would encourage you to go as soon as you can. Just get it over with, and then we'll go from there."

"So I can leave?" he asks.

Bennet signs the AMA form on his clipboard and then hands it to Ben. "This certifies that you are leaving under your own power and against medical advice. Sign here."

Bennet's tone is strong, but Ben doesn't flinch. He takes the clipboard, signs his name as a little scribble and then holds out his arm with the line in it. "Can you help me out of this?"

Bennet's phone rings again, and he snaps it from his hip, glancing at the readout.

"I have to move," he says.

"I'll unhook him," I say. Bennet nods. At the door, he gives one last, unreadable look to Ben and is gone.

"He wasn't very happy with me," Ben says, smiling sadly as I pull the line from his arm and push the rig aside.

"I'm not very happy with you either," I say, not daring to meet his eyes again. "Promise me you'll get that scan."

He laughs and looks at me strangely. "Promise you?"

"Yes. Promise me."

"I can't promise you, I hardly know you."

"Fine," I say, curtly, before attempting to bring down my trusty curtain of separation. Well, trusty until now, anyway. "Your clothes are on the dresser there. Have a good night." I turn to go.

"Caroline..."

I stop at the door and glance over my shoulder. He's still sitting on the bed. His feet dangle above the floor. His coloring is strange. I can tell that he wants to say something, but he doesn't know how. I don't know how I know this, exactly, except to say that it's almost like it's coming off of him in waves. I feel like I can sense the exact moment when he gives up and resigns himself.

"Look, I'll try to get the scan, okay?" he says. I've heard this tone before. It's the same tone people use when in polite company as an alternative to a flat no.

"Well, *really* try," I say, after another long moment where I feel like I'm staring at him like he's a mirage. It's almost like his skin is smoking. It strikes me that perhaps I need to get more sleep. Either that or maybe I have something wrong with my own head.

Then my phone buzzes and I can hear a bed alarm going off somewhere in the back, and I'm off running. It's almost forty minutes later when I finally clock out, and by then Ben's room has been empty for about thirty-nine of them.

4

BEN DEJOOLI

I'd planned on calling a cab from outside the hospital, slinking back to the rez and never talking about this little episode again, but when I get outside I see that Dad and Gam are already in the lobby. Gam is nested in a chair, puffed up in her old down jacket, and she's looking right at me when the elevator doors open. She hops down from her chair and shuffles my way, shaking her head at me. My father is at the help desk, and he looks white as a sheet. He might be the only person on earth who hates hospitals more than I do. That he even got this far past the front doors speaks volumes about how worried he must have been about me. I'm touched, actually.

Gam is now nodding her head and patting me on the side of the arm and muttering in Navajo, too low for me to understand. I grasp her bony hand, its skin paper thin.

"I'm okay, Gam," I say. She keeps nodding and shaking her head at the same time.

"Ben!" Dad says, striding over to me. "I came as soon as I heard. Danny told us. What happened? What happened to you?" I haven't seen him this worked up in years. He's borderline frantic, and I think it's best to get all three of us out of the hospital. We have bad memories of this place.

"Come on," I say, shepherding Gam in front of me. Dad follows and soon we're outside and in the car. I said I could drive, but Dad insists. He's treating me like I'm some flower, which is exactly what I didn't want, and exactly why I was hoping to sneak my way back home. It takes until we're cruising down the highway, the sun cracking over the horizon behind, before his free hand stops trembling. Gam is sitting in the back seat, nearly buried in her coat and scarf. Her eyes are closed, but I know she's listening.

"I'd been feeling off all day. I just blacked out for a bit, that's all."

"That's all? Ben. Danny scared us to death. Said they found you at the Arroyo. And I kept thinking if it was something I said, or what, and I was having these flashbacks of Ana—"

"This isn't like that, Dad. I'm not sick, I don't feel weak, it's totally different."

Gam says something in the back to the tune of *Ana said the same thing*, but I cut her off right there. Ana was anemic. She didn't know what it was like to feel well. She was always tired, but she refused to sit still. She wanted to be a normal nine-year-old girl. I just had a bad day on the job. Totally different.

"Gam, this isn't what Ana had," I say, and it feels weird even to equate the two. Neither of them is that reassured, but eventually I think they sense that I haven't had much sleep and so when I lay my head back and close my eyes they leave it be for the rest of the ride back to Chaco. I wish I could say I did get some sleep, but in my mind I keep seeing the black curtain of feathers that seemed to fall over me right before I lost it at the Arroyo. Gam starts humming something. An old Navajo song I remember her singing to Ana and me when we were little and couldn't fall asleep, our beds side by side. It was always me that worried about the dark. Ana wasn't afraid of anything. Not even of dying. She just liked to hear Gam sing. I roll my head and open my eyes to look at Gam, but she's not looking back at me. She's looking out the front window, and her eyes are small slits in the shadow of her face. I follow her gaze, and I see nothing but flat road and rolling desert hills. I'm about to close my eyes again when I catch movement in the far distance, high in the sky. A whole mess of crows streaks ahead of us, like pepper strewn across a table. I try to blink them away. I've had enough of crows. But when I open my eyes again, they're still there, and it's like they're leading our car back home. One in particular. A huge one at the head of the flock.

When we get home, the crows wheel off and away, but I still watch the sky out of the kitchen window while I manage to eat some cereal and calm my gut. I sit with Gam while she knits. Dad is off at the hardware store. Danny calls, and I pick up, and he tells me to sit out the day to recover, everything will keep 'til then.

"You know what I'mma say, don't you?" he asks.

"That I'm an idiot."

"No, you're no idiot, Ben. But sometimes you do dumb things. Can you imagine if I had to explain to your grandmother that you disappeared at the Arroyo while I was sleeping?"

"I know, Danny."

"Did you run into trouble out there?" he asks. "Tell me true."

"No trouble. I think maybe that sucker punch at Sancho's hit me harder than I thought."

Danny grunts in agreement.

"Did you find anything, at least? Was it worth it?"

Danny Ninepoint has one tone when he speaks. It's slow and methodical, like he's reading a speech. It's hard to tell if he's angry or if he's disappointed, although if I was to guess I'd say he's almost always just a little bit of both.

"No," I say, sighing. "Just a vigil and a token pile for burial."

Danny grunts again.

"Don't ever do that again, Ben. Go off without me like that."

"I know. I won't."

And just like that I know he's done talking about it. Just like I know he was done talking about the gambler, but I couldn't let it go. Danny could have said that's what I get for picking at things when they're settled, but he doesn't. He doesn't have to. He knows I get it.

"Get some sleep. Tomorrow we got some work to do."

"All right. And Danny. Thanks for looking out for me."

"Yep."

"And for dropping it now that it's done."

"Yep."

And that's that. Right now I've never been more grateful for the single-track mind of Danny Ninepoint. I take his advice and get to bed early. I sleep for twelve straight hours, and when I wake up again it's just past four in the morning. I think I have maybe another hour in me, and I flip my pillow and try to sink back to sleep again. But I think I was dreaming of the hospital because I'm in midthought when I wake up, and I'm thinking about the way Caroline looked when she asked me to promise to get that scan. She looked afraid. There's really no other word for it. And I wonder if I should be afraid too, but I feel better than I have in weeks. I just can't fathom that I have anything seriously wrong with me. Still, that look of hers lingers.

My brain is a funny thing. It's that look of hers that's on my mind when I wake up, but it's the way she held my shoulder, and the feeling I got when I held on to her hand for a moment, that ends up lulling me away and back into another solid hour of dreamless sleep.

The next morning Dad takes me to get my truck at the Arroyo. Dad drops me off but refuses to leave without me. Says he wants to follow me out. He's still handling me with care, but I see no way around it for a little while, at least until the sour taste of the whole event washes out.

I walk up to my truck with my tail between my legs. I don't want to see the smoker again, or anyone, for that matter. Thankfully, it looks like the vigil is over. In fact, it looks like the campers moved away from this edge of the Arroyo entirely. There's nobody here at all. If it weren't for the fact that my truck was still parked where I left it (and still locked, and intact, which is a blessing), I might have thought I had the site wrong. But no, this was it. In the light of early morning, the big black pit beyond the lip looks about as ominous as a sledding hill. The vigil pile is long gone too. It takes me until I walk over to where the pile was to realize I'm looking for the crow totem. I sigh, not really knowing why I'm disappointed. It's not my crow, after all. It feels right that it should be buried. Decommissioned. Given back to the earth, just like the gambler himself.

Dad honks. He doesn't like it here, and I know I'm lingering. I take one last look around the site, and it looks almost like it's been swept. Like someone took a big, wide-framed straw broom and flattened the whole place. There aren't even any footprints. That's why I stop on the walk back to my truck when I see the tire tracks. They stand out like huge fingerprints, especially to someone like me, who is trained to see them. Uneven weight—the front tread is clean but the back has displaced dirt around it. Medium width but long from front to rear. I'd say a rear-wheel drive, four-door sedan. There aren't a lot of those around here. Mostly trucks and vans and campers. If I had to guess, I'd say this tread looks a lot like an official vehicle. A town car or maybe a standard cop cruiser.

Could Danny have come by? Maybe. He thought I might have run into trouble when we talked on the phone. Maybe he came to check out the scene before I did. But he smacked my hand for coming here alone at night. He's a big bastard, but even he wouldn't be keen on jumping in his car and racing down here in the dead of night. Especially once he got confirmation that the ambulance picked me up.

I follow the tracks from where I pick them up coming out of the loose rubble, crossing over into the finer dust near the ring of the slope. They look to stop in front of the gambler's old camp site, and then there's a clear sprayback of dust and two divots. Whoever they were, they came here looking for something, either found it or didn't, and then peeled out.

I know I should file away this whole thing. Should have long ago, like Danny, but something about it won't let me close the drawer. I have this crazy desire to look for turned earth, and a creeping suspicion that even if I could find the gambler's burial pile, it would be missing one crow.

But I'm late, and I'm making Dad late for his day by wasting time, and Danny said we had work to do, so I get in my truck, start her up, and pull out. I wave at Dad on the way by, and he nods. He pulls out after me, and we leave the Arroyo behind. I check the rear mirror for crows out of instinct, but there are no black specks on the horizon. Nothing but the sharp, cold blue of a fall morning.

DANNY WASN'T LYING when he said we had work to do. Turns out it was more work than usual, it's just Danny didn't want to lay it on me the day before. As soon as I get into the station I can tell that something is up. We have this rotating group of young kids that work the front desk, another cush job staffed by the council, and usually all they want to do is talk, but today they're all business. At first I think it's me and my episode, but Danny's not a talker, and he wouldn't throw me under the bus like that. When I get to my desk I can see that it's not just me. Our district is big; we have nearly a hundred cops who work the streets and desks here, and usually the patrol guys are in the kitchen, shooting the shit, while the higher-ups gossip in their offices. The central desks generally serve more as places to sit than to work, but not today. Today everyone is glued to their seats. Today you could hear a pin drop in the kitchen. There's still a full pot of coffee. That means things are serious.

It doesn't take me long to see why the station has flipped a switch. It has something to do with the two men in black off-the-rack suits who are talking to the chief behind closed doors. I can see through the window of his office, and so can everyone else.

Danny sits down with a steaming cup of joe.

"What's all this?" I ask. "They don't look Navajo."

"They're not," Danny says, keeping his voice low.

New Mexico state patrol has come into our jurisdiction a handful of times, but never dressed like they were attending a funeral. Only one type of law dresses like that.

"FBI," I say. Danny nods.

The Feds have no jurisdiction here. The US Government checks its people and its power at the welcome sign, usually, so this is strange.

"What do they want?"

Danny looks up at me. "Rumor is they're asking about Flatwood."

Danny says this like he was reading a grocery list. Same way he says anything. But he watches me carefully because he knows what's going through my head right now. It's not enough that people like Sancho have to throw Flatwood in my face, as if I didn't already think of the man every day of my life. It's not enough for people to quiet down every now and then when I walk into the station kitchen. Now the Feds have come to remind me, and all of us, of the man I banished. I take a deep breath, and I think I smell a tinge of sulfur.

"Ben, they're not here for you. Not as far as I can see. They haven't talked about anything to me."

"I wasn't even a cop when that happened," I say. I became a cop right after that happened. Because that happened.

Danny holds his hands out low and nods as if to say *you don't have to explain anything to me.*

"Just lay low and see what it is that they want. Hopefully just a file of some sort, then they're gone. No reason to think they're here to dig up old bones."

I appreciate the sentiment, but I know in real life things don't work like that. There are no coincidences. That's why I'm not surprised when the phone at our desk lights up. Danny watches me. I know it's not for him. I pick up.

"Dejooli," I say.

"Ben, its Sani. You have a minute?"

As if I wouldn't have a minute for the captain. I look up

at Danny and then over at the closed office, behind glass. The agents are looking my way. Danny nods slowly to tell me it's okay. One step at a time.

"'Course, Cap," I say. "Be right in."

I hang up and look down at my desk, nodding to myself. Makes sense that the guy I banished would haunt me every day since. Seems quite Navajo of him. I get up without another word and make my way to the big office.

Sani Yokana is a veteran of the Chaco rez. I say veteran because he's more than just an experienced cop. He worked the streets like me for ten years, then made detective, then lieutenant, now captain. He's savvy. Nobody becomes head of the Chaco district of NNPD without knowing their way around tribal politics. Thankfully, Sani has a no-nonsense reputation and seems to have reached his position without owing too many favors, at least that I've heard of. I think it helps that he's not a member of the council and has no intention of ever being a member of the council, and has, in fact, come as close as anyone I've ever met to telling the council to fuck off while still keeping his job. He likes to run our department his way. He's a heavyset man, wide bodied, with long, grey hair that he never bands. When I walk in the office, all three men watch me. The suits are blank, but Sani gives me a pinched nod. He looks a bit piqued. I can tell that he's not exactly itching to drudge up the Flatwood case again either.

"Ben, this is Agent Parsons and Agent Douglas. They're with the FBI."

I shake their hands. Some Indians say that all white men look the same. I never held with that until now. Both are medium height, medium build. Brown hair, neatly parted. Pale complexion, not a hint of facial hair. No smile to speak of. All business. These are men whose profession it is to get in, get out, and get forgotten. They are wearing different colored ties, at least. I can give them that.

"They have a few questions to ask you about Joseph Flatwood," Sani says, furrowing his weathered brow. He's not happy having these agents in his station. I can tell before they even open their mouths that they have an air of blank-check entitlement to them. No doubt they've been trained extensively about Indian affairs, but I'd be surprised if either of them had ever set foot on a reservation before.

"Mr. Dejooli—" Parsons begins.

"Call me Ben."

"...Ben. We have an open investigation regarding Joseph Flatwood, whom we know to have been an acquaintance of yours. It's progressed to a point where we feel you might be able to help us."

I look at Sani for a long moment. He barely holds a scowl at bay. The dimple in his chin turns into a pothole.

"Council has given them free run of whatever resources Public Safety can provide," he says, strained.

Now that's interesting. For the council to buddy up with the Feds, Flatwood must really be raising hell.

"All right," I say, slowly.

"But first you need to understand that this is a classified case, and no details about what we will tell you should leave this room. It's standard protocol for an ongoing investigation."

I feel a twinge of pain behind my forehead. It's like Agent Parsons is reading from cue cards behind me.

"Okay...but listen, I haven't seen Joey Flatwood in almost six years. Not since he was banished. I haven't heard from him either, if that's what you're getting at. That's kind of the whole point."

Agent Douglas nods his head. "We know. We've been

tracking Flatwood for years now. He's been all over the southwestern United States, but just about the only place he hasn't popped up is anywhere near Chaco Reservation."

Banished means banished. Flatwood respected the council, and our laws. That was one of the worst parts of watching him go: I knew he would be gone forever. I was glad of it, and I hated it at the same time. I still remember the way he turned back and nodded at me after he passed the welcome sign going the other way. It was a reassuring nod, as if he wanted to say *It's okay, Ben*. That's what made it so terrible. Nothing was okay. My sister was gone. We'd decided it was my best friend's fault, and now he was going, too. He should have fought it, but it was like he gave up. That, more than anything, is what I keep coming back to in the middle of the night when I wonder for the millionth time if Joey Flatwood is really the reason Ana is gone. Why didn't he deny it? I scrunch up my nose to try and cut off the subtle burning smell, but it's getting stronger.

"I thought he might be dead," I say. "The way he just...disappeared like that. No word of him at all."

"Oh, he's not dead," Parsons says. "At least, not yet. He's come close to killing himself several times, though."

Parsons' textbook delivery makes me want to smack him. If Joey tried to kill himself, it's probably because of me. There was a long stretch of time, right afterwards, when I wanted to kill him myself. But the idea of him wandering the southwest, drifting in and out of depression, makes me feel wretched. I'm almost positive that he knows what happened to Ana, and I hate him for refusing to tell me, but it's been six years now and sometimes I think if I knew then how hard friends are to come by, I might have been a little slower to take the stand. I swallow down the distaste and try to match the agents' flair for deadpan.

"In fact," Douglas says, "that's what we wanted to talk to you about."

"What, Flatwood trying to kill himself?"

"And failing...when he shouldn't."

"I don't follow you."

"We have reason to believe that Joseph Flatwood should be dead, but he's not."

"You mean he's bad at killing himself?"

"No, he's quite good. He's just...still here."

I cross my hands over my chest and look at Sani, who gives me a small eyebrow shrug. "Why do you guys care if he kills himself?"

Parsons clears his throat. "Between suicide attempts he has a penchant for robbing hospitals. We started following Flatwood after security cameras in three separate states picked him up lifting pills from the medicine cabinets."

Joey Flatwood, a drug addict? That's even less believable to me than the gambler as a drug addict. Joey's grandpa used to lecture us about drugs, and Joey got a firsthand education of the mess they can turn a man into living out at the Arroyo. He never touched the stuff. We made a pact back in the day. Cut our palms with Joey's grandpa's old buck knife.

"He robs hospitals?"

"Yes. We have him on security footage taking enough to drop a man twice his size. He looked right at the camera. He's quite brazen. We also believe he may be selling what he doesn't take, to keep himself liquid and able to move."

"And this is Joseph Flatwood? Joey Flatwood? About my height, bit bigger in the chest. He's got a split lip—"

"That was repaired, but poorly. Bowlegged. Grew up in your *Arroyo*," Parsons says the word with mild distaste. "Has the tattoos on his knuckles to prove it."

"It's him, Ben," Sani says. "I've seen the tapes."

I shake my head in disbelief. "Can I see these tapes?"

Douglas looks at Parsons, who doesn't move a muscle, but some agreement is passed between them.

"If you'll help us build a file on him, yes. We'll give you access to the tapes."

"Ben, I've told them we'll give them what we have, but you don't have to work with them further. These gentlemen know where their jurisdiction lies."

My first instinct is to turn around and walk right out the door. I'd already helped the council build a case against Joey once, and I've been paying for it ever since. Now the US government wants me to help build another case, and I'm thinking how it is that it falls to me to damn a man twice. I think maybe the gods are giving me the retribution I asked for six years ago in spades, only right now I'm not so sure I want it anymore. It won't make Ana any less gone. I oughta take a page out of the Danny Ninepoint playbook and throw out the playbook. But I can't. I'm not like Danny. I just don't know why, but my book is bolted open. As surely as Dad wanders the back yard. As surely as Sancho and his ilk talk circles around Flatwood to let me know they remember. For some reason, Joey Flatwood can't be forgotten. Not yet.

"What are you gonna do with him, when you catch him?" I wasn't naive enough to think Joey could run forever. Not from the Feds.

"We're going to prosecute him on narcotics charges, breaking and entering, trafficking, and theft, and then, quite frankly, we're going to breathe a sigh of relief," says Parsons.

"Why's that?"

"Because his behavior fits certain profiles. We have reason to believe that Joseph Flatwood is on his way to hurting a lot of people."

Just then a huge crow clatters to a landing on the sill of the high window in Sani's office, and it startles all four of us. It grapples with the stubby awning for a moment, its long black claws scraping at the metal. I step closer to it, looking for a flash of red and terrified that I'll find it.

"They're all over the place these days. It's that time of the fall," Sani says.

The crow watches us sidelong, its arrowed head nearly pressed up against the glass. In profile I can see that its beak is like a six-inch shard of obsidian. It only lingers for a moment, then it drops from the sill. I can hear the beating of its wings. Still staring at the empty sky where it was, I know my answer.

"All right. I'll help. Give me the tapes and a few days to run it down. I'll tell you what I can."

"How about two days. We'd need a full character profile. What he was like growing up. How you knew him. What he was like in school. Any warning signs you might think of. And, of course, a full account of the banishment. We want your personal opinions, Ben. You knew him best."

I nod. "Two days," I say. Something about how eager these men are doesn't sit well with me. The whole story is off. Suddenly I remember the Arroyo. The tracks. The Feds roll around in just the type of town car that would leave those marks. I saw a Lincoln town car parked out front, in the handicapped spot, coming in. That would have done it. They wouldn't have any care for the gambler, of course, but there were strange similarities: the drugs, the Arroyo...the crows. Pieces of a bigger story all butting up against each other like tumbleweeds. If the Feds knew Joey grew up in the Arroyo, what else did they know? And what weren't they telling me?

5

CAROLINE ADAMS

I've been thinking a lot about Ben Dejooli, and it's kind of annoying me. I'll be working along, giving meds or helping a patient to the bathroom, and then out of nowhere he pops into my mind. I have four patients today, and one of them is a really large Navajo. Morbidly obese. She requires our specialized bed and the new hoisting system to get her on her feet so she can get to the restroom. She's also extremely rude to me and to every other person assigned to her. And a lot of people have been assigned to her. This is her sixth time gracing us with her presence in my tenure here. She's been bumped from the ER and onto the Oncology overflow. She is what we call a frequent flyer. She doesn't have cancer, but she has just about everything else. That's what happens when you're two hundred and fifty pounds overweight. You get everything.

I have no problem with fat people, but I do have a problem with mean people. Especially when we are understaffed and one of my patients who actually has cancer looks ready to code on me at the drop of a hat, and instead of tending to him like I should I have to deal with this woman and her whining for more pain meds and accusations of abuse from the staff. It's all I can do not to file her away, and just when I'm about to give up on everything—her, the Navajo, Chaco Reservation, the whole day —Ben Dejooli pops into my mind. He's looking at me with that haunted gaze, and his eyes are like dime-sized windows into the rich-clay bottom of a lake. And it gets me through the rotation and keeps me moving until I can get a half a minute in the break room to eat my granola bar.

But then, when I'm two bites in to my "dinner," my phone rings and the code alarm goes off at the same time. That means it's my patient dying, and I drop the bar and start running, along with everyone else. Mary Ellen grabs the crash cart from the manager's station and is a half-step behind me. When I get there, the CNA is already doing chest compressions, and there is more blood than I have ever seen at once pouring from the patient's mouth. This is one of those horrible times when a nurse is faced with a crossroads, and this is the longest I've ever stood frozen in one spot during a code. It feels like half a minute, but in reality it's just a few seconds. Then Mary Ellen is behind me with the crash cart and in full-blown battle-manager mode, and I can see why she's the boss.

"Get him on his side," she says, firm and cold as winter stone, as she's rolling out the defibrillator pads. All hesitation gone, I wade into the blood, jam both hands under the patient fireman style, and roll him halfway around while Mary Ellen slaps one pad to his back.

"Front," she says, and I ease him back as Mary Ellen slaps the second to his chest. He is completely non-responsive. It's like moving a bag of dirt. I place the Ambu oxygen bag over his face, but he's still breathing blood and it smears against the inner plastic like melted lipstick. It's already collecting in a pool.

"We're gonna need suction," I say. My voice is distant and small, but another nurse hears me and preps the vacuum.

"Clear!" snaps Mary Ellen, and we all step away. I take the Ambu bag with me, and blood drips from the mouthpiece in a steady line. We wait for a horrible eternity for the readout. It says "No shock advised. Continue CPR." We all move in. Mary Ellen revs the panel again while a doctor injects the IV with epinephrine. The second nurse sucks the blood from in and around his mouth then steps back, and I pump oxygen. The CNA is sweating profusely but hasn't given up on the CPR. God bless him. We're supposed to do this for three minutes before we can shock him again. That's what the book says. It feels like an hour.

"Clear!"

We step back. In the movies the patients jolt. In real life it's more of a sad shudder.

We wait for the readout. "No shock advised. Continue CPR."

We move back in.

Suck, squeeze, suck, squeeze. The Ambu mouthpiece leaves red rings around his nose and lips. They dry black just in time for another suction and then another squeeze of the bag. They're lurid on his ghost-pale skin. There is no movement under his eyelids, and all of a sudden I notice I'm quietly crying. Some detached part of me wonders when that started. How long have I been here? Minutes? Hours?

"I'm calling it," I hear, and Bennet's voice is like a bucket of cold water. He's looking at the readouts. His face is grim, but his voice is strong.

"He's dead. There's nothing else we can do. He had lung

cancer. Once the tumor bursts into the great vessels there's nothing that's going to stop the bleeding. It was only a matter of time. We knew it. He knew it."

And now that he says it, I see the blood is everywhere. It's on the patient. On the bed. On the floor. Up and down my sleeves and on the CNA's face. It's on Bennet, too. Tears roll down my cheeks, but I don't want to touch my face. Bennet looks at me, and his eyes soften. I think if he says anything to me I'm going to break down, but he just nods, thank God.

"Everyone give your roles to the nurse at the door. Time of death, three twenty-seven."

It takes ten minutes to sort out the roles for the log, and by then everyone is shaking, including me. The CNA most of all. I make a mental note to buy him coffee, or lunch. Then I almost laugh out loud at how tiny that gesture would be, all things considered, and it occurs to me that I am in a minor state of shock.

The line limps along. I step up.

"Caroline Adams. I'm the primary nurse."

Then I shuffle out. We all shuffle out in different directions like we're lost in the place we've worked for years. I just cross the hall. I'll need to clean him up and present the body to the family.

"Anybody willing to help me do post-mortem?" I ask, and it feels like I haven't talked for days. I have to clear my throat. I'm pretty sure I squeak.

The CNA nods at me, and Bennet says, "I will." I want to hug both of them then go to sleep for a week. And all of a sudden I'm thinking about Ben Dejooli again. Would he bleed like that? Probably not. If my worst fears are true and he has a brain tumor, he'd probably go out like a candle. There'd be no blood at all. Just the cancer pushing down on the nerve system until he stopped breathing. Bennet brings me back from the brink of breakdown again when he hands me a stack of wet towels. Then he and the CNA roll the patient and strip the bed. I've never seen a doctor do anything like this before, and it's the next thing that makes me want to cry. I viciously clear my throat and dab my face with the hot towel. I'm supposed to be one of the strong ones here.

I busy myself cleaning the floor and swallow down the ball in my throat. Eventually I'm under control. The repetitive swabbing movement helps. But then a strange thing happens. I don't usually go in for supernatural stuff. I believe that there's something bigger than me out there, and I guess I call that thing God. But when you've seen death like I have, you recognize it less as a scary passage or sacred departing and more as just the flipside of life. It's what's at the bottom of the sack of time all of us is handed when we come in to this world. I suppose this makes me disillusioned, but if it does, I'd challenge you to find a nurse out there who isn't. A lot of people prefer to keep the guts and gristle of life behind the skin, like our bodies are bags of magic. Doctors take the opposite extreme. Nurses, for whatever reason, are wired differently. We get in this game for the people, but we also see the guts for what they are: guts. This patient is gone. That's why it gives me pause when I feel something brush past my back while I'm cleaning the patient's face and mouth. I actually step aside.

"Sorry," I say, thinking it's Bennet or the CNA trying to get around me, even though I know it felt different. More subtle. Like a whisper. The brush of a blade of grass.

Bennet looks up at me from across the room. "It wasn't your fault, Caroline. It was stage four lung cancer." The CNA looks up at me and nods in silent agreement. He's by the far closet pulling out new sheets. Neither of them is anywhere near me. I blink at them until I realize that Bennet mistook my meaning, then go back to gently swabbing the side of the dead man's face. Then it happens again, and this time it's like I can hear the crinkle of the bed, like he's sitting up, even though he's just as still and rigid as when I started cleaning him. This time I step back, and I can feel the hairs on my forearms standing on end. Which would be understandable if I were the type to get creeped out by a dead body, but I'm not, which makes it all the stranger.

Then I swear I feel the movement of air on the damp at the back of my neck, and I find myself turning and staring at a spot in the middle of the room. My eyes tell me nothing is standing there, but there is just a hint of color to the air. Like that same strange smoke I saw on Ben's skin, but this is a different color, and it takes me a minute to recognize that it was the unique color of my patient. It snuffed out when he died, I realize this now, yet here it is again, like an echo of cologne passing by me for just a moment. And then it's gone. And, naturally, the two men I asked to help me clean and dress the room catch me staring into space like a cat.

Later, after it's all over and I've changed into my second pair of scrubs and convinced myself that the strange smoke and the soft touch of air were the result of shock, when I'm sitting back down at the table where nobody's touched my granola bar and it lies there like a sad relic of the time when my patient was still alive, Bennet comes in and sits down across from me. He's not wearing his coat anymore, and he's changed his shirt. His tie is a different color too, although it's just as skinny. It almost makes me smile.

"That was a bad one, Caroline. They're gonna do a debrief. I think you should go."

I nod. I pick up the bar, look at it, then set it down again. "Do you remember Ben Dejooli? The patient I had last week? He's Navajo. He passed out on the reservation."

Bennet nods.

"Did he ever fulfill that CT scan?"

"Not yet," Bennet says, and he seems confident in his answer. I wonder if Ben hasn't crossed his mind a time or two since that early morning as well.

I'm not surprised he hasn't gotten the scan. Not in the least. For one, he's a young Navajo man. And he's in a macho line of work on top of that, one that doesn't give him a lot of free time, from what I've seen of Chaco. And top it all off with that terrified look in his eyes—that look that practically begged me to get him out of the hospital—and you have a textbook recipe for negligence.

"He's not going to," I say, and I know it's true. That ball in my throat makes a grand re-entrance. I have to look away and scrunch up my face, so I'm sure it looks like I'm disgusted and not oddly heartbroken. It's probably better that I look disgusted. It's easier to explain away.

Bennet picks at his tie, brushes it flat. He rests his elbows on the table and lets out a deep breath.

"I wouldn't be so sure," he says.

"You work at the CHC same as I do. It's hard...with the Indians...and cancer." It's so much more than that, and my words come out sounding pathetic, but Bennet seems to understand.

"I've found that some of the Navajo need reminding. It's not their way to work on our schedule. They have their own schedule. It's been theirs for thousands of years."

"I'll never see him again," I say.

Bennet looks at me head-on, and I know that his bright-blue eyes, sharp and alive and refreshing after the horrible stillness behind the lids of the man I just saw die, can see damn near right through me.

"You're really worried about this guy," he says, but it's not accusatory. It's soft, and it's appreciative.

I nod. "I see a lot of crap out there at CHC, a lot of things that can't be helped, and I don't want to count him in that number. Somehow I think it's really important that I help him if I can."

Bennet nods again, and I notice that the sharp, aquiline blue is more than just in his eyes. It's all over him. I rub at my own eyes. The color's still there, rolling in soft wisps off of his skin.

"How about this. When are you next at the CHC?" he asks, clearly unaware that he's suddenly glowing blue. It occurs to me that I'm having a breakdown of some sort in the break room. I stare at the table and pretend to be figuring.

"Next Tuesday," I say.

"Why don't I do a little switching around and take the attending shift that day, and after we wrap up we can go find him? Nudge him along a bit."

I look at him head on. Smoke or no, that is an incredibly gracious thing to offer.

"You would do that?" I ask.

"Why not? He's a cop, right? I've been to the Chaco station tons of times working with patients who come to the clinic. I'll make an excuse to get over there at the end of the day when most of the cops are doing their own paperwork. With any luck we'll find him."

"And then what?" I ask, but I feel better than I have in weeks at just the thought of being able to address this Ben thing, this nagging fear, instead of sitting and waiting for bad things to happen.

"Well, that's up to you, but I'm sure you'll think of something," he says, and he smiles. And then I smile, and I can't help but notice that his smoke dances a bit. It makes me smile all over again, and I wonder if this is what a lunatic feels before a giggling fit.

"Okay," I say, perhaps a little too quickly.

"So it's a date?"

"It's a date."

It's only afterwards, in that night's three a.m. wonderings, that it occurs to me that maybe Bennet meant 'date' as in *date*. I actually blush, as if I was still talking to him and not alone in my bed. Probably he meant it just as a turn of phrase. Ninety-nine percent chance he meant it that way. Although doctors rarely mince words. Okay, maybe a ninety-five percent chance. And the other thing is that I could tell he was dancing without him ever moving his feet. He was dancing on the inside. I don't know what is happening to me, but if I'm going blind or nuts or having a breakdown, at least I got to see Owen Bennet dance first.

6

OWEN BENNET

If you asked me why I proposed the idea of finding this Ben Dejooli, I'd say ostensibly because I have a responsibility as a doctor to help my patients however I can, and then I'd probably add that I, Owen Bennet, personally have an additional responsibility to the Navajo people of Chaco Reservation. It's in keeping with a long line of Bennet doctors who find their practice and then find their cause. My grandfather's practice was a small pediatric clinic in Essex County; his cause was the underserved communities of upstate Massachusetts. Granddad in particular, with his black bag and his racks upon racks of black suits, would find the idea of a site visit like the one I proposed for Ben Dejooli completely normal. My father's practice was in South Boston. He did general medicine. His cause was the Southie Irish-Americans. Working class men and women who might go twenty years at a time without a checkup were it not for him.

I don't have a practice, per se, since I'm an attending at ABQ General. That didn't go over well in the family, so I doubled up on the cause. The Navajo. I work full time for the hospital and then volunteer another full day at least once a week for the Chaco Health Clinic. The sixty-hour work week is brutal, quite frankly, but it didn't kill my grandfather (although Alzheimer's did) and it didn't kill my father (he just loved whisky), and it's damn well not going to kill me.

It's for a good cause. That's what I'd tell you if you were to ask why I'm going out of my way here. But the reality is that I think I'm in love with Caroline Adams. I also think I'm terrible at hiding it.

I wish I could tell you that I'm no stranger to love. That I've had my heart broken a time or two then pieced myself back together again. That I'm stronger for it and all that. But if I told you that I would be lying. I feel that physicians are hobbled in love to begin with. My grandfather used to say that the only thing more powerful than the knowledge a doctor has is the illusion that he has even more. There has to be distance, he would say. He was remarkably cold for a pediatrician, but he was fabulous at what he did. Dad was a bit warmer, but even he told me that people don't like to look behind the curtain. They don't like to know that their physician is also a man. He is a physician first, and then a man. We may be the only profession in the world where those two are switched around. Interesting men, Dad and Granddad. You can imagine where father and husband fell on their lists.

Distance. Curtain. Practice. Cause. Is it any wonder that I have no idea what I'm doing when these feelings for Caroline slap me in the face?

Thankfully, I know what I'm doing when I make my rounds, even when I'm at the Chaco Health Clinic, where every new hire (or volunteer, as the case may be) walks around the cramped hallways with this look about them like they've stepped onto another planet. I don't blame them. I was that way, too, when I first came here nearly seven years ago. And in a lot of ways, when you step onto the Chaco Reservation you are stepping onto another planet.

Caroline was that way, too. But it's been almost five years for her, and she's leveled out. Once she hits her five-year mark she's fulfilled her grant stipulations with the US Government. She won't have to work at the CHC anymore if she doesn't want to. I've spent an embarrassing number of hours wondering if she'll leave Chaco, and then ABQ General, too. It's a decent enough place, but if you feel no obligation to stay in Albuquerque, it would certainly be easy enough to leave, too.

Sometimes I have these drawn-out fantasies where she tells me she is going to leave and it forces me to make some sort of move on her. But like I said: That's not me. It took nearly everything I had to ask her to go after Ben Dejooli with me. I felt like my heart was beating so hard it was vibrating my tie like a base string. The trick to not looking like a lovelorn sop is to keep it professional. Thankfully, that is my zone. That is where I am king. Call me Doctor Professional. That is why I've been able to work with Caroline at the CHC for nearly five years without seeming untoward or awkward. But time is ticking, and I don't want to back myself into a corner with all the rest of the kids who are too afraid to ask the girls to dance. I have to leave my zone.

The CHC isn't a MASH unit, but it's no Mayo Clinic either. It's a repurposed office building, four stories, and it has that cubicle claustrophobia about it still. We have two old conference rooms that we use for revolving-door office hours for six hours a day on the main floor. I try to get there when I can, but mostly we stock it with the resident docs. It's good practice for them. Other than that there's a small waiting room that is almost always at capacity, and then three other floors' worth of patient rooms. Just over seventy-five beds. We get about two hundred thousand outpatient encounters a year. We cram 'em in, as they say, but it's better than nothing. I like to think we do all right.

The day of our trip passes like a blur. I see Caroline occasionally, but most of the time I'm in and out of patient rooms one after another, like I've misplaced my keys and am popping in to have a look around. Here at the CHC we are strongly urged to keep patient visits to five minutes and under. That kind of thing drives me crazy, and my grandfather would most likely have spoken to every administrator there is, face-to-face, about the travesty of rushing a physician. My father knew how to work within the system better. He would have written a strongly worded letter. I simply endure. The one time I do get a free minute and Caroline is nearby, it is she who brings up our impending outing. As if it could have slipped my mind.

"Doctor Bennet," she says. "How are your rounds?"

"Never-ending. But that comes with the territory," I say, and inwardly cringe. Territory? Who am I, Meriwether Lewis?

"We're still on for this afternoon, right?" she asks, and she raises a hopeful eyebrow. She could have asked for just about anything right then, and I would have done it.

We're still getting tattoos, right?

Sure are!

We're still running away to Bali, right?

Got my bags right here!

What actually comes out is, "If you're able, yes."

"Oh good!" she says. "Yeah, I think I'll be ready at shift change. Three p.m.? Meet you outside?"

"I'll be there," I say, and she's off. She's one of the most senior staff we have now at this place, where the turnover is, quite frankly, pretty ridiculous. I try not to think what it would be like if she left. I throw myself headlong into the next patient, an emphysematous male, forty-seven, mild tachycardia, moderate diabetes risk. Suffering from light-headedness, like our friend Ben Dejooli was, but the culprit here is obvious, whereas Ben doesn't smoke and he's not overweight. I go on like this, room after room, and soon enough, work blurs my emotions, and I can pull the curtain across once more.

Before I know it, I'm waiting out in my old SUV for Caroline, and I'm putting my palms in front of the vents to try and dry them off. It's a balmy fifty-eight degrees according to the readout on the dash. A textbook New Mexico fall day. I see her walk out of the front doors of the Center, and when I tap the horn, she waves. I turn off the blasting air. I can see that she walks with a bit of tenderness, and I think it's from having to single- handedly roll that stage four lung cancer patient over during that code last week. I've been there before. You can throw your back out in those types of situations and have no idea it happened until you're in the shower that night and all of a sudden you can't reach the shampoo. My heart goes out to her. It's tough enough having to deal with a bloody code without also having it sit in the small of your back for the next two weeks.

"All right," she says, smiling and huffing slightly. "That's over."

I wonder if I should bring up the fact that her contract is up in about a month. It doesn't seem the thing to open with.

"Are you ready?"

"Ready? You act like this is some sort of war zone we're going into."

I laugh, and it sounds cavernous. I clip it short. "It's no war zone. It's a nice community. Parts of it, anyway."

"Do you know your way around Chaco?"

"I've been all over Chaco. I know it well enough."

"I've never been past the CHC."

"There's no reason for you to, unless you like to gamble. Also there's a great Mexican food place off the main drive, if you're willing to look past the tracked up floors." I scratch at my collar. I'm nervous talking now. The words keep coming. "And a bar that's pretty friendly if you go left at the welcome center and drive for a few blocks. Dirt cheap. Called the Chaco Pourhouse."

She looks at me with this barely veiled expression of amazement, and it occurs to me that I've pushed the curtain pretty far back at this point. But that was the whole idea, wasn't it? Time to move forward with my head up? Power through?

"What, you don't think doctors drink?"

"Oh, I know doctors drink. I just wasn't sure about you."

"Well," I say, and I have no follow-up, so I shrug. She's already looking out the window. I'm dreading the silence, so I turn on tour guide mode.

"The rez has parts that people are supposed to see and take pictures of and experience, and then it has parts that are best left alone."

We're driving on the main drag, north, skirting the welcome center and cutting through the nicer neighborhoods to get to the council buildings, where the police station is.

"What's best left alone?" she asks, watching a huge murder of crows that is cutting a wide circle in the sky in sync, like a flock of homing pigeons. They seem to be scanning the ground like bomber pilots and calling out landing spots.

"You don't want to go too far north. You hit some of the track bars and the row houses, and then beyond that is a place called the Arroyo. Sort of a gypsy camp for the poorest of the poor Navajo out by this big depression in the desert. I've had a handful of calls come from there, working at the CHC. It's pretty hairy." I puff up a bit here. She seems like she's interested in the rez, and I want to show her that I know it better than most white boys.

She throws me a curveball. "I'd like to go there some day," she says.

"The Arroyo?"

"Yeah. The Navajo...they're tough, but they're also, I dunno. Kinda...wonderful." She's blushing now.

"I know what you mean," I say, and I say it sincerely. "I have this bracelet."

"What?"

"I wear a bracelet. A young Navajo girl gave it to me. She was a patient of mine, back when I was a resident working at CHC. She had a goiter, very treatable but something that was literally ruining her life. It was a simple thyroid issue. That's all. But it was big and ugly, and it ostracized her. Had for years."

I still remember the day that girl gave me the bracelet. She hardly smiled. She walked up to me, set it in my hand, then she turned around and walked away, and I stared at it until my eyes started to water. That's what is running through my head, but that's a little too much, I think, for the moment, so I say, "She gave me a bracelet. I wear it under my cuff."

I take one hand from the wheel and wiggle the cuff up a bit to show her, and I suddenly feel like a child holding up a piece of noodle art, so I tuck it back in and clear my throat. I've worn it for years. It probably looks like a matted piece of string to her anyway.

"That's incredible," she says. "I had a woman come back with some food she'd cooked for me. I remember how good that felt. Also I had a grandmother cry once and shake both of my hands pretty vigorously after I discharged her. I'm hoping they were tears of gratitude. I'm almost a hundred percent sure that they were."

I look at her sidelong and can see that in her mind she's actually revisiting those tears and reaffirming her diagnosis. I laugh. I can't help it. She looks at me and smiles. She knows I'm laughing with her.

"That's pretty amazing," I say. "Nobody ever cooked for me before."

"You really care about them."

I nod. "I don't think I meant to. But it happened. Still, places like the Arroyo, or the strip out by the tracks, those places I don't care for."

Before I know it, and before I want it to happen, the Chaco Police Station is around the corner. It's hard to miss. A big, long barn structure built out of salmon-pink adobe composite. A big, chrome disk stands out front, like a quarter balanced on edge. A memorial to those officers who have lost their lives in the line of duty over the years. As we pull in to park I can see that she's nervous. She's staring blankly at the front entrance.

"Ready? Remember, it's no big deal. I'm just checking on some files, and you came along. We'll see what we can see." I shrug.

She nods.

7

BEN DEJOOLI

When I agreed to write up a report on Joey Flatwood for the Feds I knew it would be like raking over a scar that still aches. I don't do well remembering how Ana disappeared. I've tried very hard to remember my little sister as she was, running around the house, handing me odds and ends that she thought were little pieces of treasure, singing or humming to herself. The Division of Public Safety already has a formal report on the night in question, but it was written by another officer. I wasn't a part of the force yet. Essentially, what those agents asked me to do was write up a report as if I was the officer who answered my own emergency call.

I'm not a good writer. I'm good at listing facts and observations. I can pick apart a crime scene better than anyone I know, but when it comes to telling people *why* I think a thing, or *why* I did what I did, I'm at a loss for words. I'm the type of cop who acts on instincts, for better or for worse. Most of the time it does me good. Sometimes it ends up with me passed out solo at the Arroyo in the dead of night. What can I say? I've had more than my fair share of misreads, but it's the only way I know how to work. Maybe this is the reason I've essentially been running the same beat route for years. Danny passed on the chance to become a detective. He hates the desk. Says the beat is in his blood. They never even asked me, and I don't think they intend to, all things considered. I'm reminded of that every now and then when the kitchen quiets.

I have a picture of Ana on my half of the desk. Two pictures, actually. One is a five-by-nine of her sitting on Gam's lap when she was seven. Dad took it. I can see Mom smiling at them just in the corner. Ana is just about to start wriggling free, but Gam's holding her close with just a hint of a smile on her face that says she knows Ana's about to make a run for it. Ana has this gleam in her eye. She was always wanting to run. But I suppose all kids are like that.

The other picture is her fourth-grade school photo. Wallet sized. The last one she ever took. It was the picture we gave the cops. It sits in the corner of the same frame. She fooled Gam that day and convinced her to let her dress herself. She's wearing a shiny purple windbreaker with three bows in her hair, and her smile runs ear to ear.

I turn back to the blinking cursor. I start with dates. That's easy enough. I could be dead asleep and if you told me to name a date, any date, I'd say Tuesday, August 1, 2006. When I'm dead and gone you can ask my grave the same thing, and the wind'll whip the desert dust up and you'll hear it speak: Tuesday, August 1, 2006.

I start writing a bullet point list of the worst series of events in my life.

- *3 p.m., I come home for a late lunch and find Ana on the floor of the living room. Grandmother is asleep in her room. Mother and Father are out. Ana does not*

move when I walk into the house. I know something
is wrong because Ana has a congenital heart defect.

Had. Ana *had* a congenital heart defect. I could write
how all of her life I had half an eye on her. Worried sick
about that tiny cough and about the breathless way she
would come in from playing out back, wondering if she
might be dying where she stood. We'd been in and out of
the hospital countless times. Each time she cried, and each
time another dime's worth of dread of the place dropped
into my pocket as well. But I don't know how to write these
things. So I don't.

- *Ana was non-responsive when I shook her, but she*
  was breathing.

Barely. I had to lick the back of my hand and put it on
her lips to make sure it wasn't just wishful thinking. But we
had prepared for this. We had plans. We ran practice drills. I
called 911. First responders took Ana to the CHC, where she
was admitted in critical condition. The doctors were able to
stabilize her, and after eight hours she was upgraded to
stable condition. Eight hours in which I sat in a tiny waiting
room with Mom, Dad, and Gam, convinced that the last
time I would ever see Ana alive was when she was shooting
away on a rolling bed surrounded by medical staff, the
double doors swinging shut behind her, in and out of phase.
I didn't know then that later on I would actually wish it had
worked out that way. Opened and closed. Like those doors. I
don't know how the doctors saved her. Shocked her or shot
her full of something that got her heart back in sync and
going again. I didn't care. All I cared about was that she was
okay.

We moved Ana to ABQ General as soon as she was able to be moved. There they ran her through a battery of tests, again and again while we waited and watched from behind glass. An eternity later, an old, fat white man who we were told was head of pediatric medicine came out into the waiting room, stood with his hands behind his back, and told us that she needed a heart transplant. Like we could pick it up at the supermarket. Without a transplant, she would not survive the year. Until a transplant became available, she would need to stay at the hospital.

And so we waited.

Ana was a high profile candidate. Young. All of her life in front of her. Otherwise perfectly healthy. She had the whole dwindling Navajo Nation angle too, and the government likes to trumpet how much they care about us. We were told there was a very good chance she'd find a donor.

Ana was weak and slept a lot, but she understood what was happening. She was willing to climb any mountain if it meant she could have her run of the backyard again. What she didn't understand was why it was taking so long, and why she couldn't leave her bed. It was tough on all of us. At first all four of us stayed at her side, all day and all night. But when days dragged to weeks, dragged to months, we started doing shifts. One at a time. People did a lot for us. For the Navajo, blood runs deep. Gam's friends, the real old school Navajo, came to pray and perform a modified Blessingway. Our neighbors cleaned our house and took care of some of the bills. IHS insurance covered everything at the hospital, thank God, but we weren't working as much, so people organized fundraisers to help us cover daily costs. The hardware store paid Dad time and a half for every hour he worked. We were inundated with food. And throughout all of it, Joey Flatwood was there for me. He cooked me food (which was not good) and snuck in beer (which was delicious). He brought me books for when he couldn't be there, and conversation and games for Ana when he could be there.

And then, eventually, he offered to sit with Ana when one of us needed a break. For any time at all. Thirty minutes to go smoke a cigarette. An hour to go take a drive. Even a whole night if we just wanted to take a breather. He was happy to.

Ana knew Joey. He was my best friend. He'd been around her since before she could remember. She trusted him as much as any of us did. And the hospital drags on you after a while. It's like the fluorescent lights suck the moisture from your skin. So we let him in.

Joey sat in Ana's room while Dad went outside for air. And there it was. That's all I know. I wasn't there that night. I was at home applying for jobs. Thinking about if I should go to college. Thinking what it would mean if I did go to college, off the rez. How I wouldn't be looked at the same way again around here. Just like my mother. It's strange to think of now, on this side of things. I chose not to go to college, and I was still cast out anyway.

How do I put this in a police report? I can't, so the next gap in the report is about a mile wide.

- *Father returned from his shift at Chaco Hardware to find Ana gone, and Joseph Flatwood non-responsive on a chair near her empty bed.*

But he wasn't non-responsive like Ana was non-responsive when I found her. He looked like the floor had shifted under him. His eyes were open and staring at the wall across Ana's empty bed. Dad shook the hell out of him. Said he slapped him. Joey wouldn't be brought back from wherever he was. He just kept staring. Never blinking. When I got there, after Dad called me out-of-his-mind with panic, I slapped Joey too. More than a slap, to be honest. It was a full-bore knockout-button uppercut, straight to that shut-down switch to the right of the chin. When he dropped to the floor, it was the first time he shut his eyes in over an hour. Before then the nurses had been giving him drops.

He was never the same after that day. He sat in the Chaco jail for a month without speaking a word. As the chances we'd find Ana grew slimmer by the day, he sat. The police told me all he did was stare at the wall during the day and sleep at night. If you could call it sleep. They said he did a lot of screaming at night. They said if you didn't put his food in front of his face, he wouldn't eat it. It took them nearly four days to figure that out. In those first four days he didn't eat anything.

- *Subsequent examination of the security camera footage over the time frame in which Ana went missing showed nothing out of the ordinary.*

There was no recording of what happened in the room, but there didn't need to be. Her room was on the ninth floor of ABQ General, and it had one window and one door. The window was intact. The camera in the hallway showed that the door never opened. Yet Ana was gone.

- *An anomaly in the footage provided us with the only plausible explanation.*

It was weak. I knew that much, even then. It was basically what they call a "break line." It's when the camera misses some frames. It looks like a stutter step. Like the camera blinked. The Chaco detectives told me that there was a chance that Ana was snatched in that blink. I know. I didn't believe it either.

They dusted the room. They talked to every single worker on the floor at that time. They pored over every piece of camera footage, from that hallway on floor nine to every other floor in the place. Elevators too. They questioned state police outside of the Chaco border about crossings that day. They did everything. All we had was that stutter step. Either she'd been taken in that second, or she'd disappeared into thin air. 'Disappeared into thin air' doesn't look good on a police report.

- *It was determined that Ana had been abducted from her hospital room at 3:28 in the afternoon.*

The nowhere hour. The forgotten slice of the day. Nobody ever asks what you're doing at three in the afternoon.

- *Subsequent analysis of her monitoring systems showed a malfunction in the machinery.*

Malfunction is a bad word for it. The machine didn't work at all. According to the beeping box, she was stable, then erratic, then gone. It seemed to have reset itself. Nobody reported any bed alarm or crash alarm. It was as if at 3:28 in the afternoon the machine had never been attached to Ana in the first place. Her IV line hung limply from a saline bag, the needle and tape still attached.

- *Nobody reported seeing anyone other than Joseph*

Flatwood enter the room, and once he was there, he never left.

When I got to the room and found Joey blank, there was no trace of my sister. It was so undisturbed, without even a scent of her, that I was convinced they'd moved Joey into another room. Maybe if I'd sat with him right afterwards. Worked with him somehow instead of snapping and popping him in the face. Maybe if I'd convinced him to tell me what he'd done while it was still fresh, maybe I could have gotten something out of him. It's Triage 101. Every Chaco cop takes the course. The quicker you stitch a wound up, the less chance there is of a scar. I think the Chaco cops left everything split open too long. It's part of the reason I joined up afterwards. I didn't want it happening to anyone else. I'm not one to puff myself up, but I guarantee you if I had been behind a badge that day, I would know exactly what had happened to Ana.

Instead I was a terrified eighteen-year-old boy. I remember I kept running places. Up and down the halls. In and out of the front door. Around the parking lot. I yelled for her like she was a lost puppy. I screamed her name until my voice was hoarse and the police threw a blanket over me in the dead heat of August and sat me in the back of a cruiser. I didn't have a chance to look clearly at anything. And even if I'd had the sanity, I didn't have the ability. I wouldn't have known what to look for. But knowing that doesn't make it any easier. I felt like a kid who can't reach the phone when his mom is choking. When time is of the essence.

- *That day I start to see crows.*

I actually write this. I write this in the report before I
know what I'm doing, and after I write it I stare at the letters
for a moment as if they'd been spelled out on a Ouija board.
I sniff. There's a tingling in the back of my throat. Like a
drip. It smells like sulfur. My head throbs once, expands and
then compresses back. I look out of the skylights above, and
it's almost like I'm expecting to see the crow. The big crow
with the red shine to him. The one on the car. The one in
the sky on the drive back from the hospital. The one that
lives in the corner of my sight. But there's nothing but
broken blue sky. I can't look away. It's like I can feel the big
thing, right out of sight, perched on a branch and staring at
me through the wall with unblinking eyes. There's a pressure in my head, a slow-building whistling. I grip the edge
of my desk as I delete the words. Nobody needs to know
that.

"Hey." Danny Ninepoint kicks me under the desk.
"What's wrong with you these days?"

I blink. The bubble pops. Only the soft throb of a
headache remains, but I've lived with that for months now.

"It's just this report." I flick my hand at the computer. "I
don't like going back to this."

"Well, pull it together. It looks like you're the hot buck at
the dance this week," he says, nodding his head to the door.

Two white people are at the front desk, and I recognize
both of them. It's the doctor from the hospital and Caroline,
and they're looking right at me. It takes all I've got not to
swear under my breath or flinch like a spooked dog. Last
thing I need is to give any one of the fifteen bored cops
within earshot more ammo to use against me.

"You want me to go talk to 'em?" Danny mutters.

"Nah," I say. "Maybe..." Maybe what? Maybe they're here
on business? The doctor has been round before. He's

conferred with the detectives once or twice on hard cases where a Navajo ended up in the hospital. But Caroline? It's funny how her name comes to me like a letter dropping through a mail slot and plunking on the floor. Her name, and her hand on my shoulder. I remember them both quite clearly.

Like it or not, the doctor is coming towards me, walking like a stork. Out of the corner of my eye I see Danny shake his head in exasperation. I think he's tired of the parade too.

"Officer Dejooli?" the doctor asks, all business. Five or six cops turn to watch.

"Yeah," I say, defeated.

"I found a nurse who's willing to make a statement," he says, evenly.

"What?"

"The drunk driver. He came in to the ER a little over a week ago under police escort. Sorry it took so long. I want to nail that bastard as much as anybody, but it's been crazy at the hospital all week."

It takes me way longer than it should to realize that he's making all of this up to get me to talk to Caroline. He's so steady that for a good five seconds I actually think I may have processed a drunk driving case and forgotten about it.

"Right," I say.

"She's right over there. I have some other business with Sani, and I thought I'd bring her down. You know. Two birds and all that."

The cops all go back to their work. This guy is good.

"All right. Thanks."

And just like that he turns and lopes off towards the big offices. I clear my throat, smooth my uniform, and take a step towards reception before Danny hands me a notepad.

"Might want this. If you're taking a statement and all."

"Oh. Thanks."

He nods, his head already back to the reports.

Caroline smiles at me as I walk up to her, and it's not the smile of a girl who is supposed to be meeting someone for the first time.

"Hi," I say, glancing at the front desk. "I'm Ben Dejooli. I'll take your statement, if you're ready."

"I am," she says, and she clasps her hands demurely behind her back, but not before she brushes them on her pants. That's a telltale sign of clammy palms. She's nervous as hell.

"Right this way," I say, and I lead her to one of the empty conference rooms on the main level. She follows a half step behind. I flick on the lights and shut the door behind us, then I turn and just watch her.

At first she tries to be nonchalant, but she can only meet my eyes for about five seconds at a time. Then she screws up one side of her face, and for a horrible moment I think she's about to cry. When she looks up at me again I can see that she is almost as surprised as I am to find herself where she is. She looks around the room like she's lost.

"Is this about me?" I ask, quietly.

"No," she says, shaking her head vigorously. "Doctor Bennet had some files to give one of your people." She pauses and her eyes widen, as if she's insulted me. "I just thought I'd come with him to..."

"To..."

She looks up at the ceiling, giving up.

"To see if you'd ever gone to get that scan, except I know that you haven't because I could see that the order was never fulfilled. So what I really came to ask was why the hell you didn't go. There. There it is."

She's trying to stare bullets at me now. Her hands are on

her hips. She's still wearing scrubs from work. Black pants that fit her like a tarp and a blue top that looks like it was cut from paper. I think she's wearing clogs, too, and I know that sounds bad, but it's not like that. If anything it was sort of cute. Maybe more than cute.

"You came all this way to tell me to do what the doctor said?"

"Yes," she says, point blank. And that's when it finally hits me: maybe there's really something wrong with me. My whole life nobody has done anything like this on my behalf. Something as good as a girl like her coming out here to see me has to have a flipside. Everything has a balance.

"You think I'm really sick? I...I've been fine. I haven't passed out or anything since."

But as soon as the words come out of my mouth I know I haven't been fine. My head has been hurting. Now that I think about it, I don't think it ever stopped hurting. I can't remember when it didn't hurt, even just a little. It's become background noise, that's all.

"Yes," she says, softly this time, and her eyes sweep over me, over my head and arms and the skin of my hands. "I do think you're sick," she says.

"What do you think I have?" It almost doesn't come out because it feels like I have a fistful of sand in my mouth.

"I don't know. Could be a lot of things."

"The doctor said you thought it was a tumor back at the hospital—"

"I don't know," she says again, but I can tell that's exactly what she's thinking. I'm not gonna lie, the more I think about it, the more it seems possible. When you pass out and come to in an ambulance, your brain automatically leaps to the worst of the worst. You're dying. You have something fundamentally wrong with you. But when Caroline and

Doctor Bennet told me to get the scan, something in me rebelled. It's more than just how hospitals mess with me; I refused to believe it could happen to me. Cancer is so huge, so faceless. Something that you assume attacks without mercy. A dark spot inside you that sucks you away. It's not a headache. Not a momentary spate of dizziness. And yet, here Caroline is, trying not to look like she's pleading with me.

"Look, I'm right in the middle of a big case here. When it's over, I'll try to get to that scan. I promise this time."

It sounds weak, I know. To promise to try? This is exactly what she doesn't want to hear, and I can tell that her mind is tumbling over itself. But just when she looks about to come back at me there's a knock at the door, and it stills her. It's Bennet. I open the door, and he looks briefly between Caroline and me.

"I'm all set," he says. "Did you get what you needed?"

Caroline scowls, then frowns. Then she sort of deflates and shrugs, and that hits me. Bennet looks at me plainly and then nods.

"Well, you did what you could," he says.

Caroline brushes past me, and the two of them are gone in a blink. I stand in the empty conference room for another full minute, staring at nothing, trying to probe my own brain for parts of it that might be killing me. Like I said, I know I'm not *fine*. But am I *dying*? There seems like there should be a lot of ground between those two.

I end up staying at the station long after Danny and most everyone else on the day shift goes home. The night shift is half as strong, personnel-wise. On the rez there are basically two hotspots of activity. One is around ten in the evening, which the night shift takes on with fresh eyes and ears, and the other is at rush hour, about five in the afternoon. There's an old tongue-in-cheek saying around here. All of your calls essentially come from the same type of Indian: he's pissed off after work and starting shit and then drunk after dinner and starting shit.

Nobody around Danny's and my desk is scheduled for night shift, so I have a bit of space. Since nobody talks to me, I don't have any distractions, either. The shift change just sort of happens around me while I'm writing up the profile part of the report for the Feds. This is the part I've been dreading the most. Here is where I'm supposed to talk about Joey himself. I rub at my face. The only way to get through this is to just write whatever comes to my mind.

Joey was no saint, I write. *He was the only man I ever met who gave me the guts to go places that scared me and to do things I was afraid to do. He used to say that we were clipped at the knees in life just having to live at Chaco, so we owed it to ourselves to own the place. He said we'd be the rat kings. Joey never would admit it, but outside of Danny Ninepoint, I never met a man more proud to be a Navajo.*

I met Joey when we were thirteen years old, in those first days of middle school when kids hammer out the pecking order, and we decided to stick together. He lived at the Arroyo with his grandfather on his mother's side. His mother died when he was young. He didn't know his father. But his grandfather was a good man. A Navajo of the old ways. He hunted and trapped for food. He had a small herb garden in the window of his camper. He would capture water from rain, which he prayed for, and he would eat rabbit and prairie dog, which he also prayed for. He butchered them in the old way, too. Giving thanks. Never taking anything for granted. When we could, my family would pass cuts of beef and cans of food to Joey, for the both of them. His grandfather was too proud to take handouts, but Joey was more practical, and he had a soft spot for Dinty Moore stew. We ran together all throughout our teenaged years.

Looking at that last sentence, it hardly seems a fitting way to describe seven years of raising hell, chasing after cars and girls, drinking when we shouldn't and smoking when we shouldn't and what we shouldn't, usually on Joey's lead. Cigarettes that made us sick, and a couple of times peyote, that made us sicker. Swearing to watch each other's backs. Swearing in blood, smeared on our hands, dark like mud, cut with Joey's grandfather's knife, which had seemed like a sword then, and, in all honesty, probably would seem like a sword now, too. It was a huge goddamn knife. I wonder if Joey took it with him. The only one I've ever seen like it is Danny's scalp knife, which makes sense, since he has a lot of the old ways in him too.

I write, *Joey's grandfather died right around the time Ana's heart condition took a turn for the worse.* Looking back on it now, it was a subtle turn, but it was a turn nonetheless. She wasn't gaining any weight, she wasn't growing, she seemed to be shrinking, if anything. While the rest of her classmates and her friends were pushing their way up the hill into puberty, it was like she tripped and slowly began rolling backwards. But her eyes were always bright and winking, if a little softer than usual, and she laughed and ran, if a touch slower. I worried myself sick over her, playing out terrible scenarios in my mind, trying to imagine a Ben Dejooli who had no sister. I know now that I didn't give Joey what he needed then, as a friend, as a blood brother. I was selfish. His family was all gone. I still had mine, but it was going, and I wallowed in it. I don't even remember his grandfather's burial. That's how muddled I was.

We offered to take him in, have him live with us in our house, but he politely declined. He was seventeen, after all. His grandfa-

ther's camper and all that came with it, sparse as it was, was his now. Knife and all. And he knew his way around the Arroyo. He was a man now.

Still, that was the beginning of the change in him.

Joey became obsessed with death. Our conversations, whenever we met up, eventually turned to death and dying. Which I suppose is normal for a kid who has just lost his only family. Still, this went on for an entire year. Joey was there when his grandfather died. Their camper wasn't big enough for him to have been anywhere else. He said he went in his sleep, but I often wonder if his passing wasn't...uglier somehow.

I believe that this was part of the reason he offered to start watching over Ana.

The main reason he offered was because he could see the toll the wait was taking on me and on my family. But I've always felt that he was unnaturally comfortable there. In the hospital, around Ana, who was dying by degrees. I don't mean to seem like he was eager or creepy about it, not like that, but he did settle in quickly. He took one shift a week at first, just a couple of hours. He did construction day-work that started early, so he would come hang out with Ana in the mid-afternoon to give one of us a break. At night he'd go back to the Arroyo.

And there's another thing that's been bothering me, although I'm not quite sure why. Before he was banished, Joey lived in the spot where the smoker had parked for his vigil. Joey and the gambler would have been neighbors. The gambler probably had that spot for decades. He would have seen Joey grow up. There's a good chance Joey and the gambler were friends.

Something about finding these connections where they shouldn't be bothers me. The gambler and Joey should have nothing to do with each other, but they do. I just don't know how yet. I feel like I'm just outside of understanding, like I'm jumping up to get a peek through a window in my mind, looking for a glimpse of Joey or Ana, and instead I find the gambler watching me. In my mind's eye he's not dead, though. He's just silent. And staring at me dressed in dull gold and holding a turquoise crow tightly in his hand. And he thumps his fist to his heart...

I jump in my seat as a gust of wind kicks up and bits of desert sand pepper the outside of the station. The windows themselves seem to pop and settle, and the old fan that circles slowly above the main floor squeals angrily. The handful of other cops at their desks look up as well, brought out of their work, or their dozing. There is a feeling of resignation in the main room; the late night storms of autumn always signal that winter is close behind. Fall is the best season in New Mexico. It's warm and colorful, and it stretches itself like a cat, lingering in the sunny spots as long as it can. Winter is the worst. It's not cold, not exactly, but it's not warm either. It's somewhere in the damp between. The colors fall flat. The desert trees and bushes seem confused, like they don't know if they should shed their leaves or gut it out until spring.

Profiling Joey has put me in a bad frame of mind. I'm feeling twinges of the same sort of sick helplessness that tinges this entire series of events a drained sepia color in my memory. It's time to wrap it up.

The last time I saw Joseph Flatwood was the day he was banished. At the reading of his sentence.

We were on the south edge of the reservation. He had his camper on the 'out' side of the Chaco line, and representatives from the tribal council and tribal court stood on the inside. I insisted that I go, too. I wanted to see him break down. I held out hope that he might finally give me something, some precious grain of information that would let me know what had happened in the room during that camera blip when Ana disappeared, but he said nothing.

He remained silent as the court read its decision. He looked at the ground the entire time. Although I did notice that he was crying.

I feel it's important to note this in the report. He looked at me, too. I stood off of the road with Gam, who also insisted on coming. He looked right at me and his eyes were screaming something that I couldn't quite understand, but his mouth was an unwavering frown, like a horseshoe. I almost called out to him. I was either going to scream at him or plead with him, but my grandmother sensed it first and gripped my shoulder like a vice, stilling me.

And then it was over. Joey Flatwood was no longer a Navajo in the eyes of the council. The voice of the people had spoken. He was cast out. There was no great clap of thunder. No driving sheet of rain or swelling of wind, but it did feel like a cord had been cut. A musical chord in my heart, like the string of a guitar. It twanged and thumped in my mind, and then it was still. Joey never stopped watching me, even when the cops led him across the threshold, even when each man and woman turned their back upon him, one by one. I was the last. Gam had to physically turn me. I'm not sure I could have done it otherwise.

Eventually I heard him shuffle away. Heard him get into his camper, and the engine roll over slowly, struggling to life. And then he pulled away. There was no peel out. No skittering of the desert dust underneath his wheels. It was a slow, quiet rolling away. When I turned around again, his camper was a dot on the horizon, but his eyes, silently screaming at me, brimming with tears, they stuck with me long afterwards.

You could say that they never really left me.

I have to wipe at my own eyes, which I do quickly and brusquely with the sleeve of my jacket. For the first time since it happened, I find words coming to me that I never turned to before, either out of fear, or out of anger, or sadness, or all three. For years I had assumed he knew something but wouldn't tell me. Surely he knew. He was there, for God's sake.

But what if he knew something but *couldn't* tell me?

The thought triggers a massive wave of pressure in my head, and I'm forced to lay down on my arms on my desk. I sit like this for several minutes, breathing deeply, trying to get my eyes to focus correctly again. Watching my breath fog the desk. I'm not sure if I black out again, but if I did it was only for a short time, and, thankfully, I'm not the only cop sleeping at his desk at this hour. When I sit up I do it slowly, blinking heavily. There is a sour taste in my mouth and a whiff of matches in my nose.

By the time I pull myself together enough to finish my statement, it's nearly one in the morning, and by then I'm sure of two things.

The first is that Joey Flatwood saw something terrible that day in Ana's room.

The second is that Caroline was right. I need to go get that goddamn brain scan.

8

CAROLINE ADAMS

Well. That was a complete disaster.

I've been going over the trip to Chaco in my mind frame by frame; stopping and rewinding, slow motion, pausing here and there. It's three in the morning now, and I'm more convinced than ever that not only did I not convince Ben to get scanned, but I also made a complete ass of myself in front of him, and later in front of Doctor Bennet, and in general in front of God and everybody. It would be good if I just ran away. I could probably get to Arizona before my car gave out. I haven't changed the oil in a year. I haven't done anything in a year, really. And just like that, bits of my anxiety snowball into each other until I find myself in the bathroom thinking I'm going to throw up. I don't, of course, but I do stare at myself in the mirror until my nose bumps the glass, trying to find any trace of color like I saw on Ben and on Doctor Bennet. But whatever I can see on other people I can't see on me, so I pee, then get some water and get back in bed. I listen to the storm blow against the wall and let my regrets wash over me like weak little lake waves.

I think it's time I was honest with myself. I think it's time I call this what it is. I have a stupid little juvenile twelve-year-old girl crush on Ben Dejooli, and it's infuriating. I want to be rid of it. I think that's why I went to the station, to purge myself of this. This isn't normal for me, I promise. I don't want to give you the wrong impression. I don't pine. I'm not a piner.

Ben has every right to think I'm a lunatic. He should have called the cops on me. Except he is a cop. He should have called himself on me. That would have been great. But not in any sort of sexual way. Just in a sort of escort-the-crazy-cat-lady-off-the-premises type of way. And I don't even have any cats. I've often thought I should get a cat. My apartment is pretty small, but I think a lazy cat would be fine. Or an indoor/outdoor cat. Although an outdoor cat on the Albuquerque outskirts would stand a one-in-five chance of getting destroyed by a coyote every time it left the apartment. If I got a cat only to have it eaten I would need therapy. I probably need therapy already.

These are the things I think about at three in the morning.

I really hope he gets that scan. I hope because I want him to start fighting the cancer that I somehow already know is in him. Just like I know that something was in that room after that horrible code. I just know it. I want him to get the ball rolling. He's dying, and it's time to get to work.

How do I know? I can see it. I can see what is wrong with him. That's what the colors are, some sort of visual representation of what is going on inside of people. It's like how you can see when a patient is yellowed by jaundice; he has a color to him. Actually, it would be like if a patient turned yellow from jaundice and I was the only person in the world who could see it. That's a bit more accurate. Just to make sure, I asked Doctor Bennet on the drive home if Ben looked darker, kind of reddish, and he looked at me like I was joking with him.

"He looked okay to me," he said. And then out of nowhere I started sobbing.

I haven't cried since my first year on the floor. I didn't cry when my mom called and told me that my dog died. I didn't cry when a tiny dove flew into my window and I could see it flop dead to the ground two floors below on the sidewalk. I didn't cry when I had to work Christmas last year and couldn't go home and I sat in my apartment and drank out of a jug of Carlo Rossi wine watching the Hallmark channel with nothing but a ficus with a droopy star for decoration, like something straight out of *A Charlie Brown Christmas*. That was a cryable moment if there ever was one. But I didn't then. And I did today. God in heaven. And in front of Doctor Bennet, too.

Of course, he played it off perfectly. He was so kind. He patted my knee and said it's okay and let me wheeze it out while I stared out of the window and wished the radio was on a little louder. When I said I was sorry he said there's no reason to be. He's had his fair share of these days too. He didn't even call it a breakdown, which is what I'm pretty sure it was. And the fact that he was so kind to me made it even worse, of course.

I have to get ahold of myself. In general. I have to allow for the fact that some people just want to die. And there's nothing I can do about it. If they want to die, they want to die. And I think Ben maybe wants to die. He was red. He was this blackish red that was just *wrong*.

While we're on the subject of my mental breakdown, I might as well come clean with you and say that I think I've been seeing these colors in some form for much of my life. I know this now. I've been *seeing* but not *noticing*. Now I'm noticing. It's kind of like how I *saw* wedding bands on people's ring fingers all of my life, but only really started *noticing* them once I hit my mid-twenties. The colors have always been there. In a way, this is a good thing. One of the first tests we give people who think they have an abnormal growth is the longevity test. Is this new? How long have you felt the lump? How long have you had that mole? Has it always been that size? If the answer is "for a while," we can relax. If the answer is "I don't know," we nod and tell them to keep an eye on it. What we don't want is changes. And this strange color filter I have is no change. What is a change is that the colors are stronger now. By the day. And they are trying to tell me something about the person who shows them.

I do a lot of internet research over the next couple of days. Especially late at night when I can't sleep. I pride myself on my internet diagnosis skills. I'm an RN by degree, but I'm a full-blown wizard-status doctor on the internet. The closest I can come to diagnosing what I have is a condition called "synesthesia" where people associate colors with things like letters. Each letter has its own unique color. Except that's not really what I have. I see colors around people, and they don't define the people, they help describe the person at that moment in time.

One piece of information pretty much hits the nail on the head. I stumble across it around four in the morning, right about when I usually berate myself for still being awake and make myself lie down and stare at the dark ceiling, stubbornly willing sleep to come like I've put myself in time out. That's when I find this thing called 'aura sight' at the bottom of the internet.

I know. I agree. I had a good laugh about it too, even at

four in the morning. Telling someone who works in health-care that they have a psychic ability is liable to get you laughed out of the room. We don't have time for this nonsense. We're big people doing big people things. There's a "joke" that goes around the cancer floor. What do you call a cancer patient who uses a "healer" instead of a doctor?

Dead.

Not really a *ha ha* joke, but you get the point. We barely sniff at homeopathy. You can imagine what we think of this psychic crap. But that doesn't change the fact that aura sight comes pretty damn close to whatever I have. The good news is I think I've ruled out that I'm dying. The bad news is that I've ruled in that I may be a kook.

Thankfully I wasn't scheduled to work the floor on the same day as Doctor Bennet until four days after our little excursion. By then I'd gone through all the phases of over-analysis, and my internal pendulum had settled firmly into a depressed resignation that at best I'm just abnormal. When I next saw him on the floor, it was during another hectic night shift and I'd forgotten completely about Chaco and everything else in favor of trying to remember which meds I'd given to a particularly challenging bone marrow transplant patient and at which hours. In that respect my work can be a blessing. You don't get time to mope.

"Are you feeling better?" he asks me, speaking softly in the break room. He sat down next to me during my granola bar supper. Or breakfast. Or whatever you call a meal you eat at four a.m. I look up at him and see that he's still blue. I blink and rub at my eyes. Still blue. A faint, soft halo of blue smoke that seems to puff off of his shoulders and head. It's his blue. I know that now. It's genuine and caring and a little sad. I don't know how I know that, but I do. You'll just have to trust me.

"I'm fine," I say, and I'm sure it comes out sounding snippy because I'm exhausted and working when normal people are in deep REM sleep. His smoke twitches a little and darkens a shade. I have an irresistible urge to lighten it up again. Get it back to the color of his eyes.

"I never got a chance to really thank you for what you did," I say. "For taking me. Making excuses for me to be a nosy little snot. For not freaking out when I was...freaking out. In the car."

He smiles. It's like a crack in the clouds. It's working.

"No worries," he says. "I know what it's like to want to see a patient make it. Especially a Navajo. There are some real train wrecks on that reservation. You and I both know that. This Ben guy, he strikes me as a good man. I can see why you like him." He smiles again, but it's a little forced this time and his color twitches. Then his phone buzzes, and he lets out a big breath as he pops it from his side and eyes it.

"Work calls. See you around?"

"You know it."

He taps the table, looks desperately likes he want to say something, taps the table again, and pops up and out of the door.

I don't see him the rest of the week. I don't see anyone outside of the nurses who are scheduled to work my side of the unit, my patients, and my pillow. That's the way night shift is. Weeks when I work nights I'm like a vampire. When I'm not at work, I'm shut in my apartment in a pharmaceutically induced black hole of sleep with the shades drawn against the harsh late-fall sun and my noise machine humming. There's a little note on the front door of my apartment that says "Do not disturb. Night shift in progress." The landlord and even my neighbors' little kids know what it means. I am a zombie if awoken. I slept through a fire alarm once. And one other time I woke up during a fire alarm, and I'm told I actually shuffled out to the main foyer with the rest of the complex, though I don't remember it. I came to in the shower with my underwear on. I must have thought it was time to get ready for work.

At any rate, the point is that the few people I do know, know better than to try and get ahold of me when I'm on nights, because I'm a groggy mess. That's why when my buzzing phone wakes me up I know it's not a good thing, since in my state it would have to have been buzzing a long time. Multiple tries. I paw at it, grab it, and bring it close to my face. I see two screens. Both of them say I've missed five calls. It's from the hospital. This cannot be good. I steady myself and click answer.

"Hello?"

"Caroline! Thank God. It's Owen."

It takes me about ten seconds to put together that Owen is Doctor Bennet. He's Doctor Owen Bennet. I wonder if I'm dreaming.

"Are you there?"

"Yeah. Yeah, sorry, I..."

"You're sleeping, I know. And I feel like an ass, but I don't work with you for a week and I had to try and call you."

"What? Why?"

He pauses, then says, "It's about Ben Dejooli. I've had some news..."

9

OWEN BENNET

I'm sitting in my apartment, and I'm cursing my tenacity, cursing Navajo stubbornness, and drinking bourbon.

I'm not sure *where* I went wrong, but I know I went wrong. I know it because Caroline ended up crying in my car, and since then the one time I saw her she looked at me like she was in a daze, or seeing me for the first time, or something. I don't know if it was me or Ben Dejooli or what, but it was something, and now everything is ruined.

I take another swig. Who am I kidding. It was me. A doctor who has worked out here for the better part of a decade should know better than to try and push the Navajo into anything. That's rule number one. There's white man time, and there's Indian time. Indians work on Indian time. If you want to work with them, you'd better work on Indian time too. It was a rookie mistake, thinking I could make her feel better out at Chaco.

What on God's green earth am I thinking here, anyway? What is my end game? What, in my wildest fantasies, do I want to happen? Somehow I sweep Caroline off of her feet?

Convince her to stay here with me in my two bedroom apartment in Albuquerque? Maybe we clean out the second room of all of the useless gadgets I jam in there and we have babies and they grow up with Navajo kids and everyone dances the rain dance and we all live happily ever after? Is what I'm looking for basically the first Thanksgiving? I thought I was past all this. I have my practice, more or less, and I have my cause. The problem is now I have a girl. Or a dream of a girl.

I'm suddenly disgusted by the way I live. This happens sometimes. It's like a bout of nausea or a wave of vertigo. It passes, but when it happens I hate everything I surround myself with. I have no idea how to spend money. Or save money. I stuff it places or put it into stupid projects. I open investment accounts and play the markets like I know what I'm doing. I buy ridiculous gadgets like massage chairs and hydroponic vegetable gardens and memory foam pillows and microwaveable slippers. I use them for a day or a week or a month. I invest in things no sane man would invest in. Small pink slip companies from Australia that are getting into uranium mining. Drug companies that I pick at random from the complimentary pens one of their reps drops off on the floor. I have a jar full. All of these things I do. Some of them make me money. Some of them don't. I don't care. I have plenty of money. I'd have plenty of money if everything went tits up. We used to say that you could earn like a prince and live like a king in Boston. It was better than New York that way, where you had to earn like a god just to live like a man. Well, in ABQ you can earn like a man and live like a king. Especially if you have nobody to spend on except yourself.

I take another swig of bourbon. It tastes terrible. Now, you see? This is something I could legitimately upgrade.

There is no reason why I should be making a quarter million a year and be swilling plastic bottle bourbon at three a.m. in my apartment. I shouldn't be swilling any bourbon at three a.m., actually, but if I'm gonna swill, it should at least be something decent. In a house.

I don't want to give you the wrong impression. I'm not a drinker. Not a *drinker* drinker, anyway. Dad was a *drinker* drinker. Not abusive or anything, just a booze hound. That is possible, believe it or not. I only allow myself late night drinks when I have the next day off, which, if you knew my colleagues, shows a remarkable level of restraint, comparatively.

I'm going through stacks of charts. I go through a record review for every patient I have. After that I usually go to bed, but this Caroline thing has me a little off. So I go through more bourbon. Sometimes when I can't sleep I do what's called a 'dead review,' where I whip through past records in our system and pull out everyone who has died and move their files into inactive status. I get the morgue records and cross-reference them with our hospital system. There are generally a lot of overlaps. This is the definition of busywork. I am fully aware that I am doing this so I don't have to think about Caroline crying in my car because she's most likely in love with Ben Dejooli.

It's interesting when you flip through the Chaco Health Center files. I find myself lingering on pictures of the Navajo. One of the first things they teach residents that are going to CHC is that your bedside manner with the Navajo needs to be different. Clear and direct doesn't always go over so well. You have to be much more reactive; let them take the lead. Especially with the old guard. And the old guard is mostly what shows up at the Center. I'm struck by how flat their expressions are. Flat like a lake. Calm. Expansive.

There's one man in particular who gives me pause. His name is Oka Chalk. He looks haunted. He has the kind of lined, tanned face that you would instantly associate with an elder Navajo, but his eyes look like the eyes of a young man. Of a young warrior. I remember seeing him off and on at CHC for blood pressure issues related to drinking. His chart says he asphyxiated on his own vomit. The report notes drug paraphernalia on his person at the time of death, but the toxicology came back inconclusive. Positive on alcohol in the system. Well above the legal limit, but nothing that would kill a seasoned drinker. Curious. But with no living relatives and nobody to follow up, his case was open and shut. Like far too many of the Chaco cases.

I pull him from the active files and mark him deceased. On to the next. I do this for an hour until I grow weary and slightly depressed. The bourbon is swimming in my head. The night has whispered by me, and the sky is opening up to the sun. In the distance, a flock of crows stirs as the first rays hit the bare tree where they rest. They shuffle and stretch their wings like a single organism, twitchy and black. One of them caws loudly. A sharp, brief sound, like the scratching of a record. I should really be in bed. This is bad, even for a day off. I know I'll never be able to sleep long enough through the day to make up for this the rest of the week. But something in the call of the crow sobers me and draws me back to my computer.

I flip to the active files and pull up Ben Dejooli for the tenth time. I reload his chart. The scan fulfillment status goes from *N/A* to *processed*. I take the last swig of my bourbon and cough a little. I pull out my phone and call the hospital.

"Radiology, how can I help you?"

"This is Doctor Owen Bennet. I was hoping to get the results of a scan that went through."

"One moment."

The hold music sounds particularly ridiculous to me. The bourbon still burns my throat. I find I'm tapping the hem of my jeans rapidly and standing in front of the window, staring at the crows.

"This is Diagnostics. What's your patient number, Doctor Bennet?"

I recite Ben's number from memory, forcing myself to slow down. I'm not quite sure why I'm acting like a student waiting for his board results. I've done this countless times before. But in all those other times there was no Caroline involved.

"Doctor Bennet?"

"Yes."

"I'm loading the file now. You should have access momentarily."

"Thank you."

I hang up and squeeze my phone. I make myself wait for an entire minute, then I refresh my log-in on the system. Ben's file is there. And it's bad.

I see two separate causes for outright concern. The first is in the front left lobe. Three inches in diameter. The second is in the rear left lobe, one and a half inches in diameter.

I am speechless.

Multiple instances almost always indicate metastatic activity. This is not benign. The tissue surrounding the sites are in necrosis. These look like late-stage glioblastoma multiforme tumors. We'd need to radiate the sites to reduce their size before we even thought about operating.

Caroline was right. Ben Dejooli is dying.

A sound tears me away from the scan. It is the crows. They've all taken flight at once in a massive black cloak and are sweeping towards me. Right towards the window, all of them shrieking at once. They look as though they will collide with the window, and I find myself backing away, into the kitchen. I even throw up my hands before they swoop up and over the building, their calls dropping away as they gain altitude. I sit down again, my heart racing. I take out the phone once more, and this time I dial the contact number for Ben Dejooli. It's barely five in the morning, but he picks up.

"Hello?" he asks.

This is always the worst part. The part before you bring a man's entire world down around him.

"Ben?"

"Who is this?" he asks, wary.

"Ben, this is Doctor Owen Bennet, with ABQ General. I have the results of your scan."

He pauses.

"It's bad, isn't it," he says, very clearly. No one has ever said this to me before. It throws me for a loop.

"Yes. I'm afraid it is. We're going to want to get you on a treatment plan immediately."

"Like radiation?"

"Yes. And chemotherapy. In preparation for surgery. But first let's schedule a consult. I'll be there to explain everything."

He is quiet. I can only wait.

"I can't do that," he says.

"Ben, I don't think you understand…"

"I understand. I'm a dead man."

"No. Not if you choose to fight."

"And if I don't?"

"If you don't, it's my opinion you have at most a couple of months. Maybe weeks."

"Shit."

"Yes. Shit. But there are options."

"Chemotherapy? Like, the chemical kind?"

"Yes. We would radiate the tumors initially, here, at the hospital, then put you on an aggressive chemotherapy regimen with the aim of shrinking the tumors before surgery."

"Tumors? Like, more than one?"

"Yes, I believe there is clear evidence of two, and maybe one more potential site."

"Shit."

I'm standing at the kitchen counter and I hang my head. I feel like whatever buzz the bourbon gave me left with the crows and now my head weighs a hundred pounds. "I wish...I really, *really* wish I had better news, Ben."

"I can't go back to that hospital. I don't do well in that hospital."

"Well, you're gonna have to, if you want to give yourself a chance."

"No, you don't understand. I can't. And not just because of...it's also because cancer here, at Chaco, it doesn't go over well. I...it just...for the Navajo it's a mark of death."

"Not if I can help it, it's not."

"Can anything be done here? At home? At my home? In private?"

Now this is an interesting question. I rub at my face and try to get my brain working the way I know it should. We do have off-site programs for chemotherapy. And the hospital likes to appear to bend over backward for the Navajo community. I bet I could get a request for offsite delivery pushed through, given Ben's position as a policeman. I am aware of more about the stigma of cancer among the Navajo than Ben would think.

"I could probably get the chemotherapy off-site. But the initial radiation has to be done in a lab. Can you give me that? If I can get you the treatment at home?"

He pauses. "Yes. I can do that. I suppose. It's either that or die in a couple weeks."

He says this with such a cavalier tone that it chills me. It occurs to me that he has exhibited none of the usual traumatic overtones. His voice is calm and clear. No tears. No wavering. He is responsive, and not in shock. It's not unlike the discussions I have with other doctors about swapping shifts. Straightforward. Practical. I jump at the opening.

"I'll call you back within the hour, okay? Stay by your phone."

"All right."

I move to hang up, but he speaks again.

"Hey, doc?"

"Yes?"

"Who would give me the chemotherapy? At home?"

"One of our oncology nurses."

"Can I request one?"

I already know where this is going. I can't help but laugh. It's a strange, desperate laugh. Thankfully I cover the mouthpiece first.

"Caroline Adams?" I ask.

"Y...yeah."

I shake my head, but I say, "Yes. I think I can make that happen."

"Thanks."

"Ben, we can beat this. I've seen people with stage four diagnoses beat it before."

He pauses again, and I think that maybe I've finally

gotten through to him. I picture him holding his head, or covering the receiver while he gathers himself, steels himself for the battle. But after a minute he speaks again, and his voice is as even as glass.

"Yeah. I guess we'll see."

I get this uncanny feeling he's trying to let me down easy.

As soon as I hang up, I call the hospital on the off chance I can catch Caroline, but they tell me she was released early and went home from night shift two hours ago. I nearly curse out loud at the poor charge nurse, but I catch myself, thank her, and hang up. Then I stare at my phone for another ten full minutes as the sunbeams creep into my living room. Dust motes swirl about my table and my head. This is insanity. I had plenty of chances to disassociate myself from this. Let Ben be Ben and Caroline be Caroline. I know they want each other. It's like they reach towards each other when they are together. Even an analytical robot like myself can see that. Where along the line did I think it would *help* my chances with Caroline to throw her into close quarters with Ben? A terrible thought creeps into my brain, and the more I try to shut it out the stronger it becomes.

Don't worry. He'll be dead soon anyway.

And the sickness that washes over me immediately afterwards tells me something else: I do not want that. I desperately want this man to live. I want this man to live because keeping people alive is what I was born to do, but mostly because I know it would make Caroline happy. And we come back to the common denominator. And me, staring at my phone. I know she's sleeping by now, but every minute that passes is another minute of wiggle room for Ben Dejooli to back out. With the Navajo, you better strike while the iron is hot. God knows when you'll get another chance.

I pick up the phone and dial her number. Again, and again, and again. By the time she answers I'm so far beyond embarrassed that it's become a battle of wills between me and the ring tone. When she picks up, I let out a little hoot. "Caroline! Thank God. It's Owen."

She's groggy. For a second I think she's hung up on me, but she hasn't. I apologize profusely.

"I've had some news..." I say, and in the excitement it comes back to me that I'm about to tell her that Ben has late stage brain cancer. I pull the curtain across, and my face slackens. I take a breath.

"Ben got the scan. His results just came in."

She clears her throat. "You wouldn't be calling me at home if it was all clear, would you," she says, and her voice is thick.

"No. You were right. I would diagnose it as late stage GBM. Maybe stage four."

She exhales slowly, and I picture her in her bed slumping over like a deflating balloon. I think she's gearing up to shed the tears Ben wouldn't, so I jump in again.

"He wants to fight it," I say, and as soon as I do, I know that isn't entirely true. But he's willing to give it a shot, at least.

"Really?" she asks, echoing my doubt.

"I'm going to order off-site chemotherapy. Given his circumstances, I'm sure it will be approved."

"That's good of you," she says, and she means it.

"The reason I called you is that he requested you administer the regimen. You personally."

She makes a series of glottal sounds then says, "Are you fucking kidding me right now?"

I've never heard her swear before. For some reason, it

makes me smile. It is in no way emphatic, more like someone cussing in their sleep.

"No. But he needs an answer right now, and I need to get him in the books or he could run. You know what I mean?"

"Yes."

"Yes you know or yes you'll do it?"

"Yes and yes. Just yes all around."

"Okay then. I'll get it ordered up. We'll start as soon as possible. I'll get the schedule to you when you wake up."

"Let's do it," she says, and I have the strange feeling that she's looking at herself in the mirror. Self-affirming.

"Talk to you soon then."

"Doctor Bennet."

"Owen. Please."

"Owen. Thank you. All of this, it's been a mess up and down, and I've totally overextended my welcome on basically every facet of it to the point where I'm even starting to annoy myself these days."

"Caroline. I wanted to do it. I'm with you. Do you understand?"

"Yes," she says softly. "Thank you. So much."

"Let's get him healthy, then we can thank each other. Sleep tight."

I hang up the phone and stare at it for a minute, wondering what just happened to me, to Ben, to Caroline, to all of us. Then I move over to my couch and collapse into a sleep that lasts until the sun starts to set again.

10

BEN DEJOOLI

I'm a mess after the scan. If you want to know what my darkness looks like, my own personal hell, imagine an hour-long brain scan with the specter of death hanging over you, and you'll come pretty damn close. I thought it was bad coming to in an ambulance on its way to the hospital. I thought it was bad sitting and waiting to be discharged. None of those discomforts held a candle to this.

I used to feel sorry for the Navajo who balked at modern medicine. I understood why they might not feel comfortable visiting a hospital, of course, but to throw the whole thing out the window was just reckless. I still have a healthy respect for modern medicine, even after everything that happened with Ana. I saw how the doctors helped her, relieved her suffering during the bad times. But the machines and the implements and the sounds; it's not hard at all to see why a Navajo would distrust these things. They are sterile and plastic and metal. Basically anti-Navajo. And, let's be honest, they can be terrifying.

Take the CT scanner, for instance. It's a big white tube, like the mouth of an enormous bloated fish. The techs slide its tongue out and strap you on it, and then the fish eats you in slow motion while its guts churn and rotate and clank and beep and motors spin around your head in the murky light inside. Faceless voices tell you to be still. Sometimes they tell you to close your eyes. It feels like you're hiding in a closet while something terrible stalks the room outside. They give you a stick with a button on it and tell you to push it if you panic, but then caution you not to push it unless you *really* panic because it'll screw up the whole scan and you'll have to do it again.

I think I *really* panicked in the parking lot. But I gritted my teeth during the scan. I was there. I would finish.

When it was all over, I practically ran outside. I took the stairs, not the elevator. I never wanted to be boxed in in anything again. In the parking lot the sky was robin's egg blue, and I just breathed for a full minute, staring up and blinking. I thought I'd never seen anything so beautiful in my entire life. Then I moved quickly to my car. NNPD move in and out of ABQ General all the time, and I didn't want to be recognized.

I think I get an inkling of what's happening at my house before I even pull into my usual spot on the side of our street. I'd noticed a thin stream of white smoke from a little ways off that gave me goose bumps, but I was still shaken up and focusing on driving. The smoke is like a thin pole the color of a cloud. It's streaming into the sky, and it looks to be coming from my side of the duplex. I throw my truck in park and run into the house, but inside all is quiet. I push through the living room and kitchen and out to the back-yard, where I see Dad staring at Ana's pyre while a small wood fire is crackling in our old outdoor pit. He turns when the screen door slams after me. He is wearing leather breeches and is shirtless. His eyes are red, either from the smoke or from the liquor he holds in his hand. I know that in his own way he is trying to purify himself. For what is what worries me.

Dad says, "Your grandmother..."

For a terrible moment I think she's dead. It would be in line with the path that seems set out for me these days.

But then he says, "She is at the Arroyo. She has told me to bring you there."

Rather than put me at ease, this whispers along my back, and I shiver. Dad walks up to me in big, uneven steps and looks at me questioningly. He smells of campfire and whisky. It is not altogether unpleasant.

"Is she okay?" I ask.

He takes my hand the way Mom did when I was young.

"Yes," he says. "But are you?"

My spine pricks again. This is about me, not about Gam.

"We should get to the Arroyo," he says, and he walks, bare chested, to the passenger's side of my truck. He opens the door and plops himself inside, waiting.

Gam used to go to the Arroyo often when she was young. She told me she lived there for a time when she was learning the Navajo Way, which I took to mean a polite way of saying when my great-grandparents were on hard times. But she hasn't been back there in years. In fact, a couple of times she's gone off on the Arroyo as the dregs of Chaco. Once she even spat when I said Danny and I had the Arroyo rounds that week. I don't know why she would be there now, but I don't like anything about it. I hop up behind the wheel and fire up the truck.

The entire way there, Dad never speaks. As the Arroyo comes into view, the sun is setting. A bowl of heavy red light spills just over the edges and into the pit, but the light is retreating and night is moving in. I pull in where my memory tells me to, where Joey Flatwood used to live, and next to where the gambler lived and was mourned. But before I can stop, my dad taps me with his hand and shakes his head. He points beyond the Arroyo, into the rolling desert left of the setting sun. I turn to him, but he doesn't look at me. I know what's out there. That is where the hogans are.

"The hogans?" I ask. Dad nods.

"Why is Gam at the hogans?" I ask, but I know why. There is only one reason you go to the hogans these days. My palms start sweating. I flip the truck in reverse and pull back out along the main path, but where it curves towards the west I cut out along a sparse, rutted trail. The truck bounces and creaks. I slow to a crawl and keep moving forward out into the desert.

There were six hogans when I was young, evenly spaced in a long line, each separated by a good distance. Now perhaps four are usable. They are squat, rounded structures made of wood and mud, just tall enough to walk in and big enough for four or five people. Each has one door cut into it, facing the east, where blessings come from. In the center of every roof is a smoke hole where evil is expelled. Even the Arroyo kids don't mess around with the hogans. There is something about these things; they forbid it. Years ago, the six most prominent families in Chaco each had a hogan and used them regularly for ceremonies. Blessingways and chants, or just a place to gather and sweat together. As the families fell apart or mixed with others, or just got lazy, some of the hogans went the way of the dust and mud of their build. These days, the big ceremonies, the Nightway dance with all the fire and the whooping that the tourists love and things like that, all of those are performed at the cultural center in a makeshift hogan. But these: these are the real deal. Or they were, at least, once.

The hogans blink onto the horizon like beads on a table. The sun cuts across the tops of them and lays there like a red blanket. I can see that the one farthest along the line to the left is leaning haphazardly, slumped and drunken. Abandoned for a generation. But there are crows there. Lots of them. They stir with the noise of my truck and then settle again. All of them are facing me. I turn to Dad. I have this childish need to point them out to my father, like that will make them go away. I wonder when they began to frighten me. I steel myself. It's easy to lose your head when you go beyond the rez, into the deep rez, and then into the desert.

Dad points at the hogan dead center, where I see more white smoke, a single, continuous string, like the trunk of an aspen tree, pouring from the smoke hole and spreading into the sky. That's where Gam is.

When I pull up, Gam is waiting for me. She is staring at me, dressed in a heavy, poncho-like dressing gown, and she wears a beaded kerchief on her head that gathers her long gray hair. At her waist is a buckskin bag. It's the bag that seals the deal for me. If it weren't for the bag, I'd say she was out here to teach me something about my ancestors. But that's an old buckskin bag. One of a handful of things in her room she told us never to touch. That's a Singer's Bag. Gam is here to do work, and I think she's here to do work on me.

When I walk up to her, she is quiet and watchful. She looks at me like I stumbled out of the desert behind the hogans. Like she didn't instruct Dad to bring me here.

"*Hello, Dejooli,*" she says, in Navajo. She's not using my first name on purpose. Ben is a white man's name.

"*What is this, Grandmother?*" I ask.

120 B. B. GRIFFITH

"Evil is upon you. We must treat with the Holy People to expel it. Find alignment once more."

"Evil? Name the evil."

"You are sick. In your brain."

I straighten at this, come up from where I was talking at her eye level. Gam knew I passed out. She knew I ended up at the hospital. But the way she says this to me makes me think she knows more. Out of the corner of my eye, I see the crows at the abandoned hogan shuffle themselves about and then settle once more. Before I can question her, she speaks again.

"You have been marked by the white man's medicine," she says.

"Grandmother, I went because I gave my word that I would go. That is no reason to call a Blessingway."

I see two others making their way around the hogan, blessing it with pollen. One of them is big and square. His long black hair reaches the middle of his back, and his dark arms are like cable cords. He wears leather chaps over a breechcloth, and the beaded strap of his scalp knife swings about his knees. It's Danny Ninepoint.

Gam waves away my words. *"This is no Blessingway,"* she says, and her voice chills me more than the setting sun. *"There is another mark on you. A mark that runs deeper than the white man's poison."* She reaches into her buckskin bag and pulls out a handful of black ash.

"Come," she says.

In a Blessingway, the Singer essentially calls upon the Holy People to pay a visit to the hogan and bless the patient, but as far as I know it doesn't involve black ash. Another of the Holyway ceremonies does, though: the Evilway.

This is an exorcism.

Gam turns away, and I follow her toward the hogan

openmouthed. It's like I can't turn away. Dad and Gam enter the Hogan, Dad at a stoop. Gam barely needs to duck her head.

"Wait, Gam, hold on just a second," I say, in English. My Navajo deserts me when I panic. Gam doesn't hold on. Gam doesn't stop. She enters the hogan and begins preparing. I stare at the mouth of the hogan, a faint glow now visible from the small fire that will mark its center, until Danny comes around my way and stops in front of me.

"You want to wear your shirt?" he asks, so matter of fact that at first I have no idea what he's talking about. It's like he's asking me to pass the salt.

"Danny, what is this all about?"

"Your family says you're sick. And that something is coming for you. I think so too." Now that he's up close, I see fine scratches around his eyes and bigger scabs raking down his cheeks.

"What the hell happened to your face?"

He waves off my question, but his hand is marked too, like it was peppered with buckshot.

"Domestic dispute by the Boxes. The guy was hopped up on amphetamines. Fought like a bear. Bardo and I took him down."

Without his customary NNPD polish, I can see that he's weary. He looks like he's been chasing ghosts of his own. Bardo's partner retired last year. I wonder, not for the first time, if he's been picking up my slack and covering for me when I've had to make these hospital trips.

"You should have called me, Danny. I'm your fucking partner."

He waves it off again.

"If I'm sick, I need a doctor. Not a chant. This is a waste of time."

"You don't believe in the power of the Chantway?" he asks. He's not accusing, just curious.

Of course Danny believes. Danny believes as much as Gam believes. They're both from the same deep end of the Navajo pool.

"No, I mean, I do, I guess...I don't know. But this is ridiculous. How much money did this cost?" Calling a Chantway is not cheap. They require certain officiates and certain sacred objects and preparation time.

"She brought in two Arroyo men for the sandpainting. Nobody else knows. She has prepared all day."

"An Evilway? I mean, *really*?"

Danny nods.

I shake my head in disbelief. "That takes what, a day and a half?"

"Two full nights."

"This shit isn't fair to you. I know you've been working twice as hard on my account."

"I took care of it. Got Bardo and Yuska to cover our beat. Said we needed to work some things out. No big deal. It happens all the time with partners. Don't worry about me. This is about you."

My hands drop to my sides.

"Now. You want to wear your shirt?" he asks again.

I unbutton my shirt. "No, I don't want to wear my fuckin' shirt," I say, but the words have no fire behind them.

Danny takes a pinch of pollen from the buckskin sack at his waist and holds it up to my mouth. I open, like a toddler. He tosses it in and mutters a prayer I can't quite make out. Then he takes a second pinch, bigger this time, and plumes it on the top of my head. I hold back a sneeze. He nods, then continues around the hogan, consecrating. I go through the door and inside. I barely have to bend, either, but if Danny's coming in, he's coming in on hands and knees.

The hogan is hot and already hazy. A small fire made of new wood is burning in the center. It's not much bigger than a dinner plate, but it gives off a lot of smoke and not all of it escapes through the smokehole. Two old men I vaguely recognize are pouring thin streams of fine, colored sand into a mural that stretches in a rainbow around the far side of the fire. When I walk in, they look up briefly and nod. One is so old I can't tell if his eyes are open or not.

There are five figures in the mural, each drawn in a subtly different combination of simple, angled shapes and alternating patterns. Their bodies are long ovals in three colors and their arms are represented by patterned white lines and dots like Morse code. Each character stands on a thick, charcoal black line. I've been to a handful of Chant-ways in my time, both for the tourists and for the Navajo, and I can tell you that trying to decipher the sand paintings is like trying to learn another language; I can get the general sense, but the specifics are beyond me. Here, it's a good bet that at least four of the figures are the Holy Family: the Sun, the Slayer Twins (those were always my favorite as a kid), and, of course, Changing Woman. I think she's the biggest one. But this fifth one on the far right that stands apart from the Family, I can't say I've ever seen anything like it before. It's a figure all in black, made entirely of charcoal grains. Its eyes aren't sand, though; they're lumps of turquoise rock. I can't say why, exactly, but I don't like it.

The basic idea of a Navajo chant is that you want to call attention to yourself. You want the Holy People to notice you. To come on over and bless you or your family or business, or, with the Evilway, to set things right in you. I'd be lying if I said I hold by all of this. But all the same, I'd rather not call the attention of that last fella on the right if I can help it.

Gam throws me a breechcloth. I stare at it, then at her. She sighs and turns around. I strip down to nothing and affix the breechcloth over myself. When she turns around again, I hold out my hands.

"Now what?" I ask, in Navajo.

"Now we wait for the end of the sand painting. In the smoke."

She flops to sitting in a heap and carefully arrays her Singer's Bag in front of her. She pulls a plastic baggie full of twigs, herbs, and blackened wood from within it and empties it into a nearby pestle. She begins to slowly grind the concoction together. When it's a rough powder, she takes a handful and tosses it into the fire. There is no hiss or bang or colored fire, just more smoke. She adds water from an old quart jug to what remains in the mortar and keeps grinding. The sulfur smell comes on strong, but I can't tell if it's because of whatever she tossed on the fire or if it's just me. I blink rapidly, and my eyes begin to water. Neither the sand painters nor Gam take any notice of me.

I feel movement in the smoke and see Dad. He carries a crude mask made of sewn buckskin, like a leather ski mask with tiny slits for the eyes. Feathers have been sewn in at the sides and hang heavy with beads. I think I recognize it from home. As a kid I stumbled across it in the closet looking for where Mom might have hidden my slingshot from me. At the time, it scared the shit out of me. Still sort of does. Dad sits next to me and begins mixing a bucketful of ash with water and earth. Another movement of smoke, and Danny Ninepoint appears. His eyes are hard and determined. Almost manic. I can tell he's sort of getting off on all of this. Danny always loved this stuff. In his hand he carries another mask, like Dad's, but his is adorned with horsehair and woven brush around the neck. Neither of them look at me. Both stare heavily into the fire, unblinking.

"The fifth painting..." I say to Gam, if for no other reason than to break the heavy silence. She nods, still grinding. *"Who is it? Turquoise Man?"*

Turquoise Man is a strong Navajo figure. He stands with a Navajo for life. Makes him invincible. Gam sucks at her teeth. It's her way of saying *yes and no.* Gam starts to remove things from her bag. Some of them I recognize. I see the miniature bow and two ornate chant arrows. I see the bull roarer and a bunch of unravelers made of string and feathers and herbs wrapped over themselves into rough balls. There's an old bison-hoof rattle and a smooth, curved stick. But then there are other things: a wooden contraption that looks sort of like ancient brass knuckles that sprouted crow feathers. A big bone, maybe the shoulder blade of a bison, grooved and dyed dark black. A shard of obsidian the size of my hand, and then, finally, and I sense most importantly, a box made of bone, about the size of a deck of cards. This she holds with two hands and carefully sets at her feet, closest to her. Then she presses her balled fist to her chest, right at her sternum, and grimaces. I've been to an Evilway before, once, years ago. But I don't recall seeing the box. In fact, I've never seen the box before, not at any Chantway, or at any ceremony.

"Is this an Evilway, Grandmother?" I ask.

Gam sucks at her teeth.

I try to ask more, but the smoke is making my head spin a bit, and before I can speak Gam gets up. She reaches into one of her pockets and pulls out a fistful of cornmeal. She moves to each of the four cardinal beams of the hogan and rubs the cornmeal along it with a single, deliberate stroke. She holds up an oak twig in her other hand and begins a prayer song that I partly recognize and partly don't. It's beautiful, rhythmic and crooning and insistent at the same time. This is the opener. The call that lets the Holy People know we are here. It could be the smoke, or it could be just my imagination, but somewhere in the back of my head I get this strange, creeping sensation, and I picture the fifth figure, the one in black, sitting on some other plane and opening one bright turquoise eye.

The smoke is heavy now, but I feel like I'm the only one affected by it. I look around, and the two old sand painters are chanting along with Gam, putting the final touches on their work. Dad and Danny are sitting on either side of Gam, who has returned to her mortar and pestle. Dad is focused on the ashes, and Danny stares into the coals with wide eyes that are shot through with red. The smoke is as white as bone, and it's pouring through the roof like it's the spout of a kettle. Things are wavy for me. I've never had a high tolerance for anything, really. Not alcohol, not weed back when Joey and I used to smoke whatever shit hash we could buy off people in the tracts, none of it. It never stopped me back then, but it was just the way it was. Joey used to give me a lot of grief for it, even as he'd carry me home.

Both of the old men stand as one and survey their work like two regulars gossiping at the bar. They point at certain parts, nodding. They both turn to the black figure and nod silently. They move behind Gam and sit next to each other and pick up her chant in soft echoes, like the walls of a canyon. Gam nods at Dad and at Danny, and they both rise, Dad with the bucket. He sets it in front of me, and both men grab globs of ash paste and begin coating me with it.

I stand with my arms out at my sides as they coat me with black. This is in keeping with the Evilway, but even my smoke-addled brain can see differences. Gam takes the obsidian and brushes it the length of her left arm before pricking her palm. A bead of blood rises, and she moves over to the black figure and presses it upon its chest. Her hand comes away grainy with charcoal, and she touches her chest again with that same grimace, like something burns there. When I am covered head to toe in ash, Gam, still chanting, comes to me with a palmful of feathery ash. She steps up to me, then away, and blows the ash over me. Then she asks me to lie down by the fire. It's just as well. I realize that Danny Ninepoint has basically been propping me up for the past five minutes. I look at him and see that he seems addled, too. His eyes are glassy and red, but his grip is as sure as stone. He looks eagerly from me to Gam and back to me. Dad is bobbing with the chant. He is not with us, I can tell. It's like he's staring at Ana's cairn again in the backyard.

When I lie down, Gam gives me her bowl. I look in and see a black, watery mixture. I'm not really sure at this point when I stopped humoring everybody and dove into this headlong, but I'm still not about to drink something that looks like pond water without knowing what's in it. Gam lifts it up to me, and I take it and lift it back up to her and try to ask what it is, but my mouth isn't working right. My words sound mealy and thick. Still, she gets it.

"Struck wood and struck ground."

By which she means it's wood from a tree hit by lightning, and the ground around it. Lighting is bad news for Navajo. Powerful, and bad news. In some corner of my brain I know that whatever that lightning hit must have some psychoactive effect, since Gam threw some of it on the fire and now I'm feeling like I'm sinking into the pine mat they set me on. The rational part of me, the cop part, tells me to knock that poison onto the ground. But the other part of me, the grandson, the son, the brother....tells me to grab it and to drink it. So I do. It tastes like mouthwash. The rest of the ceremony I experience in flashes.

It seems like I've only blinked, but I can feel things on me now. I look down at myself, and I can see that they are several of the items in Gam's Singer's Bag. The unravelers have already been partly unraveled at my feet and shins. There are black feathers at my knees. The hoof rattle sits over my groin, and the carved bone on my chest. Altogether they couldn't weigh more than five pounds, but I could no more move them right now than fly into the night sky. The chanting is still ongoing. Always ongoing. I recognize certain words like *path* and *sky* and *wing*, but the rest is too much for me to make out. I fade again.

The next time I come to is horrifying. If I could move, I would run. I see the Slayer Twins as soon as I open my eyes. They are leaning over me, like some bizarre doctors mid-operation. A quiet part of my mind whispers that these are the masks I saw earlier, that this is Danny and my father, but the rest of me refuses to believe it. The rest of me sees the twins for who they are: *Naayee Neizghani*, Monster Slayer, and *To Bajishchini*, Born for Water. It is them. I know it as surely as I know that I am truly ill. I know it as surely as I know that the white man's scan will come back with a death sentence. These things hit me with such force and clarity that they are impossible to deny.

I watch as they shoot the chant arrows over my body. They travel slowly, but I can feel the air moving around them. Their fletching parts the smoke. The chanting gets louder. I fade again.

The third time I come around, it's like I've left the hogan altogether. The singing might as well be the sound of the wind or the rain. It isn't so much a thing being done as it is a thing that has always been, like air. I can't see the Slayer Twins anymore, nor can I see the old sand painters. All I see is my grandmother. Her eyes are closed, and she is finishing the unraveling. I can't see what she is removing from the unraveling, but at intervals she tosses things into the fire and each pops like a nut. The motion is one with the chant: the singing, the pop. I feel as though I have sweat and dried, and sweat again. Like I've broken a string of fevers.

Gam takes my hands and places a pair of painted sticks in them, presenting each to me, all while singing. Each time she looks in my eyes, I can see the concern there, the sadness. In the quiet corner of my mind I know that she knows I have cancer, even before I know. Even before the doctors know, or the scan shows it. Does she really believe she can chant cancer away? Something in her eyes tells me no. Something in her eyes tells me what this Chantway is truly about: it's about opening a path for the fifth figure.

In the thick, roiling smoke of the hogan I sense the chant reaching a climax. It's a slow build, but Gam's pitch is rising and the intervals are shortening. This is when I see her pull out the small bone box that she kept close to her. There is a tightening in the air, a pressurizing, and I know that this is the reason she chanted in the first place. To present whatever is in this box to whatever Holy People have been called to this hogan, and to present me with it, to link me to it. She shows the box to me and looks me in the eye very clearly. She is making sure I am grounded for this, not floating away on whatever smoke and potion is coursing through me. I manage a nod. The sulfur smell is stronger than ever. I get this morbid thought that maybe the smell is my brain burning, or dying, or freezing, or whatever the hell a tumor does to you, but these thoughts don't bother me like they should.

They've been muted. It's like they are being whispered to me.

Gam lifts the bone box up in the center of the hogan, and she flips it open. She reaches inside and pulls out a crow. A turquoise crow. It looks exactly like the turquoise crow that the gambler had at his vigil. She brings it down to my level, flying it over my body from toe to head. She presses it briefly against my dry lips and then over my eyes. The cut, the size, the style of the crow in flight, all of these are the same as the gambler's, but there is a thick vein of white marbling in the right wing of Gam's, and the coloring is so pure it's almost blue. This is a different crow, and yet it is not.

I try to speak to her. Try to ask her how it can be that she has the same totem as the gambler, what it means, why crows haunt me at every turn, but nothing comes out.

Gam places the crow totem on my forehead. It rests there like it was nesting. It's almost like it burrows down an inch into my brain. Everything on me feels so heavy. I just want to sleep. I want to let the crow carry me down and leave me buried miles below the earth. Just when I think I'm sunk, the pressure pops. The chanting, which was feverish a moment ago, is quieted. Like wind over the mouth of a cave. And that's when I see her.

It's Ana.

She is at the door to the hogan. The moonlight pours in from behind her. Then the sunlight. Then the moonlight again. She ducks inside, which I think is a very strange thing for a vision to do, because I know that this is a vision. A stray thought brought forth from my brain, borne from smoke and herbs and sweat, that's all. It has to be.

But it's still Ana. I call her name, but my voice only roars in my mind. I can see her turning from me, and it's like she's embarrassed. Like when I caught her drawing on the walls once with her crayons, and she turned away from me and hid them under her shirt. *Ana,* I said then. *Ana, what did you do?* And she turned away. I walked around her, and she turned back the other way. *Ana, did you draw on the walls?* A shrug. A small smile forming in the corner of her mouth. She turns like this now, in the hogan.

Ana? Why won't you look at me? You're my Ana. You're in my head. I just want to see your face.

There's that small smile, and then she turns to me. But it's not Ana anymore.

It starts as Ana, but then her warm brown eyes melt. They turn to black, and their color melts downward in two long triangles. Her soft brown coloring bleaches, fades to white in front of me like it's been baked in the sun for millennia, until what I see is a small girl with the face of eternity on her. Of Black and White. Of Absolutes.

And then whatever she is speaks to me.

Do not be afraid, my brother. All things pass.

This Ana that is not Ana, this creature, it passes from my toes to my head, and it grasps the crow totem on my forehead and yanks it out like a root.

Then all is black.

When I wake again, it is because Danny Ninepoint has poured a bucket of cold water on me. I take a huge breath, like it is my first, and then I sneeze three times. I roll and pop my neck and blink water from my eyes. Ash is running all down my face and into pools around my head.

"Welcome back," Danny says. Then he walks out of the hogan.

I sit up, calming my heart, placing myself. Everyone is gone. The sand paintings are gone. The men are gone. Grandmother is gone. There is a stale smoke smell coming from everywhere. The early morning sun creeps through the eastern door, lighting dust motes like flakes of floating ash. I sit up, and my head feels like it's twice the size.

"Take your time," Danny says from outside.

I have to crawl out of the hogan. When I do, I collapse onto the desert floor and start shivering like a dog. Danny sweeps down with a blanket.

"What day is it?" I ask.

"Dawn of the third day. Monday."

"Shit. We gotta get to work."

"Why do you think I'm here, honcho?" Danny looks at me with a straight face, but his eyes are smiling.

"What the fuck happened in there?"

"A lot."

"Danny, did you see Ana?"

"Your sister? No. But I saw other things." His eyes turn glassy for a minute, manic. That and the scratches on his face combine to make him look a bit like a junkie. It looks out of place on a man like Danny.

"Did you see Ana?" he asks.

"Sort of," I say. Danny nods. He's the only man I know who would take this as a reasonable answer. He helps me up and into my truck. He takes my keys and drives me home, where I take a five-minute shower and slam a cup of black coffee. As I'm getting into my uniform, I get a call from Doctor Owen Bennet. He tells me I'm dying.

I can't even act surprised.

11

CAROLINE ADAMS

I'm ripping down the highway with a bag of chemical poison in the back seat of my car. The pump and pole rigging sits next to me in the passenger's seat. It's secured with the seatbelt and shifts about awkwardly as I change lanes. There's no good way to move rigging. It only breaks down so much. It's like trying to pack a lamp.

The chemo itself is a sack of clear liquid, like a bag of water, but the plastic is thick and heavy. It's wrapped in a protective sheaf and secured in a bright red cooler with yellow biohazard symbols all over it. The cooler is locked in three separate places with plastic ties. I am terrified of it. You'd think after four years of chemo certification I'd get over it. You'd be wrong. The second I start to take it for granted is the day I drop a bag on the floor and rupture it and clear out the entire wing and have to go through a flushing regimen that I've heard is not fun *at all*.

Under normal circumstances I'd be going five under the speed limit, hugging the right lane, hands at ten and two, no radio on. Mom would certainly be proud. But normal has pretty much gone out the window here in the past couple of weeks. I've never given a chemo regimen off-site. I don't even like giving chemo at the hospital. But when Owen told me that Ben asked for me personally, I was all over it. I can't stop thinking about Ben, and what scares me even more than carrying a quart of cell-destroying liquid is the thought that Ben might change his mind. So instead of my usual careful driving, I'm going fifteen over the limit on my way to Chaco and praying I don't see a cop. Then I laugh out loud, because I am going to see a cop. And you can forget ten and two: my palms are so sweaty that I'm alternating them in front of the vents. As for the radio, I'm listening to a Top Forty station blaring pop music, because if it's quiet I start to think too much about what I'm doing and what it means that he asked for me personally. I need to save that for three a.m. Right now I need to do my fricking job.

Once I pass the welcome center and the CHC I'm totally lost. Owen seemed to know his way around here by heart. You'd think that after five years of shifts at the CHC that I would know my way about too. Guess not. I'm in over my head, but I don't care. I bust out my phone, but the GPS coverage isn't so good. Doesn't surprise me that these back-streets might be among the last to get digitized, but eventually I hone in on Ben's place.

Ben wanted to start treatment at his house, on his day off. He was fairly short on the phone. It took some time to figure out a schedule that worked. Where he could be alone. Apparently his grandmother is around the house most of the time, but she has a card game on Tuesday afternoons. He thought it best that nobody else was around. I said whatever he could do I would make work for me, and here I am. Before he hung up, he said thank you, and he sounded so genuine, and even a little scared, that I knew I'd make Tuesdays work.

His place is one half of a split duplex that doesn't look much bigger than my apartment. Still, outside of the main strip to Wapati Casino with its manicured desert foliage and squared landscaping and quaint houses of adobe and Spanish tiling, which even I know is for show, his place is one of the nicer I see within blocks. It's clean and simple and tended.

Ben is on the lookout for me. I can see him at the window. The curtains ruffle, and he opens the door even before I can park my car. When he walks out to me, he checks both ways down the street. I feel a bit like the ugly stepsister, and I think he knows it as soon as he comes up to me because he pauses and looks down for a second. I can see him make a conscious decision to stop being embarrassed.

"Hi, Ben," I say.

"Thanks for...for coming."

"It sucks," I say. He laughs, thank God. His coloring is better, less angry red and more like the red of a sunrise, but there's still a touch of black to him, a representation of what's frightening him. It's not a natural color. If I was to hazard a guess, I'd say it was a visual representation of the cancer. There's something else, too, about the way his coloring shows itself. It's simmering, like a heavy soup about to boil. He's putting on a good show, but he's pretty freaked out. About the cancer, sure, but it's more than that. Something has happened to him that has rattled him deeply.

"You knew the whole time," he says.

I shake my head. "Nah, I just...I get these feelings sometimes, and I...It's just hard to unsee them once I see them."

"It's funny. You and my grandmother. Between the two of you I don't know why I even needed to get that damn scan." He looks up at the sky overhead and then around at the sky behind him. I follow his gaze. Nothing but blue. Not even a cloud.

"We should get inside," he says.

He carries in the rig while I shoulder my tote bag and then carefully pull the chemo crate out of the back seat. He eyes it warily as we walk up the front steps. I wish I could tell him it's not as bad as it looks, but it is.

The front room of the house doubles as a living room and dining room, actually probably triples as a living room, dining room, and TV room. It's neat and clean and uncluttered. He's moved a well-used recliner, the green seat cushion worn to white, to an opening in front of the mantel. I set the crate down like it's full of eggs, and he tries not to stare at it while I set up the rig. Meanwhile I try not to stare at everything that makes this place his home, starting with the pictures. I see the grandmother and father in one. The three of them and what looks to be his mother in another. There's one picture in the center where he looks like a teenager and he's with a young girl. They have the same color eyes. They practically beam out of the picture frame. I look over at him as he ponders the crate and see that his eyes are soft now, no such smile behind them anymore. He sees me looking, and I panic a little and my fingers slip on the screw that tightens the neck of the rigging. To cover it up I ask him about her.

"Is that your sister?"

"Yeah," he says. "Ana. But she's been gone almost six years now."

My face flushes, and I'm sure I look as red as a baboon.

"I'm so sorry," I say, which is such a stupid thing to say, that phrase, because even if you are sorry, so very sorry, even if you're genuine, you sound canned. Just looking at a picture of that little girl, I know I would have fallen a little in love with her if she were around and smiled at me like that.

"Me too," he says, and he looks from the picture to me. "It's all right, Caroline. I'm the one that's supposed to be nervous here." He gently takes the pieces of the rig from my fingers, which feel like sausages. "I can set the rig up. I've seen a lot of them in my day. You can...do whatever needs to be done with that thing." He nods over at the chemo crate.

"You have any scissors?" I ask.

"Down the hall in the kitchen. In the big drawer."

I walk into the kitchen. It's spotless, but it has a well-used feel, a subtle layered smell of spices and oils that makes my stomach growl. I slide open the big drawer under the microwave and find the scissors, then turn to go. But I pause when I see a second room, off to the right. It looks like it was a small sitting room, but it's been converted into a tiny bedroom. I crane my neck, making sure to keep behind the refrigerator enough so Ben won't see how rude I'm being, and I see that the room is almost monastic. The floor has nothing on it. There is nothing on the walls. The bed would only accommodate two-thirds of me and is pulled hospital-tight. There's a beautiful Navajo blanket folded lengthways across it, but that's about all of the color there is to see, except for something on a small shelf above the bed: two painted sticks crossed over a worn leather pouch. The pouch is open, and the opening is facing me. Something is glinting there. It's a cold, white glint. A box of some kind. I feel myself take a step towards it, and as soon as I do a shadow drops down over the window, and I have to stifle a scream. I stumble back into the open drawer, and my butt slams it shut with a loud bang.

It's a crow, on the windowsill. And not just any crow. It's the biggest crow I have ever seen. It looks prehistoric. As it settles, its coloring seems to blur and change in the dull light of the fall sun. At first it's black as night, and then it looks shot through with red, then black again. For one terrible minute I think it's in the room, but it flaps its wings and they brush against the outside of the window with a raspy raking sound.

A cold, whispered dread falls over me, the same type of feeling I had after that lung cancer patient bled out on us, when I was cleaning his room. There's a subtle movement in the air where there shouldn't be. I almost scream again, but this time it's no jump scare. It's because the crow is looking at me. Looking right at me with an eye the size of a golf ball and as black as marble. The fact that it doesn't make a sound, not even a squawk, makes it somehow even worse. It's just perched there, on the ledge, taking up the whole sill, its head turned flush right against the window. I can see a flat, sticky disk where its eye is pushing against the glass. Its beak taps once against it with the sound of a cracking knuckle.

Then Ben is there beside me.

"Caroline? Everything okay?"

The spell is broken. I take my first breath in what feels like minutes. I look from him back to the window, but the crow is gone.

"I'm sorry, I...I thought I saw something."

He looks through the window himself, and his coloring darkens to a deep clay. It's not fear that he is feeling, but it's close, something like a mixture of dread and inevitability.

"What did you see?" he asks, but I can tell he already knows.

"It was a bird. A big bird."

He nods. "I've been having something of a bird problem lately."

I cock my eyebrow at him.

"Kinda hard to explain. C'mon, let's get this over with." He nods back towards the front room. When we get back there I notice he's held my hand for the short walk. I'd like to think it's not because he thinks I'm a snoop that he has to keep tabs on. I file it away. Prime three a.m. material, right there.

Back in the front room, I open my tote and pull out my yellow chemo gown. It crinkles like a bag of chips as I pull it on. It has matching gloves, too. High fashion in the nursing world.

"What the hell?" Ben says.

"It's standard, don't worry."

"Is that to protect you?"

"Yeah, in case something happens when I start your line."

"To protect you from getting it on your skin?"

"Exactly."

"To protect you from what you're about to put in my bloodstream?"

"That's right." I nod, then realize he's incredulous. I pause before saying, "Look, this is strong stuff. But you need strong stuff. Know what I'm saying?"

After a second he nods.

"Plus, I think hazard yellow is a pretty good color on me. No?"

He cracks a smile that is a shadow of the one in the picture, but even a shadow works for me.

"All right," I say, "let's get this show on the road."

I snip the four protective ties and open the crate. The hood bag is inside another bag labeled Cytotoxic, which I pull out like a lunch pail.

"This is Avastana. You know what it does, right?"

"Yeah. They told me it'll wipe me out. I'll puke my guts out in the short term and lose my hair in the long term." His tone is as dry as bone. I can't tell if he's joking. I never know what the doctors tell these guys, and although Owen is the best of them, docs by nature are dorks who often have a hard time not explaining things like they're a textbook. I figure I should run it down for him in plain English.

"Basically cancer is just cells that are changing way too fast. This stuff kills those cells. It also kills any cells that look like those cells. Other fast moving cells, things like hair cells that grow fast, or mucous membranes that are naturally active. That's why your hair will most likely fall out. You'll also probably get abrasions and sores in your mouth and lower GI."

"My ass?"

"Yeah. Your ass."

"So this is the red button."

"What?"

"The nuclear option."

"Yeah. You could say that."

He sits down in the old chair and deflates for a second before pulling himself together. He is getting quite dark. And not just in the coloring that only I can see. "That's pretty much what the doctor said."

"Doctor Bennet?"

"Yeah."

I nod and pull up a fold-out chair that was propped against the couch. I pop it open next to his armrest and sit down by the hanging bag next to him. It's like a big chemical sprig of mistletoe. I grab his hand, and I'm not ashamed to admit that the spark of pure, rich clay coloring that I see float from him makes me feel good. It makes me feel like a nurse.

"I'll be right here, Ben. You and me. All right?"

He squeezes my hand and looks into my eyes.

"You and me," he says. "Okay. Hit me."

I prep his vein. Every nurse judges a man by his veins. It sounds weird, but when you spend as much time fretting over hitting veins for lines as we do, and studying how best to hit veins, and reading about where we have to start lines on people when we can't find their veins, you learn to appreciate a nice, fat, dark vein. Ben's veins are crazy prominent on his arms. They look like earthworms. A blind nurse could start a chemo line on this guy. I hit his forearm vein on the first try and have to stop myself from whooping. He doesn't even flinch. I flush the IV, tape it down, and turn to the pump. I program a drip level and pull the clamp. That's that. I turn back to him and find he's been watching me the whole time.

"Now what?" he asks.

"Now we wait. It's a two-hour infusion."

"Two hours?"

"Yeah. You want a book?"

"Nah."

"I brought some cards, too. Or I could turn on the TV for you if you want."

"Nah," he says again, but he's tapping his foot. He looks a shade yellow. Nervous.

"When do I start feeling like shit?" he asks.

"With most people it's an hour or two after the infusion."

He nods, and his foot tapping intensifies. He follows the line from his arm up to the bag, and he's fixated on the pump drip like it's an hourglass. Without even meaning to, I rest my hand on his bobbing knee. The pallid mist fades away from him like vapor in the sun. Part of me feels guilty at knowing how I affect him. A small part. The rest of me is elated.

"Talk to me," he says.

"Talk to you?"

"Yeah, I...whenever Ana or I had to do hospital things, we would talk to each other. Whenever she had tests. We'd talk nonstop."

"Okay," I say, nodding. "Okay, uh. What would you like to talk about?"

"I dunno. Anything."

"What's your favorite color?"

"Red," he says, with a slight smirk.

"I knew it. All right, now you."

"Okay. What are you doing here?" he asks.

"Sorry?"

"I mean on the shithole outskirts of New Mexico. You have family in Albuquerque?" He traces the line from his arm back up the bag, his eyes wide.

"No, no family in Albuquerque, or anywhere near it. My family is from Iowa."

"So why here?" he asks, turning back to me.

"I got a grant from the government. They gave me money to go to nursing school. In return I gave them five years—twelve hours a week at the Chaco Health Center."

"Like the army," he says and starts to laugh. He nods to himself. "Dealing with the Navajo *is* kinda like a war."

"It's not like that. I had a specified term in an under-served community. It could have been anywhere. HUD areas. Inner city hospitals. Rural clinics. Anything."

"And are you glad you were sent to Chaco?"

I nod. I don't even have to think. "I knew it was the right decision the day I got a tupperware full of food from this old Navajo woman. She was a patient of mine during one of my rotations. She took the bus out to ABQ General. I don't even know where she got on."

"Had to have been in Grants City, just south. No bus system in Chaco."

"That's what I figured. She hitched her way out of the rez and then took the bus into Albuquerque just to give me food."

"I bet it was awesome."

"Oh my God. You have no idea. Best chicken I've ever had in my life. And I was new then, too. I hadn't had a home-cooked meal in months. I didn't even have pots in my apartment yet. I literally cried while I ate it all."

We're quiet for a moment, but it's a comfortable quiet. The house settles around us in the late afternoon cool.

"And then you came," I say. I don't really know why. I have this dangerous and peculiar tendency to panic around men I like, but when I do, I also have this liberating side effect of throwing caution to the wind. I think I've been in a low-grade panic since I got that call from Owen telling me Ben wanted off-site chemo and wanted it from me.

"Me?" Ben says.

"Yeah. You. You take the good with the bad when you work at the CHC. There's plenty of both, I think, but the good is quiet while the bad is loud. The bad shows up on my patient rounds late at night half-dead or detoxing. That's loud. That has a loud color. But you, you're good. And you're a quiet good. And you have a nice color, and I bet it'd be nicer if you didn't have such a mountain on your shoulders. I can see it weighing you down. I'm rambling now. I'll shut up."

For a second I think he's going to make me explain myself and my weird Technicolor Dream Vision, and then he'll laugh me out of his house and straight into therapy. But he says nothing. It's wonderful. It's wonderfully Navajo.

"All right. Your turn," he says.

"What's the deal with the crow?" I ask. I don't even skip a beat. Neither does he.

"I wish I knew," he says. Then he looks up at the ceiling like he could see through it to the sky. "All I know is that recently I've been seeing a lot of crows. But I think they've been around longer than that. You know? I think it's kind of a thing I've had for a long time around me but I'm only now coming to see it."

"Tell me about it."

"What?"

"Nothing. Keep going."

"I mean, it's late fall. This is when the crows gather. It should be normal. But it's not. "

"Because of the big guy?"

"Yeah. The big guy. And I sort of feel like they're always gathering around me. Does that sound crazy?"

I think for a second. A couple of weeks ago maybe it would have sounded crazy. Not anymore.

"No."

He lets out a breath. "That's good."

"But why? Why are they following you?"

"I think it has something to do with a gambler. And this place on the desert boundary called the Arroyo. And Ana."

"Your sister?"

"Yeah. I don't know how. But it does. And..." He squints and drops his head and then blinks rapidly. I lean in closer to him.

"Ben? You all right? What are you feeling?"

"I just feel...I feel like I'm running out of time. I had this

Evilway. It's a Navajo chant ceremony. I saw things. I'm not sure if it was good for me. I think it's speeding things up."

He's rambling now. Pouring forth. Like I've lanced a blister.

"I saw Ana. I saw her."

"What, like a vision?"

"Yes. But no. It was more. It was...terrible. She came in the hogan when..." He drops his head again, straining to remember. Then he pops up, his eyes bright with recognition.

"The crow. The totem. Or was that a vision too?" His eyes shoot back towards the kitchen, towards where the back room is. He makes a move to get up, and I have to settle him.

"You have to wait the infusion out."

He sits down again and swallows hard. "I feel strange," he says.

"I know. So do I. Let's keep talking."

So we do. Until every last drip of Avastana is coursing through his veins. We talk about our parents, his estranged but nearby, mine together but far away. We talk about paying bills and working late. We talk about night shifts and groggy mornings and old friends. He talks about a guy named Joey like a good friend, but in past tense. I don't want to make the same mistake I did with his sister, so I don't pursue it.

He looks weary when I eventually pull his line. I press a cotton ball to his vein, and he takes a huge, shuddering breath and closes his eyes.

"Weird to think of that stuff inside me."

"It's going to work," I say.

"I don't feel all that bad," he says. "Just tired."

"Give it a few hours."

"I thought you were supposed to make me feel better," he says, smiling up at me.

"I'm here to help you, not pat your head." But I pat his head anyway. Then the doorbell rings.

His color muddies. His smoke had been strengthening despite the chemo, moving to a stronger red, but it yellows with the knocking. His eyes snap to the door, then he looks at me. His eyes tell me all I need to know. Nobody was supposed to bother us. We're both silent, thinking the same thing: maybe they'll just go away.

The doorbell rings again, then someone pounds on the door. I wince at the sound.

"Want me to get it?" I whisper.

He shakes his head. "Help me up."

I take his outstretched hand with both of mine and pull him to his feet. He steadies himself and eyes the door with narrow lids. He sets his shoulders and moves over to the door. There's no window in the door—it's just a slab of wood—but there's a chain catch, and he slides it to before opening the door a crack. I hear a man's voice outside.

"Mr. Dejooli?"

"Yes," Ben says.

"It's Agent Parsons, with the FBI. I'm here with Agent Douglas as well. May we speak with you?"

"It's not a good time," Ben says.

"I'm afraid we must insist," the other, Douglas, says from behind the door. His voice is lower, just above a growl.

"Insist all you want," Ben says. "I can't talk to you today. If it's about the report, it can wait until tomorrow." Ben moves to close the door, but it thuds against a shoe.

"We found Joseph Flatwood," says Parsons.

Ben freezes.

"We need to talk with you," says Douglas, more force-fully this time.

Ben rests his head against the back of the door for a moment, then slides the catch free. He swings open the door and two men in drab suits and bad ties step inside. They have the instantly forgettable faces of government lackeys. They eye me with a clinical unease. They take in the rig and the bag without comment. There can be no mistaking what's going on here, though. I'm still dressed like a chicken, after all.

"All right," Ben says. "What is it?"

The agents look at me, and then something unsaid passes between them.

"She's with me," Ben says. "Now out with it."

I flush. I staunch a smile. Agent Parsons gives me a pitying look before turning to Ben. "Flatwood hit another hospital. In Flagstaff."

"And you got him?"

"No. He got away. Again."

I try to see Ben's color. It's hard. He's hiding it well, some-thing I suspect he is doing without thinking. The Navajo are very good at affecting a passive face when they want to.

"How?" he asks.

"We don't know. From the looks of it, he just...disappears."

"What?"

"He shoots up now, right on site. Right where he steals the drugs. He should be in a coma, but instead, he gets away."

"But you said you know where he is?"

"He drives an old motorcycle. We've had our eye out for it ever since a traffic camera picked him up in Portland. We found it outside of the hospital in Flagstaff, and we bugged it in case he eluded us again."

"Good thing," Ben says. Neither of the agents moves a muscle. "So where's he going?"

"East. Fast. His movements are erratic. He would be hard to catch, even if we wanted to."

"But you don't."

"No. We don't want to tip him off."

Ben puts his hands on his hips, and I can see that he wants to scratch at his stomach. His nausea would be knocking at the door right about now.

"I don't understand. What do you want from me?" Ben asks, and it breaks my heart to hear the hint of desperation in his voice.

"We know where he's going, Ben. There's only one major hospital on his route that's big enough for him to slip in and out unnoticed."

I go cold. "ABQ General," I say, before I can stop myself.

The agents turn to me briefly, then nod as if they were approving of the pictures on the mantel. "And he's almost there. We're just ahead of him."

"Well, catch him then. What are you standing here for?" Ben says.

Parsons smooths at his tie. Douglas scratches at his neck. Their coloring is hard to describe. It's flat brown. Almost dead. There's been very little movement until now, but at Ben's insistence a muted flash of mottled black speckles around both men. They're embarrassed. And angry about it.

"We have tried. Twice our people had him dead to rights. Twice he got away."

"You don't think you can catch him," Ben says, and I hear a hint of a smile in his voice.

"We think you might have a better shot," Parsons says.

"Me? You're kidding. What makes you think I could do anything?" He sounds incredulous, but I know otherwise. I can see it in how he sharpens, like a camera snapping to focus. He wants to see this Joey character. This friend I thought was dead. He wants it badly.

I jump in, before anyone can say anything. "Ben, you're going to be very sick soon. We don't know how you're going to react, but odds are it's not going to be good. You shouldn't leave this house."

The agents seem totally disinterested in me. Disinterested in everything but getting Ben to go with them. They're so *flat*. Like they're cutouts of men.

"I don't like them," I say. I cover my mouth for a second, then drop my hand before I look too much like a little girl. "I mean...what I mean is that if they have a tracker on him, you can get him tomorrow. Or the next day."

Or never, and you can just stay with me. And I'll talk to you. And hold your hand.

"He's getting violent," Parsons says evenly. "He assaulted two orderlies at Flagstaff Presbyterian Hospital. Hurt one of them fairly badly. He is extremely hard to take down. His strength is...outsized. We read your report. You can get in his head. Talk to him. Slow him down or distract him enough for our guys to take him down."

"Ben—" I begin, pleading.

"We don't have a lot of time, Mr. Dejooli. A matter of hours. And it's a little over an hour to get there."

I drop my hands to my sides, and my gown crinkles loudly. I already know I've lost.

"Okay," Ben says. "I'll go. Just give me five minutes."

The agents nod, then turn to leave. One of them, Douglas, turns to me and stares at me with the blank malice of a guard dog. Then he follows Parsons out. Ben and I are alone again.

"I have to go. You don't know about things between Joey and me. I... just have to go, that's all."

"You're gonna get sick."

"I'll bring a bag."

"Dammit, Ben," I say, quietly.

"I'm sorry. I wouldn't go if it was anything else. You gotta believe me."

I rummage around roughly in my tote until I find the anti-nausea medication I brought along with me.

"Here," I say, throwing it a little harder than I had intended. He catches it out of midair, and it rattles. "Take two. Then take two more in two hours. So on and so forth. It'll help, but it won't take care of everything. You're gonna feel like garbage."

He looks so grateful and relieved that I can't stay mad at him. I'm not sure it's my place to keep him anywhere if he wants to go. I can only say what I can say. I take off my gown and start packing things away while he dashes to the back. I hear him pour a glass of water and gulp the pills down, then I hear him cut left to his room. When he comes back out, he's in uniform. Hat and all. He pauses in the kitchen and looks back at the side room where I saw the crow at the window. He takes a tentative step forward and seems to be thinking. I try to fade into the wall while still watching him. He takes a few slow steps and reaches up where the bag is with the sticks. He sets them aside and slowly reaches in the bag. His back is to me so I can't see what he's doing, but he stays like this for several moments, long enough to where I'm afraid the agents might ring the doorbell again.

When he turns around from the bag, he looks spooked. He tucks his shirt in and pats at his belt, but his mind is elsewhere. He takes his hat off and scratches at his head, then plunks it back on and walks back to the front room. By then I'm all packed up.

"Thank you, Caroline," he says, but he's dazed. His color is flashing faintly, like lights underwater. He wants to tell me something, but he can't. "I'll see you...when?"

"Next week. But call me if you feel weird. Or if anything. For anything, I mean."

He nods and holds the door open for me. He follows me out, and I watch as he gets into a big black Suburban. It turns around and takes off like a rocket, and I'm left outside alone, holding the rig and the cooler.

I almost drop everything on the street when a flock of crows that had stood silent watch in the tree nearby suddenly explodes into flight in a firework of black. They take off after the Suburban, and I can still hear their keening and squawking even when they look like a floating black ribbon in the distance against the sky.

12

OWEN BENNET

We've had our fair share of bad apples visit the oncology floor. Cancer doesn't go away just because the person who has it is in prison. Cancer doesn't make a distinction between the girl next door and a violent offender. Cancer is cancer. You can debate the ethics of it from a taxpayer's perspective all you want, but the law, my oath, and my beliefs tell me that if a person needs treatment, they should get it. No matter what.

Usually you can tell a dangerous patient is on their way because the hospital beefs up security at the entrances and exits to the floor, and two guards are assigned to prep a room, do sweeps, and remove anything that could be used as a weapon. In other words, it's pretty obvious, and it sets the staff abuzz and generally creates a heightened tension that everyone could do without. It's tense enough on the onc floor as it is.

This time is different. Very different. But different because everything looks exactly the same. When I get to the hospital, it looks like business as usual. I'm the attending. I relieve the night attending. I get report. I review any material changes from the cases I prepped overnight. I get my schedule, I drink my coffee, and I start making rounds. Then I'm charting in the on-call room when the CEO, Dick Schwartz, walks in flanked by what looks like two accountants. Schwartz seems like he's about to keel over. In fact, he looks so peaked that I think he's come to check himself in.

"Hello, Doctor Bennet," Schwartz says. "Can I speak with you?"

Outside of the one day around Thanksgiving when he and the other C-level administrators hand out turkeys to everyone and shake their hands, I have never spoken with Dick Schwartz in my life. He has no reason to know my name. There are hundreds and hundreds of doctors in his employ. Now all of a sudden I'm the one feeling peaked.

"Mr. Schwartz," I say, watching as the other two check the hallway outside and close the door to the on-call room. I see a black shoulder holster under the arm of one of them. Not accountants after all. Schwartz pulls out a chair and positions himself so that his jacket doesn't rumple under him.

"We have a situation here," he says, and he clasps his hands together on the table. "Things are moving rather fast. I've only just been appraised of the situation myself by the agents here, but the gist of it is that we have a violent criminal on his way to ABQ General."

"All right. You want me to handle the transfer personally?"

Schwartz swallows.

"He's not being transferred. In fact, he's not in custody at all. Yet."

I furrow my brow. "I'm not sure I follow."

"This man, he targets hospitals for their drugs. He prefers oncology floors, for whatever reason." Schwartz looks at one of the agents, who nods. "Maybe because onc floors stock high levels of pain killers, but either way, we think he's going to end up here."

"And what do you want me to do?"

"That's just it. Nothing."

"What?"

The agent by the door steps in. "We need things to appear completely normal here. The suspect must not be tipped off in any way."

I clear my throat. "So...what, just let him roam the halls? I have a responsibility for the safety of my nurses and staff as well as the patients."

"If his other hits are any indication, you won't even see him. He's...very good. And to date he hasn't harmed anyone unless approached first, although we believe he may start to attack indiscriminately if he isn't stopped. He does occasionally go into patient rooms."

"My God."

"The sickest patients, it would seem," says the other agent, with chagrin. "He likes the ones who are dying."

"What's he do to them?" I ask.

A nurse tries to come into the break room, but is blocked by the agent, who waves her off like a fly before turning back to me. "To date he's just stared at them," he says.

"He is a severe addict, doctor," says the first agent. "If what he steals is any indication, he will not be in his right mind."

"So are we supposed to keep him here for you?"

"No," he says, and he pulls a security camera still from the breast pocket of his jacket and hands it to me. It's of a young Navajo man, squat, with that peculiar, faded look of an addict. He looks like a man who was once strong and is now retreating from that strength, as if his skin doesn't quite fit right. He wears a black leather jacket and has wild black hair down to his lower back. His eyes flash vacantly in the camera exposure.

"This is him. If you see him, stay away. If you see any of your staff approaching him, intervene. But like I said, I don't think you'll see him. That is why we won't be notifying the rest of the floor. We think it would do more harm than good."

"How are you going to catch him? You are catching him, right? Not just escorting him from hospital to hospital?"

Neither agent bats an eye.

"Let us take care of that. All you need to do is stay alert and act normal. And if either Agent Douglas or I tells you to do something, do it."

I look at Dick Schwartz for help. I don't like the tone or the demeanor of either of these agents, but I get no help from Schwartz, who looks as harrowed as I feel. Something tells me this isn't the time to get into a discussion of liability. Something tells me nothing I can say will change a damn thing. This guy is coming no matter what. But I make a mental note to step into Schwartz's office with a vengeance if we all survive this thing.

"How long do I have?"

"About fifteen minutes," Parsons says, as he reaches over and plucks the photograph from my hands.

"Thank you, Doctor Bennet," Schwartz says, but his eyes are saying *I'm sorry. These men will not be put off.*

Then all three of them sweep out of the room, and I'm left alone with the approaching storm.

I can only thank God that Caroline isn't working today.

13

BEN DEJOOLI

The agents point out the motorcycle as it approaches. We're parked in the general lot, right next to a whole host of trucks and SUVs. We look just like everyone else, and there's no way that Joey could notice us or hear us in the car, but still we talk in whispers.

It's a beautiful vintage Honda 650. Round body. Black and gold coloring. It's the bike we'd dreamed of buying and restoring as kids, even down to the offset striping on the gas tank.

"That son of a bitch," I say. The agents nod, unaware.

First thing: that Honda doesn't look like the kind of thing a drug addict would be zipping around on. Drug addicts don't restore classic motorcycles. They scrap 'em and hock 'em.

As he pops over the hill and comes to a stop at the light before the turn off, I get my first good look at him. Sort of. He's in riding leathers and boots, and he wears a red kerchief over his face. It's pinned to him above the nose by a big pair of reflective aviator goggles. It's him though. He doesn't wear a helmet, and it looks like he hasn't cut his hair in the six years since I last saw him. It nearly settles down to his seat and is as black as night.

That's the second thing. He doesn't exactly look inconspicuous.

I have to take my eyes from him because I'm going to vomit again, but otherwise I'd be mesmerized.

I've nearly filled a second grocery bag with vomit. We tossed the first one out of the window on the highway. I think next time I'll tell Caroline I need to take the anti-nausea stuff before she pricks me. I'm pretty sure the two capsules I took with water before I left are intact in that bag on the side of the highway. Still, it's not all bad. I kind of like how disgusted the agents are. These guys grate on me. They have less than zero concern about any of the human aspects of this sting, or whatever you'd call what's going on here. It's like they're getting orders beamed to their heads at the same time. Like rats on a mission through a maze, they're that focused. I feel like they'd eat through the walls if that's what it took.

Joey pulls into the general lot and coasts right up to the motorcycle parking at the front, maybe twenty feet from the double door entrance. He throws the kickstand out and steps off. He pulls down his bandana, and I get a good look at the face of a man I made sure was kicked out of Chaco forever. The man I threw from the Navajo Way. He looks terrible. He always had a squat body, but he doesn't fill it out anymore. His eyes are wide and bulging. His mouth is set, clenched, and his face is gaunt and angled to the bone. He doesn't look thin, not exactly. He looks worse than thin. He looks diminished. He looks like he's fading.

But he doesn't act like it. And that's the third thing I notice. Joey walks right into the hospital without even blinking. Not a care for the security cameras at every door. Not even a glance in either direction. This is not a man who is worried about the twenty-five-to-life he's facing if and when these suits pull him in.

The agents are on their earpieces, muttering. Parsons nods and turns to me.

"Ninth floor. Oncology. He's going up. It's showtime, Mr. Dejooli." He pops open the door.

"Remember," Douglas says, "if you can hold him, hold him. Shoot him if you have to. Just don't kill him."

Those are some pretty open orders right there. Back at the station Danny would call that "permission to start shit."

I nod. Then I'm off. I pull my hat down low, and I have to grin at the thought that I'm doing more to disguise myself than Joey did. When I reach the elevators he's already gone up. I push the button a bunch of times and wait for an interminable thirty seconds as his elevator hits nine then comes back down. When it opens, it's empty.

When I reach the ninth floor, I don't see him anywhere. I stutter step onto the floor and look around. No Joey. I go up to the receptionist, who is nervously tapping a pack of cigarettes and checking her watch.

"Did you see a guy come up here? Biker guy? Dressed in leather?"

"When?" she asks.

"Just now. Like right now."

She looks at me sideways. "Nope. You're the only visitor in the last couple of minutes."

I stare at her long enough to make her nervous. "Anything else?" she asks sharply.

I turn around and go back out to the elevators. It makes no sense. He had to have walked by the front desk. I finger the com on my shoulder. "You sure he went up the main elevator?"

"Yes," comes the reply. I can imagine Parsons grinding his teeth.

"The front desk says—"

"He went in. He's on the floor. Now you see what we mean when we say he's tricky."

Tricky my ass. Something else is at work here. He's nearby. It's like I can feel him. The sulfur has been picking up in intensity, packing deeper in my nostrils. I have to go near the corner and hold the crook of my elbow over my mouth to keep from retching. When I stand up again, I waver a bit before snapping to focus. This chemo is nasty, but then again, I was warned.

I walk back towards the desk. Then right past the desk.

"Can I *help* you?" the receptionist asks again.

"I'm here to prep a room for an inmate transfer," I say over my shoulder. I can tell she wants to stop me, but I think she wants her cigarette break more. I pass through to the main hall.

The floor is laid out like a horseshoe, the front desk at the bow and patient rooms at intervals down either rung. In the middle are a slew of computers and cubicles and lockers and whatnot for the staff. I shoot a glance down one side and don't see him. I cut across the middle to the other side, and I still don't see him. There's a fire exit at the far back, but it's alarmed. And anyway, I know he's still here somewhere. Ever since the Evilway, like it or not, I've been feeling more, seeing more, smelling more than I should be. Could be that I sweat out toxins for two straight days. Could be that I have a quart of cell-bleach in my system. Could also be that I'm dying. Whatever it is, if it helps me get this shit straight, I'll take what I can get.

I start down the near hallway, noting which doors are closed on my left and swinging my head right to clear the

computer area. I don't see him, but when I turn around, the
doors I thought were closed are open, and some of the ones
that were open are closed. It's a funhouse from hell. I really
don't want to start knocking on doors. At the end of the hallway, I find the pill case, right where the agents said it
would be.

I also find Doctor Bennet, staring at it with wide eyes
because it's swinging open like a rusty gate and with a circle
the size of a fist cut out of it.

"Shit," I mutter, and Bennet looks up at me. His eyes get
wider.

"Are you here for him?" Bennet whispers.

"Yeah. When did this happen?"

"Now. I mean just now."

"Did you see where he went?"

"No. I didn't see anything." He steps up and in front of
the case as a pair of nurses walk by. He nods weakly at their
passing greeting.

"What are you talking about? Which way did he go,
Bennet?"

"You don't get it. I was watching the case. I've been
watching it for twenty minutes. Nothing happened. I
blinked and then this."

My eyes start to water. My face feels like it's burning. I
try to hold my guts in, but I have to grab a trashcan quick,
turn away, and puke. Thankfully I have nothing left in me
now. It just sounds like I'm spitting. I turn back to Bennet,
and he's softened.

"You shouldn't be out like you are. You must be in a good
deal of pain."

"I'll be in worse pain if I can't catch Joey—"

And then there he is. I see him out of the corner of my
eye, clear as day. Dressed in black with the red bandana

pulled down around his neck. He's right there, twenty feet down the hall, staring at me. Except when I turn to look at him, he's gone.

"What? Do you see him?" Bennet asks.

"Sort of..." I say, turning back to Bennet, and then there he is again. Same spot. This time I stay still and don't turn to look. It could be that my eyes are dripping water, could be that I feel like I have a hotpot on my head, but he looks like a nightmare. His eyes are way too big, and his mouth is the same black circle shape as his eyes. The rest of his face has been smudged. Pasty skin coloring extends beyond the borders of where his face should be. And it's moving. All by itself. He looks like he's screaming, but he's not. He's standing still with his hands balled in fists at his side, and he's staring right at me. And now it's my turn to feel scared. Whatever this is, it's not Joey Flatwood. Not the Joey I knew.

Then something grabs Joey's attention, and he darts off sideways across the horseshoe to the other side of the floor. He's gone in a blink. It's like he steps through the walls. A second later, the bells and whistles go off. It's a code. I know that from the old days. Someone is dying. The Navajo people don't believe in coincidences. But even if I did, I sure as hell wouldn't believe this was a coincidence. Bennet looks at me. I nod. He straightens and rolls up his sleeves. I respect that. I respect a guy who owns up to what's coming.

"Follow the running," he says, and he takes off down the hall. We're joined by a bunch of other people in scrubs, and soon five or six of us whip around the bend and towards the blinking blue light above the room at the far end of the corridor. I put my hand on my gun. I feel like I'm gonna throw up again, but this time I'm not sure if it's all about the chemo. I strain forward and pull ahead of the wave, and I'm the first one into the room. There he is. He's leaning over the patient, his face inches from the old man's. His black hair forms a waving tent over the small figure in the bed. He's speaking. Chanting something, but it's muddled. It's not unlike what Gam was singing in the Evilway, but it sounds like it's coming from a tinny speaker underwater.

"Joey, get away from the bed!" I say, and I pull my gun. He looks up at me with a jerk, and I'm expecting the vacant black holes and the dripping oil face I saw in the corridor, but it's just Joey. A rail-thin, walking-dead-man version of Joey, but Joey.

And then he's gone.

And I have people yelling at me. I'm spinning in a circle in the room, but he's nowhere. And then I'm being pushed away, and I see Bennet calming people down and pushing me out of the room, and calming some more. People are giving orders, and I hear the whining sound of that shocker pad revving. The nurses are crowded around the unconscious old man on the bed, and I'm just outside, looking in.

No Joey.

"I think I'm losing my mind," I say out loud, just to hear my voice, just to make sure I'm still here and not dreaming. I wipe sweat from my clammy brow, and Bennet comes over to me.

"I...I think I'm worse than I thought I was. I'm seeing things," I say. I feel like I want to cry. This must be what it's like to go insane: visual hallucinations so strong you swear on your family that they're true. I get this loopy thought that maybe I died during the Evilway and this is where I ended up, doomed to chase the man I banished forever. I feel at the wall, only half sure it exists. Then I collapse against it.

"I saw him too," Bennet says quietly. I look up at him, reach for him with my eyes like a drowning man would a raft.

"You saw him?"

Bennet nods. "Ben. Can you tell me what is going on here?" He speaks very slowly, as if he's walking a thin line of sanity himself.

"Wish I could. Holy hell do I wish I could. He's still here somewhere. I can feel it."

Alarms are still blaring in the room. Bennet pops back into the chaos and then out again to check on me. He shakes his head. No Joey. Then he steps on something with a loud crunch. He looks down. He's crushed a white pill to powder under his shoe.

"He must have gotten by in all the shoving," Bennet says.

"Can you go across to the other wing?" I ask. "I'll start at the back end of this one. We work our way forward. If you see or hear anything, or think you see or hear anything, you call out. You hear me?"

Bennet nods, takes one more look at the code to assure himself it's being taken care of, then trots across the horse shoe again.

I walk down my hallway towards the back fire exit. I walk slowly, with my palms held out and my hands open, like I'm trying to catch the air. If I can't see him, maybe I can feel him.

It's difficult to focus on your periphery. Impossible, actually. So my mind's eye watches my side view while I try my best to keep staring at the fire door straight ahead of me. Every time I hear a door open or close, I look toward it in a snap, but it's just the hospital moving around me, doctors and nurses and staff going about the day. I reach the far door. No sign of him. I spin around and curse under my breath.

I listen for Bennet on the opposite side, but nothing is out of the ordinary. A small cheer comes from the code room, and nurses and staff start to file out. Guess the little old man made it after all. At least somebody is getting a happy ending here. I slump and walk back towards the front bend. My mind tells me Joey is long gone, but I still sense something in my heart. I still sense that burning darkness that came from his eyes, but it's weaker now. I pause by the door to the little old man's room, still open. His little old wife is crying tears of joy at his side, her head not far from where Joey's had been, but this time he's looking back at her with rheumy eyes. They clasp hands, thin and frail like dried flowers, but there is life there still. They have another minute with each other. And another. His wife has this sort of delirious pitch to her voice, like when you're on the tables at Wapati and you're playing on house money. It draws me a little closer to the room. It makes me smile. They don't have a care for anything but each other.

Maybe that's why they don't see Joey.

Because he's right there. In the corner of the room. And he's not some side-seen apparition this time either. No melting flesh, no dark pits for eyes. He's a flesh and blood man that I can see straight on. And he can see me straight on too. He sees me before I see him. Every cop instinct they drill into you for a time like this, when you get blindsided by something, goes right out the window. I don't react. I can't react. If he wanted to tackle me or bum rush me, he could have, right then and there. Joey was always bigger than me, and even down fifty pounds like he is right now, his eyes still have this fire to them. They aren't the eyes of a dying man. If he wanted to, he could give me a run for my money. But he doesn't. What he does do is lift a gloved finger to his lips and then move his gaze out of the doorway, beckoning.

He wants to talk.

I cock my head and squint. *You're fucking kidding me, right?*

He holds out his hands wide and bobs his head. *You know I could run if I want. You know you'd never catch me.*

It's funny how after all these years I can still read him like a book. No words required. I take a breath and purse my lips. *Fine.* Joey always got what he wanted when we were kids, why should things change now? I back out of the door and into the hallway. He follows me. We both stare at each other until we stop just a few rooms back from the far corner by the exit.

"I knew it was you," he says. And he's smiling. He looks like he wants to hug me, but he holds back. Instead he just takes me in. "It's good to see you, Big B."

His voice triggers an avalanche of memories I don't want to feel right now. Things like us screaming down the flood plain on our bicycles with the warm New Mexico night air whipping past our bare chests. I push back against them by focusing on the pack of morphine nodules I see hanging out of his bulging pockets. The audacity of this fucking guy.

"I gotta bring you in, Joey."

"You can't bring me in," he says. "I'm not Navajo, remember?" He smiles a hollow smile that reminds me of the holes in his face I saw minutes ago.

"I'm not working for NNPD here," I say.

His smile drops. "Those bastard suits?"

"They're the FBI. They don't fuck around. They want you alive, but I think there's a big gap between 'moving' and 'alive' for these guys."

"Tell me about it," he says. "You can't trust them, Ben. You don't know what their motives are."

"Shut up, Joey. Just shut up and come with me. I don't

want to hash out everything again. I really don't. I want to get you behind bars and then go home."

"They don't want me," he says. "Nobody wants me. You of all people should know that."

"Fuck you. Don't start with that shit. You brought this on yourself." I find myself gripping his jacket, balling the leather in my fist. "All you had to do was talk, you miserable piece of shit. That's all you had to do. If you didn't take her yourself, then tell us what you saw. You were in the goddamn room with her!"

He lets me grab him. He moves with my trembling arms. His face is sallow, his jaw slack, and I can see just how much weight he's lost. "Look at you," I say, and I push him back a step. "Instead of facing yourself, you've decided to wipe yourself out. You're a fucking coward, Joey. You're a coward, and I don't have room for this shit in my life anymore because it's destroying me too."

For a second, he looks like I struck him across the face, but he rallies. "You're a good man, Ben," he says. "A better man than I am. But you're such a cop. You see two points and work your ass off to draw a straight line between them. But this story is no straight line. I think you're coming to see that now."

"You're fucked up, Joey. Something fucked you up. You need help. You're an addict, man. You're knocking off hospitals and getting crazy. You've crossed state lines. That's why the FBI is here. And they don't give up."

Joey shakes his head. "Yeah, well, neither do I," he mutters.

"Let's just walk out of these doors and nobody gets shot, okay? That's what they want. That's what I want, too."

"Like I said, they don't want me."

"Well, what do they want?"

He reaches in his pocket with one gloved hand and grips something. He has it out and in his palm before I can blink, never mind draw my gun.

"They want this," he says.

It's a turquoise crow. Same as the gambler's. Same as Gam's. I can only stare at it.

"You've seen this before?" he asks. "Doesn't surprise me. Not with the path you've walked. Not with the path you have to walk still."

"Where did you get that?" I ask, my mind numb.

"I pulled it from the hands of a dead man in Colorado. Don't worry. I didn't kill him. But your friends in the suits did. I snatched it before they could find it." He smiles. "They were pretty pissed off when it wasn't where they thought it would be."

Part of my mind is telling me not to listen to the words of an addict on the run, but over the past weeks I seem to have put some distance between that part and the rest of me. A rift has opened, a rip in my fabric that started as an unraveling when Ana left me but that has been getting bigger every day and finally split down the seam in that hogan. I don't understand what Joey is saying, but I know he's telling me the truth.

"I don't know how many of these totems there are, Ben, but they want them all. Bad. And I think they'll stop at nothing to get them."

"But why? It's just a crow," I say, but I don't believe that, and he knows it.

"No such thing as *just a crow*, my brother. And they want it for the same reason I want it. Because they want to find Ana."

I step back. His words hit me like rocks. I feel bruised. I feel bile rise in my throat. The sulfur smell hits me with the force of a wildfire. My vision wavers and I hitch to the side, but Joey grabs me.

"You think I've been running this whole time—I know it. But I'm not running. I'm *looking* for her. The suits think they understand everything. That the more crows they get the closer they'll be. But they don't get it." His face is manic. His eyes glassy. "I don't either, but I'm getting closer. This shit?" He taps the vials in his pocket. "I hate this shit. But it gets me closer. The drugs, and the crow, and...and these places"—he holds out his hands to the hospital around him—"where people are battling death. Each gets me a little closer to finding her, Ben! They're all pieces of a puzzle, and they're coming together. But I'm running out of time."

"Ana?" I whisper. "Ana?" I say her name like a ward. I say it like I used to say it in my sleep before Gam would wake me and sing to me. An eighteen-year-old man weeping in his grandmother's arms.

My com crackles. It's subtle, but we both hear it. The agents are coming. I grab him by the jacket again, but my grip is weak. He pulls one leather glove off with his teeth and pries my fingers from him.

"I have to keep you here," I say, but there's nothing behind it. There's nothing in me anymore. Nothing but a rising sickness and the unsettling feeling of empty burning in my veins. He takes my fingers in his.

"I'm sorry, Ben. I'm so sorry," he says, and I have a series of flashbacks of him walking away across the rez boundary, him looking at me and weeping, but still walking away. "But time is short."

Then he takes the crow from his gloved hand and grips it with his bare hand, and he blinks out of sight. I look left and right for him, and I see him in flashes, like a man glimpsed through the crack of a door.

"Goodbye," he whispers. I feel the air part as he moves away. He's gone, and it's just me, sobbing against a wall. The fire alarm goes off. I turn my head towards the front, waiting for the agents, but instead I see Bennet, and he rushes to me as I slide down the wall. He saw the whole thing. Or enough of it anyway. It's written on his face. He's like a man who just woke up in a strange place and is looking for anything familiar to grab onto. I think I'm the same way because when he kneels down to me we grab each other, and that's when the cavalry comes in. The two agents, sure, but another three as well, and a handful of state police for good measure, guns out, scaring the shit out of everybody.

Bennet does what I can't do. He stands up in the bedlam and screams like a foghorn, "He's gone! He ran! The fire exit! Quickly!" Then he throws an arm around my back. "Come on, man," he whispers. "With me."

Bennet parts the sea of agents and cops that runs around us, and he half-carries me into a darkened patient room. He helps me onto the bed, grabs a bucket, and slides it in front of me, and I lose my guts again. I puke red, and I see red. Then I see black spots, and then I'm out.

WHEN I WAKE UP, it's like my life is on repeat. I'm strapped to another damn machine, with another damn baggie dripping itself into my veins. Except this time I don't even have my comfy lounger, and the nurse in my room isn't Caroline. She's older, and when she hears me stir, she dials a number on her phone and bustles over to my bed.

"How are you feeling?" she asks.

"Like hell. What's in the bag?"

"You're dehydrated. We're just giving you some fluids, that's all."

Then everything comes back to me, and I try to sit up. But this nurse is big, and she pushes a beefy hand down on my sternum.

"Easy there."

My head is pounding. Watching things hurts. Blinking hurts. I close my eyes and focus on not moving them under my lids, and that helps stave off another wave of nausea.

"What time is it?"

"It's just after six," says another voice, and this one I recognize. Bennet. I open my eyes a smidge and watch him through my eyelashes. "Same day. You've only been out for about two hours. Thank you, Mary Ellen. I'll take it from here."

Mary Ellen shuffles out, and Bennet closes the door behind her before sliding a small stool next to the bed. I shuffle a bit in a sad attempt to sit up, but he shakes his head and stills me with a single touch.

"Rest, Ben. Your body has no idea what's going on."

"Neither does the rest of me," I mutter.

Bennet glances at the door and nods. "He got away," he says, his voice low. "The agents and the rest of them canvassed the place for an hour before that Parsons guy called them all off. He and Douglas left without a word. Kind of a pissy couple, those two."

I let out a breath that rattles my throat, but I say nothing.

"Now why do I get the feeling that you aren't all that torn up about the dangerous drug addict's daring escape?"

"He said some things to me. Some things that rang true."

"About that rock he held in his hand? That made him invisible?" Bennet finishes with a sad laugh and creaks back in his seat. He runs his hands up and down his face a couple of times. "I can't believe I'm saying this. I can't believe I just said that without tacking on 'here's a referral to a counselor' or 'that's a side effect of the medication'."

"The crow is real. I don't know what it does, exactly, but whatever it is, it's real. It happened. But it wasn't just that. We have a history, him and me, and now I'm starting to rethink it."

"Is that good, or bad?"

"Neither. It just is. But he told me to watch out for the Feds."

"Sounds like something a criminal on the run would say."

"Nah. I get it. I get what he's saying. I never liked those two stiffs. They always rubbed me the wrong way."

Bennet is quiet, but I know he won't disagree. I know they chafe him too. The way they have blinders on. They're too cold. Too calculating. It's unnatural.

"He said the Feds weren't after him. They were after the crow."

"If it can do what I think I saw it do, it could be very valuable. It's...miraculous."

"He told me it wasn't the only one. That the Feds are on a tear to find all of them."

And then it hits me: *and I know exactly where one is.*

"Where did they go?" I ask, my voice froggy. "The Feds. Where did they go?"

"I don't know. Like I said, they just tore off. Not a word."

If they knew about Joey's crow, they could know about Gam's crow too. Joey said they'd stop at nothing. Said they wanted all the crows, and something about Ana, but that was flushed from my mind. I had to get to Gam. I grit my teeth and push to a sitting position. I see an explosion of colors, and my head feels like a sack of sand is resting on it.

"What are you doing? You have to rest, Ben."

"No. I have to go. I have to get to my grandmother. I think she's in trouble."

"You aren't going anywhere tonight, man. Even if I let you, you wouldn't make it out that door."

My eyes water with pain and frustration, and fear. Magic crows, shadow-walking people, none of these things particularly scare me, but the thought of those two men knocking on our door and Gam opening it up to them terrifies me.

"Here," Bennet says, pulling his cell phone from his pocket. "Call her. Warn her."

We don't have a landline and Gam hasn't picked up a phone in years, but I give Dad a shot. The phone rings. And rings. And rings. His voicemail picks up and says his mailbox is full. Like it's been for years. I hang up. The look I give Bennet must be so pathetically terrified that it's catching. His eyes go wide, and his pale face blanches a whiter shade.

"Isn't there anyone? Anyone at all?" he asks.

My mind races, and somehow, like it's done for the past few days, it settles on Caroline. What was she doing after my chemo? She said she was going back to the CHC to log a couple more hours. If she's still there, she'd be minutes away from my house.

Bennet peers at me and nods slowly. He takes his phone back and flips through his contacts.

"I'll call her," he says. "But you gotta explain all this."

14

CAROLINE ADAMS

I'm basically worthless at the CHC after the chemo session with Ben. I'm making my rounds, but I'm not really there. With the Navajo you really have to work sometimes to get them to open up, and I pride myself on working hard to do that, but not today. Today I'm like the dead-weight guy in the group project. Of the five of us from ABQ General who are scheduled here, I'm by far the most worthless. One of the nurses even ends up cleaning up after me when I forget a patient on one of my rounds. A nurse's worst nightmare. Don't worry, they were fine. Sleeping. Thank God, but still...

The day can't end soon enough. I feel drained. I'm not sure what to make of what happened at Ben's house, with him storming off like that with those weird men. To say nothing of the crows. I think it speaks to my mental state that I'm more worried about Ben getting into that Suburban than I am about the staring contest I had with a monster crow, or his thousand crow buddies that scared the hell out of me when I was getting into my car. The human mind is a strange thing. When something that out of whack happens,

I think my mind flat refuses to let me dwell on it. Instead it pushes it to the back. I don't forget it. It's still there, sort of waving at me, but in its place my mind swaps in other things, stupid things. Like how Ben held my hand when the chemo was first dripping into him. How he looked at me. Monster crows from hell could be swarming all around us, ending the world, and I would still be awake at three a.m. thinking about what it meant that Ben held my hand.

Naturally the days you want to end the fastest last the longest, and soon enough I'm regretting my decision to log a few more hours. I get a late admit: a young woman with severe cramping. She's been in before, around this time of the month, by the looks of her chart. A targeted birth control prescription would fix all this up, even I know that. But no, she's been prescribed a series of catch-all intrauterine devices to which she's reacting badly. Owen would have figured this out before she sat down on the exam table. I wish he was here. I don't feel comfortable talking to the attending on rotation here today, an older man. He means well, but he's from the school of physicians that believes nurses should be seen, not heard.

Anyway, the poor girl is in a lot of pain, and it's around six in the evening when we finally get her comfortable. By then I've let my charting pile up, and I'm late on my final rounds. I stop in the quiet end of the hallway and take a few seconds. I do this sometimes when I know I'm being a shitty nurse. I just stop it all and stand where there are relatively few people and roll my neck for a second. With this job, it's so easy to run and run and run, but you just can't do that because you burn out. And when you burn out, you stop being a nurse and become just another employee. And there is a difference.

On top of all of this I also have my grant fulfillment to

think about. I'm weeks away from a clean slate. No loans. No debt. Nothing. Pretty soon the CHC administration will sign off on my contract and hand me my receipt, and if I want to I can get in my car and leave everything behind me. I can't quite imagine the freedom I'd have. It gives me a strange sense of vertigo to think about it, like I'm standing at the edge of a cliff. I have to admit, it's kind of intriguing. On the other hand, it would make me a tourist. I know this place doesn't need tourists. It takes five years at Chaco just to get your foot in the door with a lot of the Navajo. I've put in a lot of work. I don't want to admit it, even to myself, but my decision on whether to stay or go is going to rest on whether Ben lives or dies.

My phone rings. I don't like to answer my phone at work because my hands are gross, and I don't want to touch it. It's usually solicitors anyway, but I'm still taking my thirty seconds, and I don't mind taking another thirty. I'm already gonna be here until seven in any case. Maybe it's my mom calling to say hi. Or that something terrible has happened. I pull my phone out of my front pocket. It's Owen. My pulse drops like a lead ball then bounces to racing. I get that feeling that you get when someone calls you at two in the morning: this isn't good, but I have to answer it.

"Hello?"

"Caroline! Thank you. Thank you."

It doesn't sound like Owen. It sounds like...but no. It can't be.

"Caroline, it's Ben. I need your help."

"Ben? Why are you...but what..."

"Please," he says, and that stops me. I can hear pain in his voice. I can almost see the black wisping off of him, coming over the line, and smoking out of my end of the phone.

"What do you need?"

"I need you to go back to my house. I'll explain every-thing along the way."

It takes five minutes and the promise of a double latte to one of the other nurses to get her to take care of the rest of my charting, and I'm out the door.

I PULL BACK onto Ben's street, but this time the crows are gone. There isn't a bird in the sky, but somehow it feels worse for their absence. The street is deserted. No cars out front. There aren't even any porch lights on.

"Are you there?" asks Ben, still on the line with me. He's told me about Joey Flatwood and what happened at the hospital. Owen is with him and chimed in occasionally, and I think that's why I finally believed his story about the crow totem. I don't believe in magic, never have, never will. Nor does Owen, I don't think. But I'm not going to sit here and tell you that I think death snuffs out a person forever. Who am I to say ours is the only plane of existence? Maybe this Joey guy, maybe he exists in a different way than we do. A way with its own rules and science and medicine. It's a stretch, I know, but I'm still secretly applauding myself for not writing both of them off as insane right off the bat. After all, I'm the one seeing colors. I'm the one that can see people's thoughts in their mist. For better or for worse, the three of us are thick as thieves in the nut house.

"Yeah," I answer him. "It's really quiet here. No sign of anybody. Wait..." I peer at the front door. It looks splintered at the lock. Uh oh. "Ben, I think the door's been forced."

I get out of my car and close the car door as quietly as I can. In the past ten minutes, it's dropped fifteen degrees. The sun has left this side of the street. I can hear both men speaking with each other on the other end. "I'm going in," I say.

"Wait, Caroline. Are you sure? They could still be there. Bennet is calling the cops. You should wait." He's a bad liar. Even over the phone. He wants somebody in there as soon as possible, and I'm the closest to hand. My mind is made up.

"If she's in there, she could be hurt," I say.

"Keep your guard up."

I put the phone in my pocket, still on the line, and push open the front door. It slides easily out, and then easily back when I make no move to go inside. Pieces of the jamb are strewn across the floor inside. I listen for any movement. There is nothing. I decide against announcing myself and slide inside, licking my lips and trying to work saliva back into my mouth. It's so still inside that a passing airplane rings loudly in my ears. A dog barks somewhere far away. Dust swirls in the low light where I'd set up the chemo rig hours before.

The place has been ransacked. A quick job. Upended drawers, flipped couch cushions. The picture of Ana and Ben sticks out from its shattered frame on the floor. I bend to pick it up, and that's when I hear a sound from the back. It's not much, but it's definitely something.

I switch tack. Time to be brave. "Hello?" I ask, and it comes out in a weak squeak. The sound stops immediately. I right the picture on the mantle again and walk slowly around the glass and debris towards the kitchen.

"Caroline? What is it?"

I jump, but it's just Ben, over the phone. I reach in my pocket and end the call. There's that shuffling again. I round the corner into the kitchen proper, and that's when I see the blood. A trail of it in a dark red line, almost black, like smeared tar on the tiles. It goes from the little side room through a corner of the kitchen and then out the back door. I look out the back door and see a man there, face down, by a small pile of rocks in the back yard. He isn't moving, and he has no color at all coming off of him. I know he's dead. I move towards him, but as I'm about to push the screen open, I hear the shuffling again and snap my head right, towards where I saw the crow through the window earlier.

And I see the crow again. Only it's inside this time, and it's in tatters on the ground, next to an old woman who can only be Ben's grandmother. She isn't moving, but the crow is. Barely. Its wings have both been broken, and its head is at an awkward angle. But it's trying to move closer to the old woman. When I step into the doorframe, it appraises me with one cloudy black eye and pauses. It blinks once, then goes back to its sad, flopping shuffle. It's terrifying, but it's in pain, and all malice that it may once have possessed has fled it. It manages to bump its sleek crown against the woman's side, and there it rests, like an old dog with its master.

The window in the room is shattered, and I see bits of feathers stuck to the jagged ends of the glass there. More feathers float lazily about in the breeze coming in. The bird still watches me, and then it squawks feebly. That's when the old woman stirs.

I step forward and pause again as the crow snaps at me and sort of gurgles. It hits me that this crow is protecting the woman. That it will die protecting the woman. And then I see the painfully slow rise and fall of both the crow's streaked chest and Ben's grandmother's chest, and I know that when the one dies, the other will die too. It's their coloring. They share it. It's a beautiful, sparkling strand of silver, like a heartstring, but it's weak and gossamer and looks like it could be snapped with the ease of brushing away a spider web.

I kneel down next to the old woman, and I can hear that she's struggling to breathe. Her neck is mottled and bruised and crumpled. Her windpipe is crushed. Blood runs from her nose. Her eyelids flutter and creep open, and she sees me. She focuses slowly, but if she is surprised to find a strange woman in her room, she doesn't show it. She mutters something softly in Navajo that I can't understand. My phone is buzzing like mad in my pocket. I fish it out and answer Ben's call.

"Ben, she's been attacked," I say, the panic wavering my voice. "Talk to her." I put the phone by her head, and I can hear Ben speaking on the other line in a near wail, but she seems to take no notice of him or of the phone. She's looking plainly at me.

"Help is coming," I say. "Just hold on," and I grip her bony hand.

"Police," she says. Then she says a name that sounds like Dejooli.

"Ben? Yes, he is coming. He will come soon. You can talk to him here, see?"

"Police," she says again. Then something that sounds like *nine-pin* or *nine-point*, and I am reminded of Ben's partner. The man who called the ambulance for him at the Arroyo.

"Yes. The police are coming. Just hold on."

The bird rests its head on her hip, unblinking, barely breathing, but watching keenly. Watching and understanding. It's such an alien feeling coming from a bird that I want to apologize to it too and tell it to hold on, help is on the way, but I stop myself. I've allowed a lot of stuff today, but speaking to a bird like it can understand me, even if it can, might be the straw that sends the camel to the nuthouse.

I pull down the collar of the woman's sweater, and I'm thinking how maybe I can open up that airway to buy her a little more time. The damage is severe. Her neck looks like a crumpled piece of tin. Still, I could get a knife and a pen. It might give us another ten minutes. Or it might kill her. I start looking around the room, and that's when I see the leather bag and the painted sticks from before, only the sticks have both been snapped in half and the leather bag has been ripped open. Next to it is a beautiful box that looks like it's made of ivory or bone. It's been snapped in two as well. The top half is upside down next to the bottom half, and inside is nothing but a handful of fine black sand. Some of it is scattered around the floor. I get the feeling that whatever was there is gone.

"I'm going to try to do something to your neck, to help you breathe," I say. I make a move to get up, but she holds me and eyes me with the same frank assessment as the bird. She shakes her head and squeezes my hand, and I realize that she is going to die here with me. The thought hits me with such force that I sit down on my rump next to her and sort of slump like an old doll. She pats me on the knee, her breath crackling like paper. She still watches me like she knows me. She is remarkably unafraid. Ben's pleading is softer, more diminished. There is a stretch of silence. He is listening, too.

"Who did this to you?" I ask.

"Police," she says, then she waves it off with a tiny brushing motion of her finger. I understand. It no longer matters. It is a thing that was done. What matters now is what happens next.

"The crow," she says. "Stone crow. He takes." I look back

at the bone box. So there was a stone crow in there. Already I'm linking it to what Ben told me about Joey Flatwood. I know it was more precious, and far more dangerous, than any mere ornament or jewel. She pulls weakly at my hand, and I lean closer. She closes her eyes and speaks in lilting Navajo. It sounds like wind whistling through trees.

"God, I wish I understood you," I say, helplessly. "Maybe Ben can—" but she quiets me with the barest hint of a squeeze of my hand.

"Wrong thinking," she says.

"What's wrong thinking?"

"The stone crow. Is important. But only guardians."

"Guardians? Guarding what?"

She drops my hand and snakes her own back up to her neck, and I think for a moment that she is looking for the source of her pain, for the source of her death. But then she slips her hands into her collar and grasps something on her chest. She carefully pulls it out, and in her hand I see a small silver bell hung around her neck with a simple leather strap. It is no bigger than my thumb. In a way it's no different from something you might see hanging on a Christmas tree, but there is a powerful weight to it that I can see with the same sight that shows me the colors. It is a weight so heavy that it is warping the faint silver strands that are what remains of her life, bowing them out and away like a powerful magnet. If we exist in one place, and Joey Flatwood another, and those that have passed from us exist on a third, then this thing that is a bell and not a bell cuts through all of those places like a hot knife through butter. I can see this just by looking at it.

Ben's grandmother sees what I see. She sees it in my eyes, and she sighs with a smile that says to me *I have chosen correctly.*

"The stone guards the silver," she says, and she hands it to me. I reach out for it. I am drawn to it, but before I can take it, she stills me with a look.

"No ring," she says, and her eyes focus to pins. I see that she has her thumb firmly on the tongue of the bell. The crow titters, and its broken wings twitch. They don't have much time left.

"No ring," she says again. "Never ring."

"No ring," I say, nodding.

She looks at me for a moment longer, and I get this feeling that she knows all about me. Knows everything I think and feel as surely as if I had lived with her in this room all of my life. She gives one final nod.

"Take," she says.

Very carefully, she transfers the bell to me. I slip the leather over her head. She lets up on the tongue last, and I clamp my own thumb over it. I feel like silencing that bell is, in all likelihood, the most important thing I have ever done in my life. I take it, and it doesn't make a sound. Physically it's actually quite light, but only because I expect it to be so heavy. It gleams a thick, milky silver color, creamier than normal silver, richer and more pure. It's also cold. Very cold. Tin-mug-in-the-freezer cold. It almost burns, but I'll be damned if I'm gonna take my thumb away from that clapper.

She nods appreciatively. Then she puts her thin lips together and shushes me.

"Secret," she says. "You, and Ben."

I nod.

She starts singing. Ben is still quiet on his end of the line, listening.

I don't know what it is she is saying, but I do know that it is a final song. A song of endings. I don't need to know the words to know that she is giving thanks. It is not sad, not particularly. It simply is, in the Navajo way. She closes her eyes, and I know she is seeing beyond herself now, bidding farewell to the path she has walked and welcoming the path ahead. It sounds like she is greeting an old friend, and when I see tears fall from the corners of her eyes, I feel that they aren't tears of pain or sorrow, but tears of joy. And I feel the same soft brush that I felt in the hospital after my patient died. The crow feels it too, because it twitches its silky black head and tracks the unseen movement of something terrible and beautiful walking through the door and over to this woman dying in front of me. The thing that walks in is the thing she sings for. The rhythm of her song slows. I press the bell tighter, holding it still with every fiber of my being, because it's burning in earnest now. It's calling out to whatever has walked into this room. It wants to be with this new thing, not with me. Perhaps it is even one and the same with this new thing. It wants to ring, but I won't let it.

I am not afraid, because I know in my heart that this thing, which I can only call Death, isn't here for me, isn't concerned with me, may not even see me. But it is here for the grandmother. There is a soft breath of air, and the silver strands of color that are the woman's and the crow's break and float away. The song is over. Both are dead. There is another movement in the air, barely a flutter, and then Death is gone too, and I am alone.

I let up on my grip and look down at the bell. I lift my thumb, but there is no longer any tongue there. The clapper is gone. Now the bell looks more like a candlesnuffer. But I know I felt the clapper when the grandmother was dying. I know it was there. I think it's still there, where I can't see it. It's just waiting.

I slip the necklace and bell that isn't a bell over my head

and tuck it close to my chest. It is still ice cold but not burning cold anymore. I would say goodbye to the grandmother, but I know that she is long gone. What is left on the floor is more one with the shattered glass and splintered wood around it than the flesh and blood she was. Ben heard the final song as well as I did, but he is talking now. Quietly. His voice sadly diminished through the tiny speaker of my phone. He is saying his own goodbye, and I leave him to it.

I hear sirens. They are close. I stand and gather myself, and that's when I remember the other body, the one that trailed the blood out of the back door. I follow it out into the back yard and come upon the man. I am expecting the intruder, but I know I'm wrong. This man has been stabbed. He has died clutching his stomach and trailing his heart's blood, but he is otherwise unscathed. He was not the one the crow died defending the grandmother from. As I bend down closer to his face, I see an instant resemblance. He has the same soft slope of the forehead and boxy cheekbones, the same soft brown skin.

Ben's father.

Did he come home and stumble upon the intruders? Did he try to defend the grandmother too? Whatever happened, when he was stabbed, he wanted to be here, out here in the back. I follow his path, the one cut short when he bled out, and I see that he is reaching for a pyre of rocks just outside of the lawn. To further confuse things, he is smiling. It's plain on his face. Not a grimace, either, or a death snarl. It is a genuine smile.

When death came for Ben's father, he was happy about it.

15

BEN DEJOOLI

The Navajo are not sentimentalists in death. My mother seems to have forgotten this. She has been away too long. She wants a fresh cut pine box for both Gam and Dad and a ceremony with speakers and eulogies and suits and ties and tears. She fights with the people of the Arroyo, with whom Gam and Dad shared their final wishes for burial in the old style. She screams at them until I have to hold her back. I see reappearing shades of the blank horror that wiped her mind when Ana vanished. She is all too used to this type of thing.

In the end, she exhausts herself and sleeps for many hours, and the people of the Arroyo take my father and my grandmother away. I help. When they are laid on the cliff, the men who carried them along with me strip and burn our clothes and sweat in a hogan for some time. I think I pass out. I find myself in a small circle of campers later, by a fire, underneath a blanket with a diamond weave of stars above me. Nobody bothers me. Nobody speaks as I dress in the clothes that were left out for me, and I find my truck and drive back to my house. On the drive out, I see a flickering fire in the distance, and I know that the Arroyo men have burned the hogan where Gam held my Evilway.

There is nothing for me here anymore. I appreciate the purification rituals that the men of the Arroyo gave me. I know that they are simply trying to wash death off of me, but the truth is, I don't care if death finds me anymore. I would welcome death, now. A clean Navajo would never set foot in a house of the dead, which is what my house has become. But I am not clean. No matter how much I sweat, I am marked. I know this now. I know this because the crows follow me.

The crows are bolder by the day. They hop from tree to tree as I walk. They soar high above me, cutting on the currents and then doubling back again to hover just behind me. They sit on the lawn of my boarded-up house with blood still staining the floor. They coat the roof like ink. They make the barren winter trees sway again with dark life. And they are completely silent. Even when I go to shoo them, they never squawk or titter. They are mourning, I think, much like I am. They are mourning the big one. The big red crow that Caroline found dead by my grandmother.

Or perhaps they are simply waiting. The way that their hundreds of black-tar eyes glisten in the hollow sun gives me a feeling like a pressure drop before a storm. Perhaps they are waiting for the thundercloud to break. Perhaps they are waiting for me.

My mom won't go near the house. She holes up at a motel off the highway while I survey the scene of the crime. By now the cops are long gone. Danny called me himself to take my statement. I asked if he wanted to walk the house with me, but he said he'd already been there and didn't want to see it again. That tells me it's bad. I asked him if there was conclusive evidence pinning it on the Feds. He was quiet for a moment, and I knew he was contemplating letting me down easy, but that's just not Danny's way.

"No," he said, simply.

Of course not. They would be pros. Still, I want to check it out. Danny tries to dissuade me, but ultimately he lets it be. He knows I have to close that door myself.

I step over the police tape and walk up to the front door as the sun is setting. It's been nearly three days since it happened, and this is the first time I've come home, although I can't rightly call it home anymore. I fish around in my pocket for my keys, and I'm surprised to find that my hand swims in my pocket now. This is a fitted uniform I'm wearing. Or it used to be. I pull out my hand and study it like it's foreign to me. Bony, thin. My fingers remind me of my grandmother's. I can loop my thumb and pinkie around my wrist. I touch my neck and find bones there too, bones everywhere. I run my hands through my hair, and it comes away in feathered clumps. I clamp my hat down on my head like it's the only thing keeping the top of me from blowing away. Behind me the crows shuffle their wings.

I step through the doorway and flick on the lights. I see what Caroline described. The place was ransacked as they searched for the crow totem. There are evidence markers strewn about the living room: little tents with numbers on them that lead me through the house like some nightmare museum exhibit. Everything is shattered and strewn except one picture of me and Ana. The frame is broken, but standing. I step over to it and pick it up. Pieces of glass fall to the ground. I barely recognize myself. I remember when this was taken. It was after I graduated from high school. We had a party in the back yard. The picture was supposed to be just of me, but Ana was messing around and shouldered her way into the frame, pushing her face next to mine. The photo has been damaged. It looks like it was scratched up during the fall, because now there are two long gashes under Ana's eyes and her face is warped. She looks a lot like she looked when I hallucinated seeing her in the hogan during the Evilway.

I almost drop the picture in my hurry to set it down. It wobbles and falls flat on the mantle with a clatter that makes me jump. I stare at it a moment longer, half expecting it to move, but it doesn't. I chide myself. The world isn't falling apart, it's just me. The only bogeyman here is the one in my head.

I follow the evidence markers down the hall, into the kitchen, flicking on all the lights as I go, just like I would if I was coming home from work and getting ready to sit at the table and eat some of Gam's leftovers or maybe try to coax Dad into a conversation and have a beer or two before watching TV until I fall asleep. But not anymore.

The blood is like a painted track. Like a dragged brush that leads out the back door. It's strange to see a thing that was inside my father on such lurid display here. It makes the murder doubly obscene. My father, for all intents and purposes, died when Ana left us. The spark that made him my dad went with her. The rest was just going through the motions. This blood would have embarrassed him. He wanted the perfect Navajo death: to leave like an old wolf, to walk out on everything and everyone without a word and sit down away from the world and die alone. Maybe underneath a tree or by a creek. His body left to nature. Burdening no one.

Sorry, Dad. Guess things didn't really work out for either of us.

Gam's room paints a picture. The shattered window, the broken bone box. There are black feathers everywhere, like little shadows. It looks like the forensics group tried to number them but gave up. Gam's quilt, ancient even when I was born, is strewn across the floor. I pick it up and fold it, evidence be damned. The medicine sticks that were used in the Evilway are broken and strewn about. There was a struggle here on more than one level. There is a dried pool of blood by the door and a spattering along the wall above it. A telltale sign of a flicked knife. So Dad was stabbed here. In this room. Somehow that brings me a measure of comfort. He was coming to help Gam.

The far side of the bedroom tells another story. There are individual droplets everywhere, and most of them are on the floor. Caroline said she found the big crow in here. If I were to guess, I'd say the blood pattern follows something that might drip from a beak.

A smudge of blood mars the linoleum where Gam's body had been. It has a Rorschach symmetry to it, as if it's been pressed, perhaps by a knee. I picture a man kneeling down here and strangling my grandmother. I trace the ground and find another mark, a streaking like dragged fingers that leads to where the bone box lies. I picture that same man, still bleeding, having finished the killing, resting his hand upon the floor not far from where I listened to Gam's final song.

There is blood on the bone box, too. It looks like there were clear fingerprints on the top of the box that were then smudged. In fact, much of the blood evidence is smudged. Now that I look for it, it's clear as day. Almost methodical: a wiped mark on the window, and on the doorframe, and on the doorknob. A smeared streak by the door and again on the screen leading out back. A big smudge in the hallway, this probably a footprint with a tread that would have helped identify the killer, now just a dirty grease smear on old wood. Danny wasn't kidding when he said the evidence was scant.

When I step out onto the lawn, the motion sensors kick on, and I'm flooded in bright porch light. I cover my eyes, and I hear crows move like the rustling of a heavy curtain. I step under the tape marking off the back porch and try to get a sense of my father's final crawl.

He came out here alone. After the killers left. You can see the gripping, ripping tracks of his progress: small scratches in the dust of the brick porch where he pulled himself with his left hand, his right hand no doubt staunching his gut wound. There is a level sweep mark there, most likely from his right arm, its elbow jutting out.

There is still so much blood. It's like a railroad track. He knew he was going to die. He knew he had minutes left, and yet some deep ember inside him, not yet snuffed, called him outside to where he was always most comfortable after Ana disappeared. He came out here for a reason. I follow his ghost out to the lawn. The blood isn't as clear here. The dry winter grass sucked it up same as water, but there is a square marker where he died, right by the edge of the lawn, where Ana's cairn is.

Or was.

It's gone now. Knocked down. All the stones strewn about the ground. Where once there was a careful stack there is now a haphazard pile.

From an outsider's perspective, it would look like nothing but a pile of rocks among a dead winter garden. Easily overlooked. But to my father this was a holy place. He tended it from the day Ana left us. Building that tiny tower from the flat rocks in the backyard was one of the last things she did, and Dad was determined to keep it as it was. I'd seen him out there in storms and in snow. In wind and in rain, checking on it, making sure it still stood. In the rare times when a few stones fell or moved, he was inconsolable. He drank heavily and repositioned it exactly as it was. That pile, a plaything to Ana, became her gravestone to him. And here it was destroyed, and not by any killer or evidence team or detective or cop. I think it was destroyed by him.

As if they hear my thoughts, a group of crows hops from the fence to the ground. They bow quickly to the grass and cock their heads, listening. But they watch me.

"What are you?" I ask.

No answer. They bow and listen.

"Help me," I say.

They start to step quickly on the grass like they're dancing. Then they stop and bow to listen. They do this several times, and then one dashes its beak into the earth, rips half of a worm from the ground, and swallows it as it watches me. Never blinking.

"Well, fuck you then," I say. It snaps its beak with the final bite and burrows into the earth again, flipping a small clump of grass away.

I turn back to the rocks. Now that I stare at them, they don't look strewn out of anger or sorrow. They look broken down and then piled again, like they're meant to fill a hole. I reach down and pick up a rock, and the crows freeze in their dance. One has a night crawler wriggling in its mouth, but still it doesn't move. I toss the stone away and grab the next in the pile, and the crows go back to work with me. I toss this stone too, and then I start digging, flipping stones away to get to the heart of the pile. That's where I find it.

It's a strip of beaded leather. The leather is worn almost to white and the beads are rubbed lumpy.

I know this strip of leather. I've known it for years. And I know the scalp knife it hung from before my father ripped it off the weapon and stashed it as his final gift to me.

I know who killed Dad and Gam, and it kills me too.

16

OWEN BENNET

We kept Ben at ABQ General for as long as we could that night. Longer than he wanted, because he didn't have a ride until his mother was able to make the trip from Santa Fe. That was maybe the worst part of the entire ordeal for me. Worse than the insanity with Joey Flatwood—that's something you deal with in your own mind, and it makes it or breaks it. Worse than watching Ben hold the phone while his grandmother died—I've seen a lot of messy deaths. But watching him sit there in the waiting room, staring at the floor, for five hours like a forgotten child—that ripped me to pieces. Just the fact that he couldn't catch a ride. Such a stupid thing that hit home like a sledgehammer. Caroline was at the police station making a statement. I tried to give him money for a cab, but he looked at me like his mind was breaking, so I just let him sit. Maybe it was best that he went with his mom. No man should go home alone to that hell.

I didn't get much sleep that night. I started drinking bourbon again. When I met the sunrise I was no more settled than I was when I tried to hand Ben cab money. And then I had to go to work again.

It's funny when you go through something like that. Something big and shattering and life-distorting, and then after it happens you wake up the next morning the same as always. You put your pants on and eat your breakfast and get in your car and take the same route to work and you log in to the same system, and all the while you want to just scream at everyone, *How can you go on like this? The world is different now!* But nobody knows. Nobody cares. People have their own problems. And who's to say a few of these people haven't come across some Joey Flatwoods of their own?

I spoke with Caroline that day, the day after Ben's life shattered to pieces, and she told me about what she'd found. About the crow and the two bodies and the robbery and the bone box. She told me that Ben's grandmother had a crow of her own. I asked Caroline what she said to her, if she knew who attacked her, or what. She said Ben's grandmother was too far gone. That she just sang her way out.

She's a terrible liar, Caroline. I think it's part of what I love about her. Probably because until right about now she's had nothing to lie about, but that night she saw something else there. I know it because when I asked about Ben's grandmother's last words she said they were "goodbye." Nobody's last words are "goodbye." Least of all a Navajo elder. I almost laughed. Fair enough. If she doesn't want to tell, she doesn't have to. I have enough trouble keeping the rational parts of my brain from mutiny with the information I already have. I'm swimming out beyond my depth here, so that first week after everything went down, I did what any sane medical practitioner does when they don't understand something: I researched the hell out of it.

I started with medical explanations for visual and auditory hallucinations of the sort that might explain why Joey Flatwood seemed to phase in and out of view. I looked for literature related to degenerative eye conditions, something akin to a temporary glaucoma-like symptom that would affect frontal vision but not peripheral. I mostly did this just to make myself feel better. To do some sort of due diligence. If it was a visual phenomenon, it would have had to affect Ben and me at the same time, and in the same way. And there's also the fact that Joey isn't an instance of ocular flashing or a visual blind spot. He is a person. A person who appeared and then disappeared. He was no hallucination. I saw Ben grab him by the coat. So what, then? Some illusion? A sleight of hand or a smoke and mirror trick? Everyone knows your brain sees what it wants to see. And yes, maybe he could have fooled me. Or Ben. But both of us? And afterwards to elude the FBI and a platoon of policemen?

There was no explaining it from a medical perspective, so I flipped the table around and tried it from Joey's end, and from what I overheard when he and Ben spoke face-to-face.

The next night I start researching crow totems and invisible men.

I go down the internet rabbit hole into some pretty crazy conspiracy websites. Eventually I know I'm just clicking through this garbage to keep myself from calling Caroline, which I want to do more than anything. The problem is there's really no reason for me to talk to her. I'm not sure what I'd even say aside from rehashing that we all broke down last night and then tacking on a *wasn't that crazy?*

I have this absurd idea early in the morning of calling Caroline to ask her on a date. After another hour of pacing the apartment and delving deeper into the underbelly of the web, I decide to table that, thank God. Essentially I'd be hitting on a girl just after a funeral, like some hornball. It's not like me at all, but then again I'm not really myself these days. I'm increasingly coming to see that whatever happened that afternoon with Ben and Joey has fundamentally changed me. It is the sum measure of a path I took up when I volunteered to attend at CHC. I gained speed on that path when Caroline stepped on the scene, and then Ben. I'm usually not one for preordination, but this kind of trend is hard to ignore. The Harvard medical student Owen, the staunch atheist, would scoff at the Doctor Bennet sitting up until the dead of night thinking more and more that it's possible that out there somewhere is a man who can disappear into space.

I stumble across a chat room on the topic of ancient cabals. The usual tropes: old orders of men and women whose job it is to shepherd the interests of humanity, typical One World Order crap that doesn't hold a candle to reason. Even the new Owen Bennet refuses to believe that the big banks are financed by aliens intent on keeping the masses from acquiring super-technology that a handful of privileged humans currently employ. That's a common theme in these whack job forums. But in my glassy-eyed state I recall a point of the conversation between Joey and Ben: Joey took his crow off a dead man. He said there are other crows. He said that the agents want to get them all.

I sleep fitfully, and I awake in cold sweats from nightmares I half remember. I start seeing things out of the corner of my eye that I know are not there. I keep a hammer underneath my pillow because it's the only thing I have in my apartment that resembles a weapon. I don't even own a good set of kitchen knives. By the end of the week, I've convinced myself I have to get off the conspiracy kick and back to the common denominator here: the Navajo connection. Ben's grandmother had a crow. Joey has a crow. The crow is turquoise, a powerful stone in Navajo lore. The crow functions as a totem, which is a Navajo token. I get out of the chatrooms and back to the academic articles where I've lived most of my professional life. This time I look up the Navajo.

I find an interesting bit about Chantways that invoke symbolism. The Blessingway and the Evilway and the Enemyway are the most famous, but there are others. Hundreds. Historians have no idea what most of them were like or what sort of function they served. The names of some of these extinct Chantways are all that survives. Names like the Hailway, the Mothway, the Dogway, the Waterway, the Big Godway, and then one that strikes me: the Ravenway. But that's where the line ends. There's no way to know what the Ravenway might have done, or been. It's lost to time along with the rest of the extinct Chantways. It's infuriating, because I have a feeling that I was getting close. Closer than aliens running JP Morgan, at least.

I stare at crows all the next day: out of windows, from my car. Daring them to make a move. But other than the fact that there seem to be an awful lot of them, they don't take any notice of me whatsoever. And as for the numbers, well, they flock in the winter, and it's just about winter.

A week goes by like this. Agonizing. Plodding. No word from Ben, and no word from Caroline. We aren't scheduled to work together for some time. I just need an excuse to call her. You'd think *I'm in love with you* is a pretty good one, but that has the unfortunate effect of making things awfully uncomfortable if the sentiment's not returned. Call me what you will. You don't have to stare at the phone like I do. You aren't the one with his heart on the line.

Then, late Saturday evening, an excuse drops right onto my plate: Ben's most recent chart, filed by Caroline on the second regimen of chemotherapy she'd delivered just the night before.

Increased visual impairment.

Reported diplopia.

Noted word aphasia.

Noted slurred speech.

Bruising on right hip and right elbow from a fall.

He can't see right, he can't speak right, and he can't stand right. Ben is getting worse.

I dial the phone. Caroline picks up on the first ring.

"Owen," she says, and as soon as she gets my name out, she starts crying. I can tell by the lack of sound, by the clipped silence that comes when you cover a receiver.

"I saw the report."

"It's worse than that. He's...he's giving up."

"We need to bring him in to the hospital, Caroline. Full time. If he's to have any chance of surviving, he needs radical radiation therapy to shrink these tumors. I don't think he's responding to the chemotherapy."

"I know that. He won't go."

"He will when he collapses."

"That's what it's going to take, I think," she says.

"What is he doing that is so important? More important than his own life?"

"He wants them."

I almost ask who *they* are, but then I already know who he wants: the people he thinks killed his family.

"He's stubborn," she says. "He has to right the wrong if it kills him. He has to restore the balance. You didn't see his house, Owen. You didn't see what I saw."

In the depths of all this insanity, it occurs to me that she is using my first name. It sounds wonderful coming from her. It sounds like she's been saying it for a thousand years.

"What did you see?" I ask.

"I...I can't say, really. I'm not sure."

So she's in shock too. The both of us adrift at sea, the mainsail snapped.

"Caroline, you have to listen to me. You need to convince him to come here, to ABQ General. You too. Both of you have to come."

"I think we will," she says flatly. "I just think it's gonna be when it's too late for him."

I swallow, and it hitches in my throat. There's no way I can make Ben come to the hospital myself. My entire career I've been fighting to get the Navajo people *out* of the IHS revolving door. It seems perversely fitting that this upending of my life should culminate in my trying to drag a Navajo back *in*.

"I wasn't crying until you called," Caroline says, with quiet pride.

"That's always nice to hear, when a guy calls a girl."

"No, I mean that I haven't just been sitting around crying the whole time."

"I know, Caroline."

"I just want to help him."

"Me too. I think it's...it's very important that we help him. However we can. Do you know what I'm saying?" I walk to the window and I stare out at where the crows massed in the tree before. It's barren, now.

"I do," says Caroline.

"You have to get him to come to ABQ. You have to try."

"I will."

"And be careful, for Christ's sake."

"You too, Owen."

She hangs up. God, I love the way she says my name.

17

CAROLINE ADAMS

Usually I'm good with patients in shock. You know it immediately. It's the vacant stare, the ridges on the sides of the eye. Anxious patients have ridges around the forehead. Shell-shocked patients have ridges around the eyes. I have this theory that it's because they're running through slides in their mind and can't turn away, can't even blink. They may be quiet, but they're having a full-blown conversation with themselves in their heads. You can see it in the twitches in the bags under their eyes.

That's how Ben looks during chemo today. His house is still a crime scene, so I administer the regimen in a disgusting hotel outside of the reservation, past the casino. The kind of place a gambler would stay with his last forty bucks. This is where I meet his mom, Sitsi Dejooli. I arrive as he is in the middle of explaining who I am.

As soon as I walk in, I hear her go, "You have cancer?" in a shrill, panicky voice. Ben moves back to sit on the brown comforter draped over the lumpy twin bed. He looks pleadingly at me for a moment, then drops his head in his hands and gives a weak nod. His mother is a small woman, thin, like Ben, and with his frame. She has the dark hair of the Navajo, but it's cut short and pixie-like around her head. She wears trim, straight-legged jeans and two-toned leather boots with thick heels. She's standing in the middle of the room clutching her purse to herself with one hand and clutching the collar of her sweater with the other. She's quite pretty, but she has that look of an older woman trying too hard to stay in her thirties. She also looks like she doesn't want to touch anything. Which I can understand.

"Cancer?" she screeches again. I get the sense she's been repeating herself. She looks at me toting my radioactive cooler like I'm here to rob them.

"This is Caroline. She's my nurse," Ben says. His face twitches. He's here, but he's not here. His color is roiling in black. It looks like clay mixed with blood. He must have seen something at the house that sapped him completely. He's barely there.

"Hi, Mrs. Dejooli," I say. She ignores me.

"No, this isn't right. You can't have...did you check with other people? How many opinions did you get?"

Ben never told his mother. Most likely never would have if his life hadn't fallen around his feet. I can see that he's not comfortable with her. He doesn't trust her. He feels like she's turned her back on him, on all of them. He thinks she doesn't love him. It all centers on Ana. I can feel this. I'm getting better at reading the colors by the day.

For what it's worth, he's wrong. Looking at this woman it's impossible not to see it. She's terrified of losing him. It's coming off of her in bursts of yellow, like popping gasoline bubbles. She wants to see him grow older. She wants to die before him. She's afraid of being alone. Which is pretty rich coming from a woman who left her entire family to carve out a new life for herself off the rez.

Ben looks over at me with unfocused eyes. He holds out a hand weakly to me, and I come over to him.

"Tell her, Caroline. I can't right now."

I sit down and hold his arm, much thinner now even than last week. I cradle it in my lap as I swab it with an alcohol pad.

"It's no mistake, Mrs. Dejooli. He has a late stage brain cancer. It's very real, and very serious."

She breaks down completely. She sits in a smoke-stained chair by the faded table in the corner and cries for basically the entire session. A couple of times she stops and looks up at me like I've betrayed her or something, then she goes back to holding her head in her hands and wiping her face with a Kleenex. I'd had such plans. I wanted to tell him myself what I'd whitewashed for the police report. I wanted to tell him about his grandmother's last minutes. About what he couldn't hear over the phone. About her calm confidence and her strange words, and, of course, about the hollow bell that hung from my neck like a ball of iced lead.

But there is no place for that. Not with his mother here. Not with the way he's lying on the bed and taking the drip and staring at the flaking ceiling like he wants to float up and through it and away. I might as well set it and forget it. I think he's forgotten about me completely until I get up to use the bathroom and he grips me by the arm for a moment. I can see he's afraid I'm leaving him. He looks lost. Like he's floundering in the deep end of his life and is about to give up and sink under. I refuse to cry in front of his mother, who is, quite frankly, putting on a disgusting little show, heartfelt or not. Tears are not what Ben needs right now.

That's about all I get from Ben this time: that one look. I wrap up my stuff to leave, and he thanks me and hugs me with a creepy finality. He made some sort of decision on that bed. Some decision that is final.

On the drive home I'm looking for any excuse to turn around, and it's Owen who gives me one. My notes. I'd submitted them to the system in my car before hitting the road while they were still fresh in my mind, and they are blatantly indicative of a worsening condition. Ben looked so bad on the inside that the diplopia and aphasia and the bruising I noticed seemed secondary to me, but of course they were huge red flags. He is getting worse. He has to go to a hospital. He needs full-time care. I just needed someone with guts to tell me to go do it, and as usual, Owen Bennet is that man.

You have to get him to come to ABQ. You have to try.

I flip my car around and bounce over the median, kicking up dust and wincing when I hear the scrape of metal on rock, but I don't care. I'm going back to him, and this time I'm not leaving without him. I turn up the radio to drown out my mind, but I still second-guess myself sick. Nothing is harder than treating a patient who doesn't want to be treated. I've seen that look before, that black look that settled over him. It's a look of pure despair that lives on the cancer floor, and you have to constantly chase it away or else it'll find a home in you. But I've also felt that tug before. That small tug that he gave me when he thought I was leaving. If you're completely gone, you don't tug like that. He has it in him to fight. If he's given up, I just gotta make him un-give up. That's all.

But when I get back to the hotel, he's gone anyway. And so is his mother. Or she's not answering the door. Either way, nothing stirs behind the shabby curtains when I slam the knocker down again and again until someone down the row screams at me to shut up.

I go back down and sit in my car in the dark and try to think. I check the clock. It's been a little under two hours since his chemo. He'll be feeling like warmed over crap right about now. There is no reason he shouldn't be on the couch or in a bed trying to sleep off nausea. It takes a lot to get a chemo patient to move. Last time it took the FBI and Joey Flatwood. This time it's gotta be something as serious as that. He looked terrified today, but there was also a cold fury deep within him, like a frozen black soup boiling at the edges of the pot. It had to have been because of what he saw at the house. That sort of scene would shock anyone, but it was more. He saw something else there. Something that he needs to deal with.

I take a deep breath and let it out, and it fogs the inside of my windshield. I grip the steering wheel. I know where he is, but I want to go back to that house about as much as I want this damn bell hanging around my neck.

It doesn't help that it's as dark as a pit around Chaco at night. On the side streets like the one where Ben lives (or used to live, anyway) the lighting is spaced way out. A lot of the streetlights are in disrepair, if they're there at all. There are bright orange cones of light every couple of blocks, but that only serves to make the homes in between darker than ever. His is the darkest of all.

It looks like everything that was once good about the Dejooli home has fled this place, and the bad that is left is seeping out from underneath. The other side of the duplex is black, too. As is the neighbor's house across the street, and the one kitty-corner as well. It makes sense, since the Navajo really hate death and the places where things die, but it gives me the impression that Ben's place is slowly infecting everything around it. I check every angle before getting out of my car and make a lame attempt at protecting myself by gripping my keys so they extend between my fingers like cat's claws. Lot of good that would do me. Probably just make me lose my keys before getting mugged.

My footsteps on the concrete are the loudest thing around. I take to creeping, and if someone were to glance outside they might think I was the one out for trouble, but nobody looks. There's nobody here at all, that I can see. But I feel Ben. I can feel his coloring like a whiff of smoke on the wind, and he's terribly weak.

The house is boarded up and locked and taped over. I won't be getting inside through the front door, so I walk around, slowly. I keep my eyes on the sky for birds, and I strain my ears for any sound as I cut through an alley that leads through to the back yard. The gate there is open, and I pause. That's when I hear the retching. It's quiet, like he's trying to muffle it, but in this silence it's still clear enough.

I peek around the corner and see Ben on his hands and knees in the backyard near where his father died. His whole body tenses with the retches and the effort to keep them quiet. Then, a moment later, he collapses on his side and spits and makes this soft mewl that rips me to pieces. I have to pull back behind the house and sit with my head against the side and scrunch up my face not to lose it. I'm supposed to be helping him. There's no excuse for this right now, not even a breaking heart. I stand and smooth my shirt and then walk out back. Ben is still on his side and doesn't seem to hear my approach.

"Ben?" I ask quietly. He tenses and turns his head to me, but he's like a lamed animal. He can't quite turn the rest of his body.

"Ben, it's me. It's Caroline."

A faint trickle of the beautiful, rich red comes back to him. I rush over, get down on my knees next to him, and brush his stringy hair from his watery, bloodshot eyes. The floodlight kicks on, and I can see just how bad he's become. His neck and head jut out like a turtle's from his hollowing body. He has vomit on his uniform.

"Caroline. What are you doing here? You can't be here," he says, but he holds on to my arm for dear life.

"Me? What are *you* doing here?"

"This is my home."

"Don't give me that bullshit. You need to be inside, warm, comfortable. With liquids and anti-nausea meds and ice cream and a terrible midnight movie playing in the background." Is that a hint of a smile? Maybe. I hope so.

"This one's pretty bad. Worse than the first one. I think I'm gonna stop this chemo stuff."

"No you're not. If you do, you'll die," I say, and I barely manage to keep my voice from clipping high at the end.

"Eh," he says. "I'm going to die anyway." He says this like he might say it's dark out tonight. "I think we both know that. It's just killing what time I have left. Which isn't much."

"We could try other regimens," I say. "Maybe...maybe you—" but he quiets me with a soft squeeze.

"Maybe nothing. I can feel it. And so can you. But I have to do something first. Here. And you need to go."

"No, Ben—"

"Yes. It's not safe for you. The people that I love get hurt, Caroline. Do you understand me? This thing begins and ends with me. Once I'm out of the way, it'll leave you alone."

Oh, I understand all right. I understand that I think that he might have said, in some roundabout, guy-like, obscure Navajo way, that he loves me. If I could see myself, I'd be leaking gold, darkness and death be damned. Talk about food for thought at three a.m. I'll be chewing on this one for years.

"Caroline? Do you understand? You have to go. He'll be here soon."

I shake my head again, and he tries to interject, but I stop him by putting my face right in front of his. "No, Ben. This didn't begin with you. And it won't end with you either. Whatever is happening here, it's an old thing. Very old. And it's bigger than you and me."

Ben tries to shake his head. "He's got Gam's crow, but I got something of his. Something that is important to him. Something he wants back," Ben says, and he holds out an old beaded lanyard of some sort. I don't quite understand him, but there's no time to hash it out.

"Yeah well, I got something else important," I say, and my hand touches the cold metal resting on my chest. "And I need to talk to you about it—"

But that's when we hear the sound.

It's a strange whistling. Low, and in pockets, like the sound of a staff being waved through the air, followed by a small pop, like a ball hitting a glove. It's out on the street first, and then closer: *whistle, pop. Whistle, pop.* Then, impossibly, it's inside the house, without a door opening or closing. Both of us can hear it, low and muffled, but there.

Whistle, pop. Whistle, pop.

Moving from room to room. There's a haphazard crash then, and some rough shoving of furniture from Ben's grandmother's room. We can hear it loud and clear from the backyard because her broken window looks out on us.

We can see it, too. Or him, rather. A massive dark shape straightens and turns towards the window, and two black glints of eyes blink once then stare solidly at us. There is a flash of teeth, either a smile or a snarl.

"Too late," Ben says and shuffles back to sitting. His hand goes to his gun and there is one more *whistle, pop.*

Then he's there in front of us. Like he stepped out of the air itself.

"Hello, Danny," Ben says.

Danny's a massive Indian in full war paint, his face dyed red from his forehead down to below his eyes, and his long hair is straight and as smooth as black water. He is shirtless despite the cold, but he steams like a bull, and all along his arms are spots and whorls of paint. He wears buckskin chaps and has bare feet, and in his hand is a knife the size of my forearm. It flashes in the moonlight as he adjusts his grip on it.

"Ben," he grunts. As if he ran across us at the supermarket. His face is as telling as stone.

"Forget something?" Ben asks.

Danny nods slowly. Ben holds out a leather string of beads. Danny looks at it and laughs. It's a great, booming laugh. One that I can tell is seldom used, since it sets Ben on edge as much as it does me.

"No. Not that. I no longer concern myself with trinkets of this realm. They mean nothing to me."

"What?"

"Where did they put out your grandmother, Ben?" Danny asks, his voice quiet.

Whistle, pop, and then he's there in front of Ben. He shoves me aside with as much care as he would a curtain of beads. He grabs Ben, heedless of the gun, and pulls him up to his face, his feet dangling in the air. Ben's eyes are wide with shock. Danny's so close now that I can see that what I took for spotted markings are actually scabbed tears and claw marks. I remember the dead crow. The crow that didn't go quietly.

"I have no time for this, Ben. It calls to me. It is near. I must have it. I believe your grandmother was the Keeper. I must know where they put her out for the cliff burial. Perhaps the crows took it from her body." His eyes are full of madness, brimming in the darkness. He never raises his voice, but he speaks each word carefully and each one drips with malice.

And then Ben spits in his face. "Fuck you. You're insane. You killed her, and my dad, and now you want to desecrate her burial? You stole her totem, Danny," Ben says. He pulls his gun up and places it between them, right at Danny's gut. "But now you're gonna give it back."

Danny looks down at the gun with mild interest.

"Always fighting. A rookie, but a fighter nonetheless. You would have made the circle stronger. But you are dying, so you are worthless to me. Your grandmother was strong, too. She fought, too, but she was old. No longer fit to be the Keeper. Your father was a loose end. Always at the wrong place at the wrong time."

He ticks each of them off like he's reading a grocery list.

"The gambler was unfit. Flatwood is too," he says.

Ben peers into his eyes with growing horror, looking for any light, but he can see as well as I can that there is none there. "You killed all of them," he says.

"Not Flatwood. Not yet. But I did convince you to banish him while I continued my search for the bell. He's an industrious rat, though, and he found a totem despite his banishment. But I will find him and take it. Then I will have three. Triple the power. Better to find the bell. It took me years to find my first totem with the gambler, and then your grandmother's dropped in my lap at the Evilway. Things are moving faster. More becomes clear to me every day."

"But why? Why?" Ben asks, and his color fades, guttering.

"We are the first people, Ben. And we will be the last. A

Navajo must be the Keeper of the Bell. A *worthy* Navajo. Strong in the old ways. Not an old crone, or a hopeless addict, or worthless trailer trash like your friend Flatwood. Me. It must be *me*." His voice is a fervent whisper now. Like a muttered chant.

"Go to hell, Ninepoint," Ben says. And then he fires his gun.

Whoosh, pop. Danny flicks in and out of existence at the same time. Ben drops heavily to the ground, and a moment later Danny is standing just as he was, unscathed. He looks down upon Ben and narrows his eyes.

"You would have killed me?" he says, and his tone is tinged with surprise. "*You?* You would have killed *me*?"

Ben looks blankly at his gun, then up at Danny. He swallows and tries to kick away, but Danny is there, grabbing him by the lapel and jerking him up to standing.

"Fool. I have two crows. I am untouchable. And now I must kill *you*," he says. "It is only fitting. In the end, I'm just bringing about the inevitable."

It all happened so quickly—in the span of half a minute. The gunshot is still ringing in my ears, and everything around me, the very black of the night itself, seems to sway and hitch. I wonder if I'm having a panic attack or passing out, but when Danny Ninepoint grabs Ben, everything snaps back into focus. I throw myself at Danny. I don't care how big he is. I don't care how strong. I don't give a shit who this man is, or about the crow totems or even about the bell. All I know is that nobody should speak to Ben like that. That condescending "*you*," as if he were less than human. Nobody should speak to anybody like that, but especially not to Ben, a guy who is ripping precious days from the jaws of death itself just to set things right, a man who cares nothing for himself and everything for those around him. That is the type of man who deserves the most respect. Buckets full of respect. Not a fucking "*you?*"

I catch his knife hand on the windup. He wants to slash across Ben's throat, but I grip him by his arm like I'm climbing a tree, and he hitches mid-swipe. I pull down his arm and try for the knife. I manage to turn it in his hand a bit and yank it free. I feel a quick, cold pain across my palm, then a terrible running warmth. The knife falls to the ground. He goes for it, but I grab at his face, flinging blood, dark and glittering in the moonlight, all over him, and press my bloody palm into his eyes.

"You bitch!" he says, and he backhands me. I stagger back. I feel like I took a frying pan to the head.

"Unclean," he says, wiping at his face. He mutters more, but I can't hear him. My head feels like someone poured boiling water over it. My hearing is wavering, and my face stings like fire. He picks up his knife again and wipes my blood off on his chaps. "I'll deal with you afterwards," he says, then turns back to Ben and points a finger at him as if Ben were a child. "You should have come alone." He steps towards him. Ben is watching me with blank shock, his hand loose around his gun. He sits like a worn teddy bear: slouched, tipping. Danny grabs Ben's hair and grimaces when a tuft of it comes off in his hand. Ben looks up at him. Then beyond him. Danny pauses.

That's when I hear it too. It's a tittering sound. And the wavering in my vision is back, but this time it's not from any slap to the face. The entire night is moving.

"What's that?" Danny asks.

Ben's blank stare falls slowly back into focus. Then it's Ben's turn to smile.

"You're wrong, Danny."

Danny's face shows a crack of fear. Faint, but there. He looks around himself as if he's lost. He can hear it, too.

"What...what are you doing? What are you saying?"

"I said you're wrong."

"Why?" Danny asks, looking all around to pinpoint the source of the sound we're hearing, but it's no use. It's the night itself, oozing black.

"Because I was never alone."

There's a brief stillness then, an expectant hush when I can hear everyone breathing. Then, from out of the darkness, three sharp calls of a crow, and then the night explodes around us.

I didn't see any birds because there was nothing to see *but* birds. Crows everywhere. They painted the roofs and weighed down the trees. They bowed the wires and covered the fence lines. They'd sat still as stone upon the grass and the dirt, watching the three of us until that very moment, and then every single one of them flew right at Danny Ninepoint.

He's there one moment, and then he's not. But this time he doesn't disappear. The crows won't let him. They cover him like tar, raking at him and slashing and tearing, and only his screams can be heard. Then even his screams succumb to the rush of feathers, a sound like the shaking of a forest in the wind. I hide my head, I scream, I scramble to Ben. He holds me, and I bury my head in his arms as the black vortex rages around us.

And then it's gone.

When I look up, there is nothing but blood on the grass and feathers floating in the air. And there, on the ground where Danny had stood, are two small stone crows. One that had belonged to the gambler, and one that had belonged to Ben's grandmother. We watch in stunned silence as one black feather floats to the ground in front of our faces.

I turned to Ben. I want to kiss him. To tell him he's saved us, somehow, by calling down the night. He's figured it all out. I am in his arms. This is the perfect time for a kiss. This is textbook. This is it. If it's ever going to happen, it's going to happen now.

But Ben is crying. He is in a ball sobbing quietly to himself on my shoulder and saying their names over and over again. All of them: Gam, Dad, Ana, Joey, and yes, even Danny. All of them. So instead I just turn towards him and hold him.

And that's when the agents come.

They walk slowly into the floodlight, one after the other, stirring tufts of feathers with each step. They have eyes only for the crow totems. Each snatches one with greedy abandon, their eyes glimmering. As they touch the totems with their bare hands, they flicker a bit in and out of focus, and terrible grins spread across their faces. I'm beginning to think they don't know that we're here, but then Parsons speaks.

"Thank you, Mr. Dejooli," he says. "We'll take it from here."

Then both of them blink out of existence.

18

BEN DEJOOLI

She saved me from the knife. From Danny's huge knife. The knife that's hung at Danny's side as long as I've known him. The same knife that Danny would casually click in and out of its sheath when things got tense on calls. He used to use the bone handle to crush beer cans at station BBQs. He once plucked a two-inch splinter from my palm with the tip of it. Caroline stopped that same knife from ripping my throat open. That's my first thought when I wake up in the hospital bed.

The second thought is that it was a lot of work on her part to buy me another couple of days. Don't get me wrong: the last thing I wanted was to get killed by my two-faced partner. When I go, I can count him being swallowed by a million crows among the top five most beautiful things I've ever seen in my life. Ana being another one. Caroline being another. I would have missed that sight if it weren't for her, but part of me wonders if she shouldn't have bothered.

The other two in my top five, in case you're wondering, are kind of like memory snapshots. One is of a sunrise. Danny and I were coming off a nightshift one warm summer night two years ago. I had the next two days off. We were driving the fringes, the northern border of the rez, just flying across the desert in the cruiser, and the sun was rising over the sand and it painted the whole thing purple. It doesn't sound like much, but it was. If you were there, you'd have thought so too. The way things ended up with Danny doesn't change that sunrise. That picture. That's forever.

The second is a snapshot of a bonfire out at the Arroyo. It was a Saturday night, and I was with Joey Flatwood. Both of us were fourteen, tearing circles around the fire pit while our folks drank beers and talked and sang. I have this picture in my mind of us running around and around like a long exposure of light in the dark, and we're leaving these phosphorescent firefly trails behind us. Even when I banished Joey, even when I thought he knew what happened to Ana and was keeping it from me, nothing could ruin that picture either. That's forever, too.

It's funny how you take stock of these things when your life is coming to a close. You don't really do it because you're getting all sentimental, either. A lot of it is boredom. There's not a lot to do in a hospital bed when you're waiting to die.

I'm pretty far gone, now, I think. There isn't a lot of pain. The morphine drip killed all that, along with most of my hospital phobia. Funny how high-powered drugs will do that for you. So I'm not nauseous anymore and I'm not aching, but I am sort of being packed away. I feel like I'm being swaddled, slowly, from the feet up. I lose chunks of time. First it was hours, but the chunks are getting bigger. Half a day? A whole day? All I know is that the times between when I open my eyes are getting longer, and I suspect that when I actually die it'll be just that: the time between when I open my eyes will be forever.

I can't really talk anymore, but I can think, and I can

listen. I know that people are here with me. And that people are coming and going. Caroline has been the most constant. She holds my hand and speaks to me about everything, and I suspect that she knows I can listen. I think she can see more than most people. Can understand more. It's like she can sense when I surface, even if I don't open my eyes. She whispers to me about the bell. She doesn't know what to do with it. I don't either. She says it's mine, by rights, but I don't think it is. I don't think it's anybody's. I don't think it even belongs here at all. I can feel it, resting on her chest. It has this dull hum that seems to get stronger as I get weaker. She tells me that I'm flipping through the pages of my life. Setting the numbers in order. She whispers to me that she wishes she could be in there with me, flipping the pages. She wishes she could see it all. I can feel her tears, hot, falling on my cheeks, before she wipes them away. It feels good, to have someone cry for you. That may sound like an asshole thing to say, but it's true.

Mom is here too, although less frequently. I don't blame her. I think her mind is breaking. I think it cracked when Ana died, but now it's breaking. She'll have lost everyone, when this is all over. I think she's learning that it's one thing to push everyone away when they're still here and it's another thing to have them disappear altogether. She talks to me, too, although she sounds off. She talks about the day Ana disappeared. She says it was just like this. Over and over again she says that: *Just like this. Just like this.*

"It's happening again," she says, when I float back. She's panicky, and her hand is trembling as it holds mine. I want to help her. She was dealt a heavy hand of grief in life and she folded with it, gave up early on, but I'm not sure I can begrudge her that. She couldn't deal. Is that her fault? I'm not sure I could deal, either, if I was her. Maybe that's why I joined the force. Not because I was dealing with Ana's loss, but because I wasn't dealing with Ana's loss. I spent my days patching up other people's problems instead of dealing with mine.

I manage a squeeze, and she latches on to it. I open my eyes and mumble, "S'okay, Mom." Kind of a stupid thing to say, especially given that pretty much nothing is okay. But there's nothing she can do about it. I expect her to break down or something, but she doesn't. She gets real close to me and says, "Stay, Benny. Stay here."

That's pretty rich. I don't exactly feel like running these days, Mom. But she's serious.

"Ana didn't stay," she says. "You must stay. No matter what Gam or anyone says."

Gam's gone, Mom. Dead. Ana's dead, too. And I'm going. I hope she gets the help she needs, my mom. This is going to pretty much destroy her. Is it bad that I take just a tiny measure of comfort in the fact that I won't be around to see it?

I get the sense that Caroline's right. I've been flipping through my book, setting the pages in order, but here at the end there are a bunch of blanks. The pages are there, the numbers are right. They're the end, but there's nothing on them.

Not yet, anyway.

Something is coming. Something has to happen for me to close my book. It's why I'm not dead just yet. It's why I can still hear them. I'd heard that right before people die, some of them get really lucid. Sort of come back for one last big push. I think that's what's happening to me. I think I have one last big push stored up, and I'm terrified to think of what it's for.

The people around my bed are like pieces shifting on a

combination lock. Doctor Bennet, Caroline, Mom, they need to be here, I feel it, but one is missing, and when that fourth shows up, I know it is time.

Joey Flatwood.

It's late at night when he comes to me. I hear the *whoosh, pop,* and for one horrible minute I think Danny is back. I actually open my eyes. It startles me back to the surface, almost above the surface. *This is it,* I think. *This is the push. This is the end.*

Joey is stunned, looking at me. He's like a bull charging into the china shop only to find it's a butcher's. He reaches one trembling hand out towards me, and it hangs in the air.

"Jesus, Ben. I mean...Jesus."

"Hello," I say. It comes out a croak.

Caroline stirs in the chair next to me. Mom stirs in the makeshift bed next to Caroline. Doctor Bennet walks by the door. I know he's done that many times, many more times than he needs to, always with the pretense of checking my vitals or reading my charts, but I know it's more than that. I wish I had more time to get to know the good doctor. I think we'd have liked each other.

When Bennet sees Joey, he stops still, looks back and forth along the hallway, then steps inside the room and closes the door.

The gang's all here.

"This is bad," Joey says, staring at me as he walks over to my bedside.

"Well, it's not good, Joey," I say. I try to smile. My lips are goopy from Vaseline.

Joey looks from me to the other three, who watch him carefully, but everyone seems to know to stay quiet.

"No. I mean they're coming," he says. "They know about the bell. They think you have it."

"Who?"

"The agents," he says, then he freezes and pricks his ears. He looks over his shoulder at the door. He turns back to me, and I can see that he's genuinely afraid.

"It's here, isn't it? I can feel it, too. It pulls at the crow."

We are all silent. Bennet looks at me. I have to make a conscious effort not to look at Caroline.

"It's here," I say, at last. Then I ask him a question, very carefully, because I know a lot hinges on it. "Do you want it, Joey?"

He looks at me without blinking, and he works his jaw around.

"No," he says. "No, I don't think I do. I don't think anyone can have it. Especially not them. It's too...too much. Too dangerous. Too...everything."

"What is the bell?" Caroline asks quietly. Joey flicks his gaze over to her. He zeroes in on the leather strap around her neck, and I know he knows. I know he knows it's right there, with her. But all he does is nod. And right then I know something else, too: Joey had nothing to do with Ana's vanishing. Far from it. In fact, it wouldn't surprise me to learn that from the second I banished him, Joey spent every waking day trying to make sense of what happened to her, just like me.

"It's what took Ana," Joey says.

"What?" Mom asks. "What?" She's getting louder. Bennet tries to quiet her, but she ignores him. She runs to Joey, grabs him with both hands, and shakes him. "What are you saying? You can't just say things like that. You can't just come in here and say things like that." She slaps him, and he takes it. "What do you *mean*?" she wails. She is unraveling. Bennet grabs her with both arms and pulls her away. I hear movement outside.

"I don't know," Joey says, and I see that he's crying. "I don't fucking know. It's all I've ever wanted to know. You have to believe me. Ben, please. I don't know how. I don't know why. But that bell took her away from me right before my eyes."

"I believe you," I say, and I sound stronger than I have in what feels like weeks. The push is upon me. The crest is here. "Joey, I really fucked up, man. I really fucked up, and if you never forgive me, I understand."

"It was Danny, Ben. Danny planted the seed. Danny brought the hearing. Danny pulled all the right strings, with the council, with your family, with your heart. He wanted the bell for himself. He knew I wanted it too. But I don't want it like he did."

"Nah," I say, and it's a sort of wail. The beginning of a cry. "Nah. I fucked up. I did."

There's a subtle shift in the air, and we all feel it. A *whistle, pop* from down the hall. There's shouting outside the room. They're here. Joey turns to me. His eyes are swimming, but his teeth are gritted.

"I want you to know, man. I want you to know that you never stopped being my best friend. Never. Not when you screamed at me at the hospital that day she disappeared. Not when you spoke against me in front of the court. Not when you stood and watched me cross that line out of Chaco. Never. And you never will."

Bennet locks the door. Joey looks at him. "Locks don't matter," he says, and just then there's a *whistle, pop* and one of the agents is there. It's Douglas, the bulldog one with the stained teeth. His face lights up, and his eyes are like tar-dipped coins.

"Here you are," he says, staring at me with wild, hungry eyes. He sniffs the air. "And it's here, too."

Joey steps between us, and I see Bennet position himself in front of Mom and Caroline.

Douglas snaps away, and then in a blink he's back with Parsons, who looks fresh from a conference call, as always. Both of them stare at me, unblinking. They suck in the air as if mad for the scent of the bell.

"Where is it, Mr. Dejooli?" Parsons asks. He's like a schoolteacher giving an unruly pupil one last chance. But Joey steps in between us.

"It's not for you to have," Joey says. "You don't know what you're doing. The crows are meant to protect the bell. To keep it secret. And safe."

Parsons and Douglas turn to Joey as if seeing him for the first time.

"It will be safe," Parsons says. "With us. And only with us."

Douglas steps towards me, but Joey holds out his hand and stops him. Douglas bumps into it and stares at it like it's a tumbleweed bumped against a fence.

"Back off," Joey says.

Douglas looks back at Parsons, who cocks an eyebrow. Then both of them laugh. It's not a good laugh. It's the strange, low laugh of the far gone, and I know there is nothing we can say that will stop these two men. Douglas unbuttons his jacket with one hand.

"Don't do this," Joey says. "None of us knows what that thing can do."

"It's more powerful than any crow. More powerful than all of the crows," Douglas says, with strained patience, reaching in his pocket. "And if the crows can do this—" He grasps the totem in his bare hand. In a hissing blink he's behind Joey, right next to my bed. He reeks of sulfur, like a pack-a-day habit of the devil's own cigarettes. He grabs the sheets of my bed and throws them off, his eyes wild and probing. "—Then we must have it," he says.

There's another pop, and suddenly Douglas goes sprawling back into the door, splintering the jamb and throwing it open with his bulk. In his place is Joey once more. It's like Joey left us and then came back at a charge and checked Douglas straight in the chest. Parsons looks impassively at him. Douglas looks ridiculous, sitting like a child in the doorway with both legs out. He nods to himself and cracks his neck.

"I said back the fuck off, suit. Both of you," Joey says.

"Impressive, Mr. Flatwood," says Parsons. "I'll admit, you know your way around the crow. But then again, you've had more time with yours."

He doesn't sound impressed. He sounds pleased, actually. One look at Douglas confirms it. He's smiling, too, from the floor. They both look like prize fighters at the title bout.

"Last chance, Mr. Flatwood. All of you. Give us the bell, and we'll let you live," Parsons says, as Douglas stands and dusts off his jacket. "For a little while, at least," he adds, looking at me with a wan smile.

Joey starts to speak, but I beat him to it. "You aren't worthy," I say, surprising myself. Thinking of Gam. Thinking of Caroline. Gam carried it all her life and never said a word. Caroline carries it now, as it's supposed to be carried. As a burden. A quiet burden. I don't know exactly what this bell is, but I know that's how it's supposed to be worn: heavy and soft. As if he can hear my thoughts, Joey looks back at me and nods. It's a thankful nod. It's like he's come back. Like we've seen each other in the airport and hit the bar, and it's all the same. In my mind another page is written and numbered, and it has everyone here on it. I'm that much closer. I have minutes. Minutes until I'm gone. But there's one more page yet to write.

My words hit Douglas. He seems to me like the idiot of the pair. Proud. Quick to anger. His bureaucratic smile turns to a snarl. There's a puff of air as he slips out of space, and I know he's coming for me. For my neck. For my face. And I can do nothing. I am passing from this world, and if it's Douglas that does it or the poison cells in my brain—six of one, half dozen of the other.

Whistle, pop, and he's there, in front of me. But so is Joey.

Douglas brings his hand down, ripping through the air, trying to grab at my throat, but Joey stops him with a sledge-hammer blow to the side that sends him sprawling again. Whatever plane the crows flip them to, it seems like Joey gets a running start before they flip back. Joey is not a big man and the drugs have drained him, but somehow he's hitting like a fire hydrant. Joey doesn't even blink before he throws himself at Douglas again. Douglas tries to phase out, but Joey catches him. What happens from there is like a movie seen in snapshots, like frames have been removed from the reel of a fistfight. They dance around each other, pummeling each other. They flip in and out of sync, coming back bloodied and torn. Douglas reaches for his gun at one point, but Joey grabs him and phases both of them out before he can fire. This time the blood comes back before they do, spraying out like whipped washing, and then they are with us again, Douglas's head snapped back and his mouth split and Joey grazed at the shoulder. They blink out again, and a piece of a tooth is all that remains, clattering to the floor in their absence. I smile grimly. Joey always knew his way around a fistfight. I suppose an existential fistfight is still a fistfight.

But then there's Parsons. He watches the popping,

whooshing, sucking explosions with a cold smile, like he's hanging over the pit of a dog fight, and then he begins to walk toward me, adjusting his tie, sniffing at the air. Bennet swipes at him, but he phases in and out and takes no notice. Bennet lunges forward again, and again comes up with air. Parsons stops at the head of my bed as calm as a Sunday morning while Douglas and Joey rip at each other like desert coyotes.

He is disturbingly gentle as he brushes my scrub top apart and pulls my palsied hands flat. No bell. He sniffs the air again, then he turns to Caroline. I try to scream at him, to lunge at him, to do anything. But my time is up. I'm being packed in. I can feel the weight upon me. The first words on the final page are being written, and I can see them in my mind. They say, *A crow flew down the hall.*

Which is insane, because we're in a hospital. And yet there is the crow. It passes across the open doorway at normal speed, but everything else seems to have hit a time pocket. No one else notices it, and I know that this is because no one else can see it. Then, in a blink, everything catches back up.

I look back at Caroline, who is gripping the bell under her shirt like it's pulling her down to the ground. Parsons walks towards her like a golem. He reaches for her, but Bennet throws himself towards him, and this time Parsons doesn't phase out. He's done with dancing between our two planes. He's been snake charmed by the call of the bell, and he doesn't count on Bennet's reach. His haymaker staggers Parsons, who looks at Bennet as if he's just arrived. Bennet takes advantage and slams his shoulder into Parsons, pushing him away, battering him back, putting distance between the agent and Caroline. He's pummeling Parsons' face bloody, and I think for one glorious minute that we've done it, that we've beaten them. Then Parsons takes out his gun.

"Unworthy," he says, echoing the madness of Danny Ninepoint as he levels it at Caroline.

Bennet throws himself in front of the line of fire just as the gun blast echoes and we hit another time pocket. And on cue, there's another crow. This one makes a sloppy landing out in the hallway in front of the door, flapping and hopping to a standstill in the time it takes for the bullet to leave the chamber. The crow stares at me. The sulfur hits me like a smoke ring to the face. People are caught in mid-scream outside, but they are like shadows of themselves— bugs rolled in sap, caught in time. Then there is another crow. It flutters down from the top of the splintered door, much more gracefully than the first, and then another that seems to swagger into the room. This one ponders the bullet leaving Parsons' gun with a cosmic cloud of gunpowder—a misshapen lump of lead that inches forward even as it spins over itself, like a curve ball in slow motion.

If I could reach out I could grab it, I could pluck it from the air like a lazy bumblebee. But I can't reach out. There is a weight on me that I know has stopped my lungs, and I will never breathe again. That was the last one, the final breath. I've taken in all of the oxygen that will ever reach my blood. I can only watch as Bennet dives in front of Caroline with his eyes closed, and I can't help but admire him. What a strong, crazy bastard he is. I know he loves her. Loves her madly. I also know he is worthy of her. It's a slow motion game of angles and trajectories between him and the bullet, one that was written out long ago, and the crows hop up on my bed to watch with me. They rest on my headboard and perch on my feet. There are many of them—first ten, then twenty, then thirty. They gather around and watch with me as the bullet, in a game of millimeters, misses Bennet's heart and rips into his shoulder. And then they all titter, like an applause. I want to jump up and hoot.

I turn towards Joey and Douglas, locked around each other's necks like lions on the savannah. Joey has him. I turn back to Parsons, who is frozen in an implacable look of dismay. We've been slowed by the thousandth now. His look is such that he knows that was the only shot he had, because I can feel the last page of this story being inked, and I know it ends with this: *Ana.*

Ana walks through the door after the crows. She walks with the same girlish bounce she always had, and the crows move aside for her. One sits on her shoulder and bows its head to her. She is pale, so pale, paler than she ever was before. And she wears a child's dress of black and lace that is resplendent one moment and tattered the next.

And she is smiling. And illusion, vision, demon, or nothing at all, when my sister smiles like that, I've never been able to resist it. I smile too.

"Hello, brother," she says.

"What are you doing here?" I ask.

"I've come for you," she says. "At last."

"Am I dead?" I ask.

Ana cocks her head in such a perfect imitation of how she used to listen to us when we tried to get her to come in from the back, or eat her dinner, or close her eyes to go to sleep, that it's as if the years of her absence never happened at all.

"No," she says, after a moment. "Not yet. But I can wait."

She steps over to Bennet, the bullet still ripping the sinew of his shoulder. She grabs at the rippling air that marked its passage as if she could stop it, but her hand passes right through. And that's when I see that Caroline is with us in the pocket of time. She looks up at me with huge eyes. Blinking wildly, she takes a staggering breath and touches her own face, as if to confirm it's still there.

"Am I dead?" Caroline asks.

Ana listens to the air again, and it chills me to the bone. Such a childish expression, like she's listening to a tin-can phone, but I'm terrified of whatever is on the other end.

"No," she says, nodding to herself. "Not yet."

Caroline stands heavily. She lifts her head as if it is yoked. Then she freezes. Very carefully, very slowly, she reaches down her collar and grasps the bell. She pulls it out and over her like it is a link of iron chains. She holds it out in front of her and opens her palm.

"The clapper. It's back," she says.

Ana nods cheerfully.

"It only appears when someone is dying," Caroline says.

"Yes," Ana says. "My brother is dying."

She hops up, scattering the crows, and she comes to the foot of my bed. Her little head barely reaches over the footboard.

"Is this really you, Ana?" I ask, my voice hoarse.

Ana listens to the invisible wind again.

"Yes, and no," she says.

"How?"

"Because I am Ana. But I am Death," she says, and she smiles. It's pure and young and good. But there is something in her eyes. Something just as natural as the smile, but far blacker. She walks around my bed, trailing one small finger, and now she looks embarrassed. She scrunches up one side of her face as if she's about to cry.

"I missed you, Ben," she says, nodding at the truth of it.

I start to weep, and I grab her to me. She lets me take her in. I feel as though I'm leaving my body. I know I have seconds left, but seconds stretch. I smell her hair. I kiss her forehead. I wrap my arms around her tiny frame, and she hugs me back, giggling. "Ana, why didn't you come to me before?"

"Silly," she says, smiling up at me. "Because you weren't dying before. I can only take the dead people away."

The air chills again. And when I look at her I see that the deep black is leaking from her eyes again, just like it did when I saw her in the Evilway, when the chant breached our two planes.

"It's almost time," she says, and the black leaks like tears from her, dripping down in triangles from her eyes.

"But how, Ana? How did you come to take all the dead people away?" It's all I can think to ask as I watch the child in her morph, turn darker, blacker, longer. But she still has that same puckish voice as always.

"I rang the bell that Gam gave me," she says. "That's how. She told me to keep it very secret, and if I felt like I was going away, to ring it. So I did."

Caroline looks at the bell in her hands, bowing down her arms with its unseen weight. Ana ponders it, then nods.

"That's it," Ana says. Then she laughs with a strange, unsettling darkness. "I saw her pick it up from my bed after I left it. Careful. If you ring it, you have to take dead people away too."

The page is almost done, the ink almost dry.

"Ana," I say. "Are you tired?"

She thinks for a second, then shakes her head.

"Are you lonely?"

She nods.

"Are you ready to go?" I ask, because I know now. I know what the bell is and what the bell does.

She looks at me for a second, then throws a fierce hug

over me. I can feel her changing, feel her moving, but inside all of it is my little sister. The girl I've dreamed of seeing gives me the hug I've dreamed of getting. The one that I used to weep over when I woke up before it happened. It's happening now. She holds me. And she is warm, and small, and she is Ana. She is finally here. And she and I come to an understanding then.

"I'm ready to go now," she whispers.

And that's when I look at Caroline.

"Can I have the bell?" I ask.

She shakes her head vigorously, throwing tears left and right. "No." She knows, too. She knows what happens if I ring the bell. She knows what I become. "No. You're going to live. You're going to get better. You're going to beat this, and we're going to live together and have kids and dance around the fire together and grow old and die holding each other's hands." She shakes her head again. "No. Absolutely not."

"Caroline," I whisper. "Look."

I turn towards my vital monitor. It's flat. No beats. Nothing. I am sitting up talking to her, and I am lying down dead at the same time. We've caught a window, but that window is closing. I listen carefully, and I can hear the flat buzz of the machines in the time outside of our time. I hear the alarm of the code. I see the soft pulsing of the blue light outside of my room. It's slow and subtle, but it is there.

"Caroline, I'm already gone," I say. "In a heartbeat I'll be beyond you forever anyway."

Caroline hears the sounds, she sees the lights. Ana looks curiously at us, her face melting further and further.

"Hurry," Ana whispers. "Please hurry. Or I have to take you."

"Please, Caroline," I say. "Ana isn't meant for this. She

was thrown into this. She needs to go home with Gam and Dad."

"What happens to you?" Caroline asks, weeping. Snotting. She sniffs and coughs and cries, still holding the bell like it's a ten-pound stick of dynamite.

"What happens to me?" I ask Ana.

"You become me," she says, as if that explains everything. "It's a lot of work," she adds, knowingly. And in a blink her face has become that of a monster. Her eyes have dripped down to nothing. Her face is two strips of terrible black ripped through an orb of pure white.

"It's time," she says, and her voice is changed too. It is layered beyond itself into endless echoes. She reaches for my hand. For the first time in my life, I refuse my little sister.

"The bell, Caroline. Last chance. If I go with her, it's all over."

Caroline sobs, but she stumbles forward, her thumb in the bell. She falls onto me, and my hand grasps the bell. Our lips find each other, and we are given a kiss outside of time that lasts longer than the lives of many people. It lifts me. It unwraps me. And then it is over.

"Goodbye, Ben," she says.

"Goodbye, Caroline," I say. "Go. Live."

The thing Ana has become grasps my hand with cold finality, but I ring the bell first, and the time that had been slowed truly stops.

In a blink Ana is herself again. She laughs and jumps and stretches—and she begins to fade. I am not afraid of this. I know this is what is supposed to happen. It's a one in, one out policy.

"Goodbye, Ana," I say. "Say hi to everyone for me."

She giggles and spins in circles and runs up to me and

grabs me around the waist, but her grip is like the brushing of a feather.

"It's hard," she says. "What you go to do."

"I am sure."

"You'll do good," she says, nodding. Then she pushes back. "Remember," she says, pointing at the machines that blare and the flat lines. "You're gone too, Benny. When the bell rings again, you come to be with us."

She fades and fades. Soon she's just a smile. "Love you, Benny. See you later."

"Love you, Ana."

Then she has truly passed. In the silence, one of the many crows that nobody but I can see hops onto my shoulder and turns to look at me. He ruffles his feathers and stretches himself, and somehow he seems to grow, and grow, and shocks of red tinge his feathers until I recognize him once more.

"Hiya," he says.

"Hello."

"Time to clean all this up, I'd say," he says, nodding at the slow motion spectacle that is happening around me. Bennet is about to hit the floor. Joey and Douglas still spar for each other's necks. Parsons watches with cold fury.

"Ben? Where are you?" It's Caroline. "Ben?" But her voice slows, matches the pace of the world around us as she passes out of the pocket of time and we are gone to each other.

I stand.

All of my pain is gone. Everything that marked my understanding of the world is gone. In its place I have what I can only describe as a black map that is marked with pins of light. Millions upon millions of pins of light, more popping into existence all the time, but as soon as they do, they start to fade, each in their turn, by infinitesimal degrees. And I am there, with each of them. But I am here, too, completely. I am where I need to be, exactly as I need to be. Because I walk the map, and I tend to the lights when they are dim enough. I have been called Death before, but I already know that's not accurate. Better to call me the Walker.

Where I once lay, the covers softly cave. My body is not there. My body is gone. Nothing remains of me on the plane where these humans stand, screaming and fighting and bleeding. I am separate from them. Separate and alone. And yet I remember. I remember them. All of them. I see the agents, but I do not feel anger towards them. I mark their time. I can measure the strings of their lives.

I see my mom. She is screaming in madness, and her string is weak, fraying. I am troubled by this only in the sense that I know it is not yet her time.

I see Owen Bennet. He is bleeding, but he will survive. His string is stronger than he shows. Stronger than he knows.

And I see Caroline Adams and am shocked by the force of feeling that swells within me. The crow cocks his head at me, and the light brushes his beak such that it seems to smile.

"You don't lose everything of yourself," he says. "Kind of a curse, though, because you can't do anything with what remains."

"She's special."

"I'd say so," the crow says. His voice has a bit of a drawl to it. If you were to close your eyes and listen to him, you'd think a twenty-something beach bum was talking to you.

"Look at her string," I say. "It's beautiful. Colorful."

"I'll take your word for it. She does have that glow though."

"I have to save her. These men will hurt her."

"Can't do that."

"Why not?"

"Direct interference. Strictly off limits. Them's the rules."

"Rules? Horseshit." I take a swipe at Douglas, who's still moving at a snail's pace. My arms pass right through him.

"Told ya," says the crow.

"So she's going to die..."

"Not necessarily."

"What?"

"It's the bell they want. Not the girl."

"But I can't give them the bell."

"Oh, you can't let them have the bell. That would be a terrible idea. You're right. They suck. What you can do, though, is take it out of the equation."

I look at the bell in my hand. I see the clapper is fading, and my grip on it is slipping as well.

"Quickly now. Once the clapper's done for, it's back in their plane again. Those bastards will snatch it up, and that's all she wrote."

"What do I do?"

"If I were you, I'd take it out back and chuck it as far as you can."

"Out back?"

"Way out back, if you catch my meaning."

I think I do. I focus beyond the hospital room and grab on to the map of lights, but this time I also step into it. It's like opening up a heavy trap door at the bottom of my mind, and jumping in. The lights zip around me and spin wildly, and I start to scream. It's like falling in a dream, but endlessly. There's no waking up from this one.

"Stop flailing around, dumbass. Your little sister got it on the first try," says the crow. He's flapping his wings next to me, keeping steady with my head.

So I stop. And the lights settle around me. I see them for what they are. I'm floating inside a map of souls. The bell is still in my hand, but it feels lighter and lighter.

"Get rid of it, man! Throw it!"

"But where will it go?"

"Who cares? Not here!"

So I wind up and throw it. I throw it forever. It's like a golf ball in space. It sails and sails and sails, and then it's gone, like a coin disappearing into the ocean.

"Where did it go?"

"Somewhere else on their plane. Don't you worry about that bell. Worrying about the bell is my job. Frickin' thing has a propensity to show up at inopportune times. To say the least. The point is, I'll find it, and if I know these two scumbags, you bought your friends some time. Look."

The crow flips in the air with all the grace of a flying rag, but he manages to turn around and look back where we came. I follow him, shakily, like I'm turning around in close quarters on a bike.

I see nothing but the soul map. Billions of lights pulsing in an orb around my head.

"Where'd they go?"

"You tell me, bro. You saw their threads. You can find them again."

"How?"

"Hell if I know. I'm just the bird. You're the Walker. That's why you get paid the big bucks." The crow titters.

He's a wiseass, but he's been helpful so far, and even though he sounds flip, I get the feeling he really believes in me. I'll chalk that up to being related to Ana, who I can already tell he was fond of. I focus on the threads I saw back in the hospital. It's hard to picture all four of them, though, so instead I think of only one: Caroline's. It shimmered like a rip of sunset through campfire smoke, if the fire burned in every color of the rainbow: flare red, sparkler white, gas-rich blue, the green of flaming sap, and more— purples and pinks and so many shades of white I don't have the words to describe them, from soft to hard, all burning at a million degrees. This was her line of life.

And then I see it. I reach for it, and in a smashing blur I'm back in the room. Standing by the bed. My clothes ripple and still. I notice that the hospital gown is gone. In its place is a uniform, not unlike my NNPD getup: crisp slacks and a trim buttoned shirt, but it's pure black. I don't wear shoes. I can see the veins in my feet, and in my hands. They are very thick and very clear, and they pulse black.

There are many crows still in the room, including the one that talks to me, and all of them turn to watch me. I hold my hands out to the one that speaks and show him the pale underside of my wrists and the black veins there. He shrugs.

"Comes with the territory. The soul map is a powerful place. It leaves its mark. Only you can walk it for that long and live. And me, of course." He preens his glossy feathers, and I see the red marks there more clearly than ever. "What do you think of your new threads?"

"Not bad."

"Ana figured you'd like 'em. All right, get ready now," the crow says.

"For what?"

"As soon as the map closes, we're back on their time."

The window into the fiber-optic cityscape of the soul map is closing like water going down a drain. As it spins away, time catches up with itself. And then, with an audible pop, the commercial break is over.

And the agents scream.

They scream louder than Bennet does, because they know the bell is gone, and they see that my bed is empty, which can only mean one thing. They missed their chance.

"Where is he?" Douglas screams, frothing. He forgets about Joey entirely and runs to my bed, ripping up the sheets. He passes right through me as he throws the monitoring equipment aside. Joey looks at him with his hands still out, stunned and panting.

"You know where he is," Parsons says, his gun still trained on Caroline. I snarl, helpless to intervene. "He's right here. But he's beyond us, now."

Douglas takes a mad swipe around the room. I can't even feel the wind of his passing. The code alarm is blaring and people are running into the room and then out of the room at the same time, once they see the gun. Douglas tilts his head, sniffing, as if chasing the noise. Parsons turns the gun on Joey, then on Bennet, keeping all of them at bay.

"I can still smell it," Douglas says. "The bell. But it's fading."

"Better than nothing," Parsons says.

Without another word, Douglas snaps out of mortal view, and a shade of him flits by me, only this time I think I can feel a touch of wind. Then he's out of the room, and then out of the hallway, and soon out of the building entirely. On the trail of the bell.

Parsons looks around at the mess and then turns briefly towards where Caroline has run to Bennet, who's bleeding on the floor. My mother is screaming in her madness. Joey watches him carefully, his hands still out, waiting for Parsons to shoot, but instead Parsons spits in disgust. He holsters his weapon, and I breathe a sigh of relief. Then he speaks to me.

"I know you're here, Mr. Dejooli. I know about the bell, not everything, but enough to find it again, no matter where it is. I know about the map, too. Is it beautiful? I can almost picture it. And one day it will be mine, with all of the power that comes with it. So don't get used to it. You may have rung the bell, but you're still a two-bit cop to me."

His flat, vanilla gaze melts slowly into a wicked smile. "The bell is out there. I can feel it. When I find it, I'm coming for you."

In a flash, he's gone. But I can watch him still. When he flits out of his realm, he's a shadow in mine, but he cannot see me. He is passing between our realms when he grabs the crow totem. He is neither here nor there. Soon enough, he's gone too.

The big crow is tapping his beak against the metal of the bed in mocking applause. "Hear that? He's gonna getcha! What a dick, am I right?"

He's joking, and I smile, but I'm still unnerved. Parsons and Douglas know more about where I am and who I am than I do, and it bothers me. Those two aren't just going to go away.

All around me the room has exploded into action again. Police and doctors and nurses swarm about, treating Bennet and shuffling my mother and Caroline out and under blankets and into locked rooms.

Joey becomes a shadow, and I know he's holding his crow and is invisible to those around him, but I can see him.

"Ben! Are you there?" he yells, but his voice is muffled and whipped, like he's screaming into a gale force wind. I can also tell that it's hurting him, flitting between realities like this, and suddenly I know why he was taking the drugs.

They help with the pain of phasing out. Allow him to walk in shadows for longer than he should.

"Go, Joey! You'll kill yourself!" I scream, but he can't hear me, or see me. His crow shines like the sun in his hand.

"I'll watch over the doc and the girl! Don't worry! Those fuckers won't touch them!"

I can't help but smile at his bravado. Old school Joey, right there. The first flicker of it I've seen since this whole mess started years and years ago. As if he can sense me, he smiles too.

"I'm glad it's you, buddy. I hope you said goodbye to Ana."

I nod to him. He was right. He found her after all, even if he couldn't see her.

Then he's out of the room in a flash, and it's just me and the crows. I'm surrounded by people, but I can't touch them. I can't speak to them. I feel terribly alone. It's like the first soft pressure of a crushing weight that threatens to drown me, but then the big crow is there. He flies to my shoulder and settles there as if born to it, and I feel instantly better.

"It's not so bad," he says. "Ana was a good Walker, very good. But I don't think she was the one we need now. It's good that you let her go."

I turn to him, puzzled. "What makes a good Walker?"

"All in good time. We'll start simple."

"I can already feel that I need to be in places."

"People die," says the crow, shrugging his shoulders. "It's the one constant on this plane."

"Then I will go to them," I say.

The crow nods. It's a sort of excited bob that makes me smile again.

"What's your name?" I ask.

"Don't know. I've had countless names."

"What did Ana call you?"

"Well, she called me a lot of things. Flappy, Blackie, Birdie, Dummy, mostly Birdie. When she got lonely and reached for me sometimes she'd call me Ben," he says quietly. "Or Chaco."

"Chaco," I say. "I like that one."

"Chaco it is then, chief."

The lights are calling me, they are fading, and they need me to tend to their end. I know I can do this. It's what I am meant to do.

"Well, Chaco. I think my time is done here."

"For now..." Chaco says.

"Then let's get going. We have work to do."

I reach out my black-veined hand and press through the air. A pinprick of darkness appears, and I swirl the matter that makes up this plane like I'm spinning batter in a bowl. The soul map whorls into view, bigger, bigger, until it is all that is in front of me, staggering and infinite.

"I like the swirl move," Chaco says. "Nice touch."

I gaze flatly at him. "Try to keep up," I say, grinning.

Then I'm off.

19

THE WALKER

When I was dying, I spoke of life as a book, of our experiences as a series of pages fluttering to an eventual close. Now that I'm on the other side of it I can tell you that's not true. Not exactly, anyway. The idea that each of us has a book to write, and then once it's done we shelve it in the great library of existence, that's ludicrous. No story is separate. If you could see this map, this beautiful, glowing map, you'd understand that.

I've walked the map a bit by now, and I often catch myself thinking about how I could explain this to you, or to Caroline, or to anyone. The best I can come up with right now is this: you know those huge fiber optic cables that span the oceans like enormous ropes? Imagine one as wide as the sun, and cut it in half so you see the countless individual fibers pulsing with light. That's about as close as I can get to describing it. Your life isn't a book: your life is a string of light, wrapped up with every other string into infinity.

I walk these strings. I walk the rope. Sometimes Chaco joins me, but mostly I do what I do alone. When a thread is breaking, I'm called to it. The life it belongs to can see me then, although I don't know what they see when their eyes are opened in death. Sometimes they call me the names of people they knew, or loved. Sometimes they weep. Sometimes they cheer. The old are happier than the young. The old often cheer. The young are often heartbroken. I can understand. It's hard to let go of life. Even if it sucks, it's hard to let go.

I do not frighten them, for the most part. Perhaps they expect the cowl and scythe. They get me, instead. Or whatever their impression of me is. On a handful of occasions so far I have had people run. The first guy I actually chased, too. The old cop instincts kicked in, and I ended up running down a beach after the guy for half a mile before I remembered I could slow time. Good thing, too, because he was a young guy and I hadn't used my lungs for quite a while by then and was out of shape. In a footrace he would have kicked my ass. As it was, I pulled the fabric of time down a notch and walked right up to him. He screamed the whole time, screamed bloody murder with nobody to hear but me. These runners are the only people that I've seen so far that are truly afraid when I come for them. Everyone's afraid of death until they die, then the hard part is over. The ones who are *still* afraid when I come are the ones that know that whatever lies beyond me won't be good to them.

What lies beyond me? Wish I could tell you. I walk the rope, and I can't drop off the sides. But something does lie beyond me. I get whispers of it when I work. Rustlings from beyond the veil, and not all of them are good.

It came naturally, what I do. In a nutshell I clip the fading string of light and pack it away into the rope. Sort of like cosmic sewing. Left alone, the string will fade and weaken, but it will hold on. Like I said, life is pretty tenacious that way. Thing is, it's not supposed to linger once it's faded past a certain point. It's bad if strings linger. It upsets the order of things. It's unnatural, and its unnaturalness calls to me, tugs at me until I walk the rope and find it and clip it.

No scythe, either. Not even a pair of store-bought scissors. I use my fingers. Pointer and middle, I tease it out of them, and I snip it. There is no pain. It actually feels quite tremendous for the both of us, like finally sneezing after waiting what seems like a lifetime. After I clip a string, a seam opens in space, not unlike when I open the soul map, but it's red and it billows like a curtain. I can't walk through. I tried. Something stops me. All I can do is usher them through. Sometimes I hold their hand and send them off. Sometimes I just point. Sometimes I have to shove. But they all go through the veil eventually.

I'm getting better at it. The first couple of snips were disasters. There was the runner, and then there was this young kid who wept and wept and wouldn't go through the curtain. The longer you wait, the bigger the curtain gets, until it takes up everything. This only scared the kid more, and I'm not ashamed to admit I panicked a little myself. I started getting pressed back, and the kid screamed until I basically tossed him in. Just kind of picked him up under the armpits and chucked him through. Not my proudest moment, but it worked. And like I said, the veil gets you in the end. It's just a matter of how you go through it.

At first I got backed up. Way backed up. Think about it. People die every second on earth, but there's just one Walker. It took me a while to figure out how to split myself. To be in many places at once. The key is to not think about it. Just let it happen, smooth your mind. The stoners we used to bust out by the Arroyo were closer to transcendence than I gave them credit for, because that's what it is I do. When I stop thinking of myself as being in one place, I allow myself to be in every place. I sucked at it for a while, still sort of do, but I'm getting better, thanks to Chaco.

Chaco's a strange thing. I'm learning about him just like I'm learning about everything else. Slowly, but surely. First, he's not a bird. Not exactly. There is only one creature like him, just like there's only one creature like me. I think the best way to describe him would be as a 'thinning.' There are animals on the earth that are 'thinner' than others. Animals that are just more aware of what is beyond the earth plane. I'm sure you know what I'm talking about. Cats are probably the best example. When they sit and stare at walls, do you really think they're staring at walls? Nope. Crows are another. Sloths also, believe it or not. Elephants have some capacity for it, and wolves. There are others, too. Many of them. Chaco can take on any of their forms. He just likes the crow the best.

He's been helping me when he can, but mostly he's been looking for the bell. Or rather, waiting for someone to find the bell and become the new Keeper. Chaco watches over the Keeper, just like Gam's iteration of Chaco watched over her and gave its life for her in the end, to protect her from Danny Ninepoint and allow her to pass the bell to Caroline. I was a little disappointed to hear that Chaco served the bell, not me, because I thought he was like my sidekick, sort of like every wizard has an owl. He put a short end to that line of thought though, by laughing his ass off when I tried to give him an order.

I asked him how all the crows killed Danny Ninepoint, if they weren't ordered to do something like that. He said they killed him because they loved Ana, and Ana loved me, and they knew Danny meant me harm. He said this like he was explaining that the sky was blue. Good enough for me. They came in in the clutch, and Chaco does the same. He almost always comes when I call for him, but I try not to call him unless I need him. But right now I need him. I need his help to get the crow totems back from the agents.

See, it turns out that just like there are thin creatures, there are also thin *things*. The crow totems are one of these thin things: they exist on more than one plane. In the case of the crows, they're on the earth plane most of the time, and on my plane when they're activated, but only briefly. We're talking seconds. And seconds I can't slow down. Chaco had always known it could be done, he just hadn't seen it, and it's no wonder, because it's hard as hell to get the timing right.

I couldn't tell you how long I followed those two agents. I stepped out of time for quite a while, practicing my grab while they crisscrossed the globe looking for the bell. Chaco tells me it's almost impossible to find the bell on its own, but once it presents itself to a Keeper, the race is on. For now, though, it's sort of dormant. He tells me they'd literally have to stumble across it.

Still, I can't even chance a stumble. Even a blind squirrel has a shot at a nut, and the more I follow them, the more it becomes clear to me that I have to keep the bell from them at all costs. They have strange ideas. Unnatural ideas. They have a sense of the map, and the veil, although I'm not sure how. They speak of forcing the veil. Of bending the map to their will. Cutting strings that aren't fading and sewing fading strings back to strength. I haven't been on the job long, but even I know that stuff would spell disaster.

Chaco assures me these things can't be done. But I'm not so sure. He's the thinning. He doesn't deal with the strings or the veil or the map. I'm the Walker; I do. I learn new things every day. Just because I can't do something now, like cut a healthy string, doesn't mean it can't be done. It's just that I have the good sense not to try it.

I know if I can take their totems, it will at least slow them down. There are others on earth, as many as twenty that I know of, but most likely more, so the agents could theoretically get another pair. But it won't be easy. I know a little bit about who carries these crows. They call themselves the Circle of the Crow, and they're sworn to protect the bell. Joey is one of them, but there are others, and some of them make Joey look like a punk. Safe to say, the crows won't be easy to replace, even by a couple of lunatics like the agents. So I practice the timing, and I learn to find the subtle signs that the two of them are jumping. I learn to read the fabric of their plane so I'll know when the crow begins to part it. And I wait. I know I'll get one shot at this. I'm guessing there are ways to protect the crow even during the phasing. I don't want to tip them off.

When the agents meet up together to sniff out New York City, a big task that requires both of them at once, I know my time has come. They are walking down the street— prowling down the street, is more like it—and even the hard-eyed New Yorkers know to move out of their way. Humans have a sense of when not to mess with people that could get them in trouble. More than I give them credit for. They range from dull to Caroline-status, but everyone has at least something of what you might call a sixth sense. Everyone knows to leave the agents alone to their dark work.

Everyone except me.

I keep pace with them. Walking backward, keeping a measured distance. They know nothing of me. Not until they phase out, that is. Then they see me there for half a heartbeat. I know they see me there because they pause, but that is all it takes. It's like a baton passing gone wrong. They try to jump forward in space, but I snatch the crows from their hands. One in my left, one in my right. Their bodies pass through me, untouchable, but the crow totems are thin, and for that one moment, they're as real on my plane as they are on theirs. I pluck them from their hands like flowers, and the agents tumble back to the New York City sidewalk in a heap. Parsons knows immediately what has happened, and I see the hate burn silent within him as he scans the empty air in front of him. Douglas screams and swipes madly at the air, and an entire sidewalk full of people crosses to the other side of the street immediately. But all the spitting and swearing and raving in the world can't help him now. Once I bring the crows to my side, they're lost to him. I couldn't bring them across again even if I wanted to. I and everything with me walk the rope. I can observe their world. Nothing more. Unless the bell rings.

Parsons quiets Douglas and says, "Patience, patience." He looks around at the empty air, passing blindly over as I pump my fists in the air.

"There are other crows," he says quietly. "Other ways."

"I'll be ready!" I scream, right into his face, but he can't hear me, and eventually they turn away. I know that's not the last I'll see of the agents. I have the feeling that Parsons in particular is the kind of guy who only gets more pissed off when you needle him. I remember his golem stare, and I shudder as I watch them walk away, side by side.

Now. What do I do with these two crows?

I call Chaco. I use the two-fingered whistle he taught me, but I think he's just messing with me. I think he knows when I need him, he just wants to make me spit through my fingers. I'm not a good whistler. I can hear him careening through time even before I take a breath. He blows through the soul map and pops out in New York City. He flares his wings and settles on my shoulder.

"What can I do ya for, chief?" he asks.

"Any luck with the bell?"

"Not yet. But I've narrowed it down. When it finds a Keeper, I'll know. I'll be the first there. Although let me tell you, they're gonna have to work pretty damn hard to beat your grandmother. That old lady could kick some ass."

I nodded. Chaco often talks about Gam. He's been through thousands of Keepers, but he keeps coming back to Gam. Sometimes I wonder if Gam didn't have all this in mind when she gave Ana the bell. She was patient even for a Navajo, which basically put her at guru status. Me ending up here, with this gig, at this time, this is exactly the sort of long play she would drum up. The thought makes me smile, but it also worries me. Gam never did anything without good reason.

"I wonder if you could help me," I ask Chaco.

"Maybe. That's eighteen favors to zero now. I'm keeping track."

"Yeah, yeah. Listen. I can't pass through to the human plane, right?"

"That's why you dragged me all the way here? I was in a pretty awesome beach town, my man."

I ignore him. "But you can, right?"

He quiets.

"I know you can, Chaco. You did it with Gam. And I saw you too, back when I was Ben. A couple of times. One time you shit on my car."

He titters in what I can only assume is a bird laugh. "Yes. Yes, okay? I can. When a Keeper is declared—"

"But what about now? When there's no Keeper."

Chaco pauses.

"I dunno, bro. It's not good to mess around with the rules of this place. You don't want to piss off what's behind that curtain."

"Please. I have to get these crows to the other side."

"You mean to the girl you love and the doctor."

I pause. Am I that obvious? I suppose so.

"You know you can never be with her," Chaco says. "You know that, right? I mean, there ain't no *way*—"

"Yeah, yeah. I get it," I say. And I do. I think. "But I know they would be great allies of ours. Both her and Owen Bennet. I think you know this too."

Chaco puffs up in a birdish sigh. Then he bobs his beak. "Yes. I think so too."

"So you'll do it? You'll cross over?"

Chaco eyes me with cold calculation, then squawks in frustration. "I can tell this is going to be a hell of a run, with you."

"Chaco—"

"Yes, Walker. Yes, I'll carry the crows," he says.

I hold them out, one in each hand. He snatches them in his claws and then takes off in a whirl. I watch him rise, rise, and then blink out of view.

20

CAROLINE ADAMS

I magine going to work again like it was just your typical Monday after meeting Death herself in a patient's room.

Imagine falling in love and then watching the one you love taken from you. Not even into death, but into something else. Something just as distant, but even less understood. And then the hospital gives you two working days off to pull yourself together, and then it's Monday and you're back at work again, answering your phone, helping your patients to the bathroom, administering meds, all while trying to ignore the fact that your world has fundamentally changed.

Owen is a hero. I expected nothing less. He was borderline adored on the floor to begin with, and then he got himself shot in my place and that just threw the entire hospital into a frenzy. The CEO met him personally. They gave him a ceremonial key to the complex at a big dinner a week later that was attended by every C-level executive. I think I was the only nurse. It was surreal. I thought they only did that stuff in movies. In typical Owen Bennet

fashion he demurred and shrugged adorably through everything, one arm in a sling, the other resting softly over it.

The aftermath of the shooting went by in a blur of police
questioning, mandatory counseling, and cleanup. There was
no way Owen or I could tell the truth about what happened
in that room. We'd be committed along with Sitsi Dejooli,
Ben's mother, so we kept our lie simple. Two men claiming
they were FBI agents barged into Ben Dejooli's room. Owen
Bennet and I confronted them, and Owen took a bullet for
me. Then the two men took Ben from his bed and disappeared. The agents never showed up on camera. All the
police had was our testimony, as well as that of two nurses
who were the first on the code. They said they saw at least
one man in a suit, which would have been Parsons, but
couldn't say what happened to him. When they turned back
around, he was gone, along with Ben.

The police put out an APB for the agents, but there was
no trace of them. We were told the FBI had no record of
employing an Agent Douglas or an Agent Parsons, and they
declined further comment on what they deemed a state
matter. The bullet markings didn't match anything on file,
nor did any of the blood samples found. Not surprising.

It's also not surprising that this series of events was
finally what broke Sitsi Dejooli's mind. She wouldn't
respond to anybody: not the police, not me or Owen, not
anyone. But in her quiet, staring pondering I sensed a
certain measure of peace. I could see it in her coloring, too.
Her yellow is tinged with a soft pink now, barely there, but
consistent. It looks like the color of a woman who has seen
more than her mind will allow. Rather than fight it and
make sense of it, her mind has simply decided to close itself
for a time. I'd be lying if I said part of me doesn't envy her.
She recovered at ABQ General for two days. The only words

I ever heard her say after the whole ordeal was her verbal consent to a transfer upstate to Los Alamos, where the Navajo Nation had arranged for her to live in a step-up care mental facility indefinitely. She turned her back on the Navajo, but it would appear that the Navajo hadn't turned their backs on her. The Council said it was the least they could do, given her loss. She was blood, after all.

And all the while I had a decision looming. I had entirely forgotten about it until I received the papers in the mail. My five years were up. My debt was forgiven. If I wished to stay at ABQ General I was to notify my nurse manager in writing by the end of the week. If not, they wished me well, thanked me for my service at the CHC, and would be happy to write a reference on my behalf wherever I decided to go.

Check the box yes or no. Sign your name. Drop it off with your supervisor. Three simple steps that will define the trajectory of my life. It's enough to make you laugh out loud. They clearly don't know me. I am not good with decisions. I sweat over dinner plans. So I made lists: a pros list and a cons list. The old high-school approach.

Pros:

- The job is pretty good. Not wildly good. Not something I wake up every morning super jazzed for, but pretty good. Good enough, I decide.
- I'm already here. I'm settled. I have an apartment and a car, and I know the city.
- I can work at the rez. Which makes me feel like I'm doing something worthwhile. And I like the Navajo. For the most part.
- Owen Bennet.

I've avoided thinking about my feelings for Owen, because they're all wrapped up in crazy right now. But the bottom line is he would give his life for me. He proved that much back when Parsons tried to shoot me. I know what that means. Ben told me that he loved me. Owen showed it. To think that the world was within two inches of swapping him out for me is insane. It makes me go beet red and feel slightly ill at the same time. Let's be honest, of the two of us, he is the one you want on your team. He's Owen Bennet. I'm just...me. I put *x2* next to his bullet point. Then I crossed it out and put *x3*. He deserves to be weighted more heavily.

Cons:

- If I keep it up here for much longer, there's a
  good chance this is where I'll play out the rest of
  my days.

I'm nearly thirty. All the girls say it gets harder to make stupid choices after thirty, even if they might make your life better in the long run. Things like traveling or nursing abroad. ABQ is okay, but let's face it, it's not exactly Paris.

- Ben is dead. And it's hitting me way harder than I
  thought it would.

I knew he was going to die. I knew the second the chemo regimen didn't stick. I had weeks with him to prepare myself, but it still hit me like a dump truck because I loved him. I hope I let him know that, but the more I think about our time together, the more I'm afraid I fretted so much about whether or not he loved me that I missed a chance to tell him I loved him. Typical.

- Ben isn't gone.

I put this on as a con because it's an argument against me staying here. I wake up in the middle of the night sometimes and for a split second I think I can still feel the soft pressure of his hand. I have to tell myself that whatever happened to him, he is beyond me now. I am slowly coming to peace with that—but I still want to know what happened to him. What it means. What the bell is. And I don't think I can do that if I stay here.

So there you have it. I stare at the list, two columns. It's hard not to call it what it is: Ben vs. Owen. Ben's dead. Owen is alive. So why is this so hard? At three in the morning it's easier to convince myself that I need to go. Nothing seems right around me anymore. The shadows of that day haunt me. The Ben factor has a heavy weighting, too. So heavy I'm not sure it can be measured. In the end, it's enough to make me check the 'No' box. I decide to pack it up. But then, the next day, I run into Owen as I'm about to hand in my resignation. I think he knows what I'm doing. I think he was on the lookout for me.

"Caroline," he says. "Wait. Please." He reaches out for me, and his fingers flutter briefly towards my hand before he drops his arm and looks at the ground. "You're leaving, aren't you," he says.

The *Bennet x3* flashes in my mind. He looks so sad. Like the resignation letter in my hand is a personal rejection, when it's not. This place is all screwed up for me, now, that's all.

"I wish..." He grits his teeth and shakes his head. "I wish I was better at this. I wish I could stop you. Ben could have. I know that."

"Owen, please..." My mind is already full up on regrets. If Owen throws his hat in the ring, I'll never sleep again.

"No, I understand," he says, smiling sadly. "He...he was special. I just hope that I let you know..." He stutters and smooths at his white coat. "I hope I was able to make myself clear, that you are special too. I know he thought so. But so do I. I hope you know that."

I can't take this. These men have ruined me. I want to do the cowardly thing. I want to run away.

"I can't stop you. I know that," he says. "But I also can't help but think that if I had more time. If we had more time...maybe I could."

I'm crying as I push the letter through the slot. He watches it like it's the tail end of a train carrying his life away from him. It clinks inside the box with a hollow ping. I want him to shake his head and shuffle away. I want him to get mad at me, give me a disparaging look, even. But instead when I look back up at him he's still there, smiling sadly.

"Can I at least walk you to your car?" he asks.

Dammit, Owen. Of course you can walk me to my car, you beautiful man.

We're quiet on the walk out, our hands shoved into the pockets of our coats against the first real winter wind of the season. I turn to him, and the wind cuts at my face and streaks my tears sideways. "I wouldn't have left without saying goodbye to you. You know that, right? I owe you my life, Owen."

He shrugs. "I believe you," he says. At my car we pause. "I was thinking," he says, struggling. He puffs his coat out from the pockets.

"What?"

"I was thinking of doing something crazy and stupid. But I'm not sure I can."

I want to draw more out of him, but there's a subtle ringing in the distance, just barely sounding above the wind and a ripple in the sky draws our attention to the horizon at the same time. He steps closer to me, so we're shoulder to shoulder. I know he feels it too: something broke through.

"Not again," he says.

"No. Look."

There, on the horizon, is a black speck. And it's growing.

Still, Owen pulls his hands from his pockets and angles himself in front of me, even after we watch as the speck grows into a bird, a huge bird, with a dull glint of red upon its head. A bird I recognize. A bird I saw die.

"How the hell?" I begin, but then I know. Somehow Ben is behind it.

The bird flies in near silence. Slowly, languorously flapping its wings like an ancient beast, which I suddenly know it is, in one form or another.

"My God, it's huge," Owen says. "Is it coming after us?"

"No. Not in that way. I don't think it'll hurt us."

Now it's careening out of the sky, slowing, and dropping down straight for us, and I'm rethinking what I just said. But in an instant it flares its wings and pulls up before flopping rather unceremoniously on the hood of my car. It sort of tumbles down the windshield and then manages to stop itself on the bonnet by gripping a windshield wiper in its beak. It shakes its head, and I swear if I could hear it talk it would be telling us to keep that landing between the three of us. I can't blame it, though, because I see it's got something in both claws. Something it deposits on the hood after a preliminary, twitchy look about itself.

With one final glance at both of us, it lets out a deafening trio of *caws* and swoops up into the sky. I can feel the wind from its wings on my face as it's up, up, and out. I feel that distortion again, like a popping bubble: the world's cabin re-pressurizing. And it's gone. In its place are two crow totems, side by side, touching wing tips.

We stare at them, dumbfounded. Owen is the first to speak. "Well, that's about all the providence I need."

He picks up one in his gloved hand, and tucks it in his pocket. "I believe the other is for you," he says.

I pick mine up as well. It seems to hum, in a way only I can hear. It feels right. I grasp it tightly, protectively, then I tuck it away. When I look up again, Owen is watching me carefully.

"That stupid thing I was thinking," he says. "I think I can do it, now. Maybe."

"Maybe?"

"I can't stop you from leaving," he says. "But I was wondering if you'd let me leave with you." He cringes a bit, looking slightly ill with anticipation. "It doesn't have to be like that, or anything, of course. I'd just...it's just that I have this strange feeling. And it's been growing stronger. And it's that Ben, or whoever he is now after all that happened to him...I don't think he's gone. He's just changed. And I think he'll be needing our help. Am I weird in thinking that? Am I going insane?"

I shush him by basically running into him. Before I know what I'm doing I've thrown myself into his arms and am hugging him. No passionate kiss. No longing look into anyone's eyes. The last time I expected that to happen things didn't work out. I'm done with perfect moments. From here on out, I'm just going to work on taking advantage of whatever moments I'm given. Perfect or not.

Owen puts his arms around me in delayed shock, and even that thought makes me want to giggle like a teenager. But I compose myself and step away from him, holding both of his hands in mine like I'm physically keeping him here with me. If things are about to go down, there's nobody on earth I'd rather have on my side than Doctor Owen Bennet.

"No," I say.

His face falls.

"No no no. I mean *no* as in 'no, you're not crazy.' Yes to everything else."

He looks back up at me with a wry grin, still hesitant.

"Sorry. I always screw these kind of things up."

He lets out a big laugh. I've never heard him laugh before, I realize. And as he does, a flock of crows flies by overhead, an enormous flock—hundreds of them, blotting the sky like dribbled ink. They seem to catch his laugh as one, and all of them call out against the winter wind together.

Maybe it's just a coincidence. But I doubt it.

ACKNOWLEDGMENTS

Several people helped me out at various stages of this novel, and I'd like to take a moment to give thanks. First and foremost, to my wife, Emily, whose experience as an oncology nurse proved invaluable in crafting the perspective of Caroline Adams. I'd also like to thank Emily in general for her patience and fortitude in being married to a writer. That can't be easy.

I'd like to thank my editor Laura and the editing crew at Red Adept Publishing, along with Kit, my beta reader, for their work in polishing the story. They all have eagle eyes.

In writing the Navajo lore, I drew in part upon the research and essays of Leland C. Wyman ("Navajo Ceremonial System") and R. W. Shufeldt ("Mortuary Customs of the Navajo Indians"). I also learned from Tony Hillerman's work; his *Joe Leaphorn* novels are an education in the Navajo culture in and of themselves.

Finally, I'd like to thank you, the reader, for taking a chance on my book. Whether or not you liked *Follow the Crow*, please leave a review to help others decide on the novel. There's more to come, and if you'd like to be notified when I have another book out, you can join my mailing list here: http://eepurl.com/SObZj. It is an entirely spam-free experience. I promise.

I can also be reached over at my digital home: bbgriffith.com.

Feel free to drop me a line. I'd love to hear from you.
Happy reading,
-BBG

ABOUT THE AUTHOR

B. B. Griffith writes best-selling fantasy and thriller books. He lives in Denver, CO, where he is often seen sitting on his porch staring off into the distance or wandering to and from local watering holes with his family.

See more at his digital HQ: https://bbgriffith.com

If you like his books, you can sign up for his mailing list here: http://eepurl.com/SObZj. It is an entirely spam-free experience.

ALSO BY B. B. GRIFFITH

The Vanished Series

Follow the Crow (Vanished, #1)

Beyond the Veil (Vanished, #2)

The Coyote Way (Vanished, #3)

Gordon Pope Thrillers

The Sleepwalkers (Gordon Pope, #1)

Mind Games (Gordon Pope, #2)

Shadow Land (Gordon Pope, #3)

The Tournament Series

Blue Fall (The Tournament, #1)

Grey Winter (The Tournament, #2)

Black Spring (The Tournament, #3)

Summer Crush (The Tournament, #4)

Luck Magic Series

Las Vegas Luck Magic (Luck Magic, #1)

Standalone

Witch of the Water: A Novella

Made in the USA
Middletown, DE
29 June 2023